FRANZ KAFKA

THE METAMORPHOSIS *and* OTHER STORIES

With an Introduction and Notes
by Jason Baker

Translated by Donna Freed

George Stade
Consulting Editorial Director

BARNES & NOBLE CLASSICS
NEW YORK

JB

BARNES & NOBLE CLASSICS

NEW YORK

Published by Barnes & Noble Books
122 Fifth Avenue
New York, NY 10011

www.barnesandnoble.com/classics

Kafka's stories in the original German were published in the following
years: "The Judgment" and "The Stoker" in 1913; "The Metamorphosis"
in 1915; "A Message from the Emperor," "In the Penal Colony," "A Country
Doctor," "An Old Leaf," and "Before the Law" in 1919; "A Hunger Artist"
in 1922; and "Josephine the Singer" in 1924. Donna Freed's
translations of these stories first appeared in 1996.

Published in 2003 by Barnes & Noble Classics with new Introduction,
Notes, Biography, Inspired By, Comments & Questions,
and For Further Reading.

Introduction, Notes, and For Further Reading
Copyright © 2003 by Jason Baker.

Note on Franz Kafka, The World of Franz Kafka,
Inspired by Franz Kafka, and Comments & Questions
Copyright © 2003 by Barnes & Noble, Inc.

The Metamorphosis and Other Stories
ISBN-13: 978-1-59308-029-7
ISBN-10: 1-59308-029-8
LC Control Number 2003102536

Produced and published in conjunction with:
Fine Creative Media, Inc.
322 Eighth Avenue
New York, NY 10001
Michael J. Fine, President & Publisher

Printed in the United States of America
QM
12 14 16 18 20 19 17 15 13 11

FRANZ KAFKA

Franz Kafka was born in Prague in 1883 into a middle-class Jewish household in which he grew up with feelings of inferiority, guilt, resentment, and confinement. He was the eldest of his parents' six children; two brothers died in infancy, and he had three sisters. Franz's domineering father expected his son to take up a profitable business career that would ensure social advancement for the family, as well as a successful marriage promising the same. His mother was submissive to her husband, always siding with him in matters concerning Franz. Toward her son she was alternately fawning and neglectful.

Kafka earned his doctorate in law in 1906 but decided against practicing, to the disappointment of his father. Instead, in 1908 he took a position at an insurance agency, which left afternoons and evenings open for writing, and at which he remained until 1922— two years before his death.

Kafka's literary method follows the logic of dreams and other unconscious processes, and his stories read like allegories without an established point of reference. Kafka's best-known story, "The Metamorphosis" (1915), in which he translated his experience as family breadwinner into a parable of alienation, transformation, and ultimately death, epitomizes his style. During his early writing life Kafka was introduced to the writings of Friedrich Nietzsche, Charles Dickens, Fyodor Dostoevsky, and Thomas Mann, and became part of a literary and philosophical circle that included Oskar Baum, Martin Buber, and Felix Weltsch.

Kafka had significant relationships with several women during his brief life, notably Felice Bauer, to whom he became engaged in 1914 and 1917; Julie Wohryzek; Milena Jesenská-Pollack, his Czech translator, with whom he became involved in 1920; and Dora Diamant, a young Polish woman he met a year before his death. Kafka's sporadic literary career was in part fueled by these relationships, which varied in degree of dysfunction, and in which he vacillated emotionally, paralleling his mother's behavior toward him as a boy.

Diagnosed with tuberculosis in 1917, Kafka saw the publication of a limited number of his works during his lifetime, including "The Judgment" (1913), "The Stoker" (1913), for which he received the Fontane Prize in 1915, "The Metamorphosis" (1915), "A Country Doctor" (1919), and "In the Penal Colony" (1919). In 1924 Kafka asked his confidant Max Brod to burn his remaining unpublished manuscripts. Instead, Brod dedicated the rest of his life to the full publication of Kafka's works. Among these are the novels *The Trial* (1925), *The Castle* (1926), and *Amerika* (1927). Franz Kafka died on June 3, 1924, near Vienna.

TABLE OF CONTENTS

1846   Fyodor Dostoevsky publishes *The Double*, a work that will greatly influence Kafka's story "The Metamorphosis."

1850   Charles Dickens publishes *David Copperfield*; Kafka will imitate the novel's style in "The Stoker" (1913).

1870   Leopold von Sacher-Masoch publishes *Venus in Furs*, which lays the foundation for masochism and has an enormous influence on Kafka.

1883   Franz Kafka is born on July 3 in Prague to Hermann and Julie (*née* Löwy) Kafka. The family is Jewish and middle-class, and speaks both German and Czech. Franz is the eldest of his siblings; his two brothers die in infancy.

1889   Franz begins elementary school at Fleischmarkt. His sister Elli (Gabriele) is born.

1890   His sister Valli (Valerie) is born.

1892   Franz's sister Ottla (Ottilie) is born; of all his family, Kafka is closest with Ottla, for whom he plays the role of protective older brother.

1893   Kafka begins his studies at the German gymnasium in Prague, where he forms a friendship with Oskar Pollak, who will become a respected art historian and introduce Kafka to the writings of Friedrich Nietzsche. He also meets Czech-born poet, playwright, and novelist Franz Werfel.

1899   Kafka reads the works of Arthur Conan Doyle, Charles Darwin, Knut Hamsun, Baruch Spinoza, and Jules Verne. He forms a friendship with Hugo Bergmann, who will become a leading thinker in the Zionist movement. Kafka begins writing, although none of this early work survives.

1900   The Germans first test the zeppelin.

1902   Kafka meets writer and editor Max Brod at Brod's lecture on the German philosopher Arthur Schopenhauer. Brod becomes Kafka's most intimate friend and eventually his

interpreter, translator, biographer, and posthumous publisher. They discuss the works of Charles Dickens, Fyodor Dostoevsky, Gustave Flaubert, Hermann Hesse, Hugo von Hofmannsthal, Thomas Mann, and August Strindberg. Kafka's literary circle also includes dramatist Oskar Baum, existentialist and influential Jewish thinker Martin Buber, and philosopher Felix Weltsch.

1903   Thomas Mann publishes *Tonio Kröger*, a favorite of Kafka's.

1904   Kafka begins writing the surreal story "Description of a Struggle," his earliest surviving work.

1906   Kafka receives a doctorate in law from German-speaking Karl Ferdinand University.

1907   Kafka begins writing "Wedding Preparations in the Country," a novel that he will abandon but that contains the germ of "The Metamorphosis"; both involve the transformation of a human character into a lowly, despised creature.

1908   Shunning the practice of law, Kafka secures a position at the semi-governmental Workmen's Accident Insurance Administration, where he works until his retirement in 1922.

1910   Kafka begins to keep a regular diary, a decision that lends discipline and seriousness to his writing. The performances of a Yiddish theater group from Poland captivate and inspire him; he later adopts a dramatic structure for "The Metamorphosis," dividing it into three parts, like acts of a play.

1911   By night Kafka does his own writing, and by day he compiles insurance manuals and policies. He develops a friendship with Yiddish actor Isak Löwy; Kafka's father, without knowing Löwy, compares him to vermin, a metaphor that features heavily in Kafka's fiction, especially "The Metamorphosis." Hitherto indifferent to his parents' religion, Kafka studies Jewish folklore and becomes fascinated by his Jewish heritage, an appreciation that will increase throughout his life. Gustav Mahler's Ninth Symphony, *Das Lied von der Erde* (The Song of the Earth), is performed for the first time.

1912   Kafka meets Felice Bauer, from Berlin, when she visits

Max Brod's family. An extensive correspondence ensues, in which Kafka attempts to at once woo Felice and keep her at arm's length. He feverishly composes "The Judgment" in a single September night; of all his literary accomplishments, Kafka finds this the most satisfying. Soon after, Kafka completes "The Stoker," the story of a young German immigrant that later becomes the first chapter of his novel *Amerika*, and "The Metamorphosis," his tale of a man literally and symbolically transformed into an insect. Thomas Mann publishes *Death in Venice*.

1913   "The Judgment" and "The Stoker" are published. The second Balkan War begins. Kafka meets Felice's friend Grete Bloch, with whom he corresponds, writing mostly about Felice.

1914   Franz and Felice are engaged, but within a month the engagement is broken. Archduke Ferdinand is assassinated at Sarajevo, setting in motion events that culminate in World War I. After a two-year period of creative sterility, Kafka writes the parable "In the Penal Colony," followed by "Before the Law," a sketch from his novel in progress, *The Trial*.

1915   "The Metamorphosis" is published. Kafka receives the prestigious Fontane Prize for "The Stoker."

1916   He writes a series of stories that will be collected and published in the volume *A Country Doctor* (1919).

1917   Kafka begins learning Hebrew. He becomes engaged to Felice Bauer a second time; diagnosed with tuberculosis, he ends the relationship. Kafka takes a leave of absence from his job, and his diary entries cease. The Balfour Declaration approves the establishment of a Jewish national state in Palestine.

1918   Kafka studies the metaphysical writings of Johann Wolfgang von Goethe, Søren Kierkegaard, Arthur Schopenhauer, and Leo Tolstoy, and continues his exploration of the Old Testament and Jewish folklore. He writes aphorisms based in part of these studies.

1919   *A Country Doctor* is published, as is "In the Penal Colony." In the wake of the Treaty of Versailles, the Nazi party is founded in Germany, as is the Fascist party in Italy. Kafka becomes engaged to Julie Wohryzek, the daughter of a worker in a synagogue. Kafka's father objects on social grounds and convinces Kafka to break the engagement. This action, more than any other, precipitates Kafka's most autobiographical work, "Letter to His Father."

1920   Kafka meets the Czech writer Milena Jesenská-Pollak, with whom he becomes romantically involved. Milena translates several of Kafka's works into Czech. She ends the affair in August.

1921   Kafka starts writing the stories that will be collected in the volume *A Hunger Artist* (1924), centered on the difficulties an artist faces in coming to terms with human society. While seeking to restore his health at the Tatra Mountains sanatorium, Kafka meets Hungarian medical student Robert Klopstock, who becomes his friend and physician.

1922   The insurance agency grants Kafka's request for early retirement.

1923   Kafka meets Dora Diamant, a Jewish socialist twenty years his junior. He moves to Berlin with her, hoping to devote himself fully to writing. Kafka asks Dora's father for her hand in marriage but is rejected based on a rabbi's counsel, perhaps because of his deteriorating health.

1924   *A Hunger Artist* is published. Kafka's rapidly declining health and his lack of money force him to return to living with his parents, a humiliating experience for him. He dies on June 3 in an advanced stage of tuberculosis of the throat in a sanatorium in Kierling, near Vienna. His last words to Robert Klopstock are "Kill me, or you are a murderer." Before his death, Kafka asks Max Brod to destroy all of his unpublished manuscripts.

1925   Disregarding Kafka's request, Brod begins publishing his friend's work, starting with the first of Kafka's three unfinished novels, *The Trial*.

1926   Brod publishes *The Castle*, an account of the futile efforts of a man to be recognized by the authorities.

1927   Max Brod publishes *Amerika*, an immigrant's adventures in a baffling new country.

1933   The Nazis ban Kafka's work and hold public burnings of his books.

1940   Grete Bloch, who had met Kafka in 1913, claims to be the mother of his child, a boy who died at age six and about whom Kafka had known nothing.

1942 The Nazis remove Franz Kafka's sisters Elli and Valli and their husbands to the Lodz ghetto in Poland, where they die.

1943 Kafka's sister Ottla, because of her marriage to an "Aryan," is exempt from Nazi deportation. Disdaining the preferential treatment, she divorces her husband and chooses to be led away; she ultimately is taken to the concentration camp in Auschwitz, where she dies.

1944 Grete Bloch is beaten to death by a Nazi soldier. Milena Jesenská-Pollak dies at the women's concentration camp at Ravensbrück, in Germany.

1952 Dora Diamant dies in London.

1960 Felice Bauer dies in America.

INTRODUCTION

FRANZ KAFKA'S FICTION DOESN'T make sense. Kafka was no doubt aware of the resulting awkwardness, and perhaps he hoped to hide from future readers when he asked his confidant Max Brod to destroy all his unpublished manuscripts upon his death. Kafka's writing is on the one hand specific and realistic, and on the other incomprehensible. His literary puzzles resemble the unreal landscapes and structures of M. C. Escher's drawings and lithographs. Actually, Escher's imagery offers a useful way to visualize Kafka's literature. As if leading the reader up and down endless staircases of logic, Kafka focuses on multiple dualities at once, all of which crisscross in three dimensions. Rather than a linear argument, Kafka writes a spiral one, which often makes readers dizzy, if not seasick. Interestingly, metamorphosis was one of Escher's favorite subjects, and three of his most famous woodcuts share this title with Kafka's novella. Metamorphosis, Anthony Thorlby argues, is the theme implicit in all Kafka's prose ("Kafka's Narrative: A Matter of Form"; see "For Further Reading"). Kafka's content is somehow incongruous with his form, and as a result, the language must either undergo a metamorphosis itself to accommodate his pen, or perish—and sometimes it does both. At its best, Kafka's prose is re-formed into a new mode of signification; at its worst, his words are deformed, depleted, meaningless. In striving to fit his impossible situations into the feeble vehicle of language, Kafka knowingly embarks on a failed enterprise. He attempts to express the inexpressible.

The metamorphosis of his writing, Kafka's real accomplishment, takes readers to a place at once familiar and unfamiliar. Intrigued by this immediacy, critics have celebrated Kafka for his "universality." This flattery overreaches perhaps, but the term "universal" was not picked by accident. Kafka's fiction examines a universe largely unexplored in the literature preceding him, one full of implications that venture into the remote regions of human psychology. It's a universe with different rules than those governing our reality. And there's no map.

But Kafka's universe nonetheless resonates deeply with who we are and who we've become. Early readers who hailed Kafka's universality had never seen their lives in books, and they had only dimly recognized the "Kafkaesque" as an unnamed thing. Kafka was among the first to describe bourgeois labor and its degrading impact on the soul. In his fable "Poseidon," Kafka even portrays the god of the sea as consumed with tedious, never-ending paperwork. Kafka brings to mind a vocabulary of images— an endless trail of meaningless forms to be filled out, a death apparatus to rival Poe's pendulum, a man wearing a bowler hat, a gigantic insect. Thanks to interpretations like Orson Welles's film version of *The Trial*, Kafka's universe has expanded to include rows of office desks, oppressive light, and snapping typewriters. Kafka understood the trajectory of bureaucracy, and his literature predicts the nightmarish corporate world we live in today.

Kafka's fiction, though concrete in its particulars, suggests an array of interpretive possibilities. "The Metamorphosis" alone has inspired Catholics to argue a case of transubstantiation, Freudians to extrapolate Gregor's castration by his father, and Marxists to infer the alienation of man in modern society. Kafka's descriptions vacillate between realism and allegory—a narrative style best described as parabolic. But unlike a traditional parable with an easy moral, Kafka's parables resist successful comprehension.

This volume has as its parentheses Kafka's two best-known parables, "A Message from the Emperor" and "Before the Law." They both illustrate Kafka's near-nauseating ability to describe infinite regress. "A Message from the Emperor" checks any firm interpretation with its simple but devastating phrase "or so they say" (p. 3) in the opening line, which calls into question the tale's validity, as if the account is rumored. Additionally, the "you," the second person, has dreamed the whole thing up (p. 3). This second piece of information not only contradicts the first, it turns the parable on its head—why would someone, especially "you," which seems to refer to the reader, dream up something so unnecessarily complicated, especially when it concerns something as momentous as an emperor's message? This "you" can stand for Kafka himself—a writer who saw an infinite corkscrew of obstacles spiraling before him, and yet felt compelled to record his own deliberate steps. "Before the Law" also features an Inferno-like layering and again pits an unsophisticated character against an implacable system, unknowable in its complexity. Though the man from the country never recognizes it, his defeat by the Law, capital L, is a foregone conclusion. The Law's only purpose is to shut out the man and, in so doing, to destroy him.

Kafka's parables are epitomes of his larger works ("Before the Law," though published first on its own, is actually part of *The Trial*). Their shortness only concentrates the reader's perplexity. Robert Wenniger claims that Kafka's father engendered in Kafka a disparity between language and meaning. In fact, silence was Kafka's typical response to his father. By writing incomprehensible texts, Wenniger argues, Kafka assumes the role of the father, an authorial position over the reader (Wenniger, "Sounding Out the Silence of Gregor Samsa: Kafka's Rhetoric of Dyscommunication"). This leaves the reader confused and vainly searching for meaning. Of course, Kafka shares this privilege with many of the world's great writers, whose work is often a challenge to interpret. In "On Parables" Kafka writes, "Parables really set out to say merely that the incomprehensible is incomprehensible, and we know that already" (*The Complete Stories*, 1971, p. 457).

In Kafka's formulation, the parable is used by the sage to gesture toward something larger than, or invisible to, himself. The need to make this gesture is innate. But the parable dissolves the moment we understand it; the gesture would not be beyond language if it could be defined. We *lose in parable* the moment we pin things down to an accessible meaning. Realizing it is impossible to discuss or interpret Kafka without losing in parable is the first and perhaps only step we can take.

Kafka's parables not only fall apart once we interpret them, they are impossible to put into practice. If anything, his parables guarantee the failure not only of his characters, but of readers wishing to abstract any lessons applicable to their own lives. Failure, it seems, is Kafka's true subject. To get at this conundrum, we must explore discretely the dichotomies Kafka himself conflates—dreams versus reality, idleness versus work, vermin versus human, child versus adult. For Kafka, each of these antagonistic pairs represents an authorial relationship. It is possible to lump the lowly—dreams, idleness, vermin, child—on one side, and the authority figures—reality, work, human, adult—on the other. But ultimately this equation is too simple, for Kafka himself fails to pick a side. He calls both sides into question and finds them equally detestable. Unbraiding Kafka's authorial relationships is the only way to find out why.

Dreams—and, perhaps more importantly, nightmares—held a singular influence over Kafka and his writing. Kafka's nightmares are so natural, so convincing, that they creep into the reader's mind almost subliminally. He metamorphoses reality into a new, insidiously darker one, often within a single sentence. In "The Judgment," Georg's father throws at him an old, unfamiliar newspaper (p. 64), an actual object that evidences a deception, staggering in its elaborateness—Georg's father has been feigning his infirmity, only pretending to read his newspapers, for years! In "The Metamorphosis," Kafka speeds time ticklessly: "It was half past six and the hands were steadily advancing, actually past the half hour and already closer to three quarters past" (p. 8). Later, the head clerk arrives at the Samsa flat to investigate Gregor's tardiness, *at the moment of his tardiness*. Even if Gregor's absence from work was judged grave enough to send the head clerk himself, the event remains absurd. Somehow, the head clerk would have had to foresee Gregor's lateness and taken an early train to show up at the flat just minutes after Gregor should have been at his office desk.

In "A Country Doctor," the sudden, ominous appearance of the groom is punctuated by his mysterious knowledge of the maid's name and his tacit intent to ravish her. Following this, the doctor is whisked away in his newly harnessed trap, as if beyond his control, completely unable to assist his maid, who locks herself in the house: "I hear my front door splinter and burst as the groom attacks it, and then my eyes and ears are swamped with a blinding rush of the senses. But even this lasts only a moment, for, as if my patient's courtyard opens just outside my gate, I am already there" (p. 124). The ten-mile distance between the doctor's village and his patient's house, the reality that precipitated the need for strong horses in the first place, evaporates.

Nightmare-turned-reality is the power of "The Metamorphosis." Gregor Samsa is a different animal, a unique figure even among canonical supernatural tales. Without the permanence of

Gregor's monstrous form, we would be left with something like the absurd comedy of Gogol's "The Nose," in which Kovalyov's nose leaves his face to prance about the town disguised as a state councillor but in the end returns to its proper place unchanged. Without Gregor's inimitable subjectivity, we would be left essentially with the horror of Oscar Wilde's *The Picture of Dorian Gray*, in which the painting of Dorian becomes monstrous while Dorian himself remains ageless, until the fey moment when the two destroy each other, leaving only a moral behind.

Instead, we arrive at a story that cannot claim the supernatural as one of its elements. The mystery of "The Metamorphosis" emerges in one of the most famous, and most variously translated, lines in Western literature—its first: "As Gregor Samsa awoke from unsettling dreams one morning, he found himself transformed in his bed into a monstrous vermin" (p. 7). This is marvelously funny. Instead of waking up from a nightmare, Gregor wakes up into one. Reality, the only balm for bad dreams, is significantly less reassuring when you wake up hideously disfigured. But in Kafka's fiction, the rational and the irrational intertwine menacingly. Often these irrational elements spring from the minds of his characters and manifest themselves physically. Ideas are metamorphosed into reality, with little effort on the characters' parts. Here Gregor's idea, originating in his "unsettling dreams," has followed him into the real world. The echo and confirmation of this reality comes in the second paragraph: "It was no dream" (p. 7). Unlike Lewis Carroll's Alice, who, after transforming several times, wakes up, Gregor's most bizarre adventure is real, and has only just begun.

Kafka treats the bed, representative of both illness and idleness, as the birthplace of these irrational ideas. The first sentence introduces Gregor not only in his nightmarish form but also ensnared in his bed, as if caught in the grips of tangling irrationality. Gregor spends most of the first section of "The Metamorphosis" trying to extricate himself from his bed: "in bed he could never think anything through to a reasonable conclusion" (p. 9). In viewing the chaos of his legs waving in the air, Gregor tells himself "that he could not possibly stay in bed and that the logical recourse was to risk everything in the mere hope of freeing himself from the bed" (p. 10). By escaping, he hopes to shut out the irrationality of his new form and return to his old self. We learn that Gregor was unrelentingly reasonable as a human; the head clerk booms through the door, "I have always known you to be a quiet, reasonable man and now you suddenly seem to be indulging in rash eccentricities" (p. 14). For a brief second, Gregor even entertains simply sleeping it off (p. 7) or resting in bed in hope of a cure (p. 10). Here he employs a reverse logic, an irrational hope that the bed will magically restore his "unquestionable state" (p. 11). It does not. In fact, Gregor's human form isn't restored once he's free from bed either. But his irrational belief that it would be was itself generated in the bed. This divides Kafka's universe into the irrational—dreams, notions deriving from the bed—and the rational—reality, working, family. The surreality of Kafka's fiction consists in his constant traffic between these two realms.

In Kafka's story "Wedding Preparations in the Country," Eduard Raban fantasizes about splitting into two forms: one, to remain in bed all day, dreaming; the other, to go forth and conduct the business of the world. Interestingly, Raban envisions the "bed" form as a large beetle, the worldly self as the shell of his human form. Raban thinks to himself,

> I would pretend it was a matter of hibernating, and I would press my little legs to my bulging belly. And I would whisper a few words, instructions to my sad [human] body, which stands close beside me, bent. Soon I shall have done—it bows, it goes swiftly, and it will manage everything efficiently while I rest (*Complete Stories*, p. 56).

Kafka differentiates the two tales by treating Raban's splitting as "pretend," and Gregor's transformation as real. But in truth, Gregor invents his transmutation just as Raban invents his. The metamorphosis does not happen *to* Gregor. It's something he consciously—or perhaps more aptly, subconsciously—wills upon himself. Gregor thinks of himself as "condemned to serve" (p. 11), as trapped. When Gregor makes his first appearance before his family in his changed form, he reveals his total willingness to give up his job: "If they were shocked, then Gregor was no longer responsible" (p. 15). This passage betrays Gregor's premeditation and points to the idea that Gregor *wanted* to change into a monstrous vermin—something incapable of working in an office. While not consciously desirous of his new form, he's sentient of his situation and very much in control. Of course, in attempting to shirk his responsibilities and escape the confines of the office, the lonely hotel rooms, and his family's flat, Gregor confines himself even further; his room becomes his sole domain, and eventually even it metamorphoses into a storage closet.

Kafka's metaphor of a man's transformation into vermin is unique not only because the change comes from the man himself, but also because it critiques modernity and the impossibility of living functionally within it. In this sense "The Metamorphosis" stands as one of the greatest indictments against work ever written. Gregor's impetus to transform reflects the illogicality of working life, the impossibility of sustaining a work ethic. After the novella's fantastic first sentence, Gregor searches for clues that might explain his newfound condition. After ignoring the overwhelming evidence of his new body after the briefest of perusals, Gregor looks about his room. Out his window, he perceives dreary weather, which causes him to feel "quite melancholy" (p. 7). It is typical Kafka for a man, who has most recently discovered he occupies the form of a monstrous vermin, to feel saddened by the weather. But this melancholic whim extends beyond Kafka's humor and points to Gregor's chronic dread of mornings. It's a prelude to his vitriolic damnation of working life:

> "Oh God," he thought, "what a grueling profession I picked! Traveling day in, day out. It is much more aggravating work than the actual business done at the home office, and then with the strain of constant travel as well: the worry over train connections, the bad and irregular meals, the steady stream of faces who never become anything closer than acquaintances. The Devil take it all!" (pp. 7–8).

Gregor does not mince words: grueling, aggravating, strain, worry, bad—all followed by an imprecation. Deeper still, the diatribe is prompted by a "faint, dull ache" (p. 7) in his side. How telling that Gregor, who has so recently lost his familiar, human form, should notice an ache and immediately think of his job. Whether this pain merely reminds him of the rigors of labor or is a soreness actually caused by it, Gregor innately associates work with pain.

The ritualized actions listed in Gregor's exclamatory account of his job give the impression of a thoroughly regimented lifestyle. Because we never know Gregor in his human form, we have to piece him together after the fact. It seems Gregor's human self was like most of us at some point or another—weak, afraid, submissive to corporate and familial pressures. He lacks the space for creativity, and even irrationality. Immediately upon his awakening, Gregor's gaze falls upon the illustration of a woman that hangs in a frame he carved with his fretsaw. The pride and enthusiasm he has for his gilt frame is evident, and it resurfaces when he protects it from his sister and mother (p. 33) in their unwitting attempt to strip away the only proof that Gregor was once human. The picture represents Gregor's single creation—or in Marxist terms, the one product he is allowed to keep. For Gregor, work precludes the possibility of creation; in the life of a traveling salesman, the gilt frame is the exception rather than the rule.

But why go to the trouble of changing into a monstrous vermin? Why didn't Gregor just quit his job? For Gregor this was impossible: "If I were not holding back because of my parents, I would have quit long ago" (p. 8). A loyal and loving son, Gregor feels obligated to pay off his parents' debt. Simply quitting would betray that loyalty. After his transformation, Gregor overhears his family discuss their bleak financial situation and feels "flushed with shame and grief" (p. 27). He despairs of the prospect of any one of his family members, especially his sister Grete, working to make ends meet. Gregor blames himself for spoiling the quiet life he had previously provided for them. He knows firsthand the impersonality, the lifelessness of modern labor, and he shudders at the thought of his family experiencing it.

The family members do indeed get jobs, and as they do so, they complete the reversal of Gregor's metamorphosis. The transformation of Gregor into vermin, and his resulting abdication of the breadwinner role, forces the Samsa family to transform *from* vermin. The family members, who have lived parasitically off Gregor, change into tired, silent, and empty people who more and more resemble the pre-insect Gregor. They must work even when they are at home to accommodate their three boarders, and thus they degrade into obsequious servants. Eventually the sister is resolute in her decision that Gregor must be gotten rid of: "We all work too hard to come home to this interminable torture" (p. 46). Here, because the family's day is filled with the torment of working, the additional strain of Gregor becomes unbearable. Their inability to disengage from work in the evening deprives them of the only possible respite from labor, and life without some kind of rest is torture. The worst irony is that taking care of the verminous Gregor is a filthy chore. Gregor, by escaping work, has not only forced his former dependents into labor, but has *become* work: disgusting work that only his disgraced family can perform.

Kafka returns again and again to the idea of vermin—the revolting nomads who communicate like birds in "An Old Leaf," the dehumanized, emaciated hunger artist, the strange mouse people, among whom even Josephine barely distinguishes herself, and the man from the country in "Before the Law," who by the end holds the fleas in the doorkeeper's fur collar above himself. Max Brod actually refers to "The Metamorphosis" as Kafka's "vermin story" (*Franz Kafka: A Biography*, 1960, p. 18). Additionally, Kafka regularly inserts *himself* in his fiction, giving his characters names like K. Some critics have even connected the two short *as* of Samsa with the identical vowel construction of Kafka. Vermin is in the eye of the beholder, and Kafka clearly sees a self-resemblance.

For Kafka, thinking about vermin was a way to understand the universe, and his own place in it. "A Message from the Emperor" begins by describing "you" as the emperor's "single most contemptible subject, the minuscule shadow that has fled the farthest distance from the imperial sun" (p. 3). The "you" lives in shadow like a rat or a cockroach. Further, this shadow darkens against the authorial source of light, "the imperial sun." The lowliness of vermin is created by a hierarchy, at the top of which is an amorphous, omnipotent authority. Kafka's short parable "The Emperor" echoes this idea: "When a surf flings a drop of water on to the land, that does not interfere with the eternal rolling of the sea, on the contrary, it is caused by it" (*The Basic Kafka*, 1979, p. 183). Interestingly, Kafka again chooses a laborer to play the role of vermin.

In Kafka's universe authority and vermin are natural enemies, and each gives rise to the other. In "Letter to His Father," Kafka addresses himself in the voice of his father, Hermann:

> There are two kinds of combat. The chivalrous combat, in which independent opponents pit their strength against each other, each on his own, each losing on his own, each winning on his own. And there is the combat of vermin, which not only sting but, on top of it, suck your blood in order to sustain their own life (*Dearest Father*, p. 195).

Herr Kafka represented the ultimate figure of authority for Franz, who here accuses himself of operating on the level of vermin. Moreover, this passage lashes out against the inequality intrinsic to an authorial relationship. Kafka's suspicion of authority governs every word he writes. Throughout his life Kafka committed himself to many things—intellectualism, vegetarianism, teetotaling, Judaism, a string of women—but his subscription to each of these was never total. Once Kafka came to regard any philosophy as nothing more than a system of rules to be enforced, a dogma both bigger and smaller than himself, he withdrew from it.

In Kafka's story "A Report to an Academy," the narrator, who five years previous had occupied the form of an ape, has been transformed into a human. In this tale it is difficult to draw a black line between the narrator's two selves; the differences are subtle. The narrator's tone implies that his gradual transformation from an ape into a human represents an improvement. But Kafka questions this authorial status of humans. Driven by the desire to escape his cage, the ape observes his observers; the narrator writes, "it was so easy to imitate these people" (*Complete Stories*, p. 255). Thus Kafka diffuses the differences between animals and humans. In so doing, he extends the reader's natural sympathy for human characters to include vermin, and applies the reader's natural aversion to vermin to humans instead. In Kafka's fiction, it is possible for humans and vermin to function as mutual metaphors, and though the dichotomy between vermin and human remains, it becomes increasingly difficult to choose a side.

Gregor Samsa plays host to the conflict between vermin and human in that he does not disown his mind as he does his body. Throughout the novella, he retains his human consciousness, memory, and ability to understand human speech and intentions. Because of his residual human perception, Gregor never sees his armor-plated form as even *potentially* liberating; instead his inhabitation of an insect's body is tortured and guilt-ridden. Wilhelm Emrich argues that the impersonal nature of modern life prevents Gregor from recognizing the freedom of his "prehuman" form (commentary in *The Metamorphosis*, Bantam edition, 1972). Instead Gregor views it as monstrous, alien, and other. During Gregor's initial reconnaissance of his room, he seeks solace from his former humanity; his gaze falls upon his work samples, his desk, his gilt frame. He all but ignores his new, unsightly form. Gregor hungers obsessively for the explainable; his absolute need to hurry off to work represents a severe form of denial, itself a human tendency: "What if I went back to sleep for a while and forgot all this foolishness" (p. 7). He courts rationality out of an obligation to his former self. But his feigned, humanlike demonstrations are silly: trying to stand upright, speaking to his parents and the head clerk, returning to work.

Upon seeing his unpacked samples, Gregor admits to himself that he does not feel "particularly fresh and energetic" (p. 8), an absurd notion for a man-size insect to ponder. He presumes the change in his voice to be caused by a severe cold, "an ailment common among traveling salesmen" (p. 10). But Kafka does not let Gregor off so easily. By positioning the head clerk at the bedroom door, Kafka keeps the reader from believing in Gregor's self-delusion. Upon hearing Gregor speak, the head clerk says, "That was the voice of an animal" (p. 15). Gregor's metamorphosis is real, and his efforts to deny it are frail.

In "Wedding Preparations" by contrast, Raban dreams of frittering away his days in bed. His weightless disposition comes from his ability to indulge in his irrational side. The pre-vermin Gregor would have considered such an activity frivolous. Before his transformation, Gregor never gave in to distractions other than fretsawing. He stayed home each night and busied himself constantly, "reading the paper or studying train schedules" (p. 12). Kafka himself worked at the same job all his life. At his office, he wrote tracts such as "On Mandatory Insurance in the Construction Industry" and "Workers' Accident Insurance and Management." In the evenings Kafka remained cloistered in his room, where he worked on his various manuscripts. By contrast,

Gregor has no such dedication; he's learned to suppress his personality, to submit unconditionally to authority. As the head clerk has it, Gregor's reasonableness derives from not indulging in "rash eccentricities" (p. 14). In fact, Gregor champions himself for his impersonal habit of locking the doors at night (p. 9). For Kafka, an oppressive rationality and the human experience, at least within the modern bourgeois value system, are synonymous. Gregor, who is fluent only in rationality and is loyal to the human social ideal, is tortured by his insectival state.

Consequently, Gregor fails to see that he's capable of conscious irrationality. The metamorphosis seems a mistake, a wrong turn, a trap out of which the only escape is death. Walter Sokel goes so far as to say that Gregor's true form *is* death (commentary in *The Metamorphosis*, Bantam edition, 1972). Perhaps in this light Gregor's insect form represents a slow death, a chronic, fatal illness. Kafka saw his tuberculosis as a liberation; interestingly, he called it "the animal." Further, Kafka found his passages on death to be his most compelling pieces of writing. But "The Metamorphosis" is more than a tale of suicide. For if Gregor is ultimately dead in the first sentence, what is the point of reading further? There must be a glint of hope for his salvation—and there is. If Gregor is capable of turning himself into a monstrous vermin, then he can change back. He just doesn't want to.

It is guilt—that most revolting of all human sentiments—that prevents Gregor from embracing his insect form. Out of guilt, Gregor chooses not to relinquish his role of family provider. Though he laments his obligation, he never gives it up. In the final section, Gregor considers "the idea that the next time the door opened he would take control of the family affairs as he had done in the past" (p. 39). Rather than the absurdity of Gregor's earlier denials, here Kafka focuses on Gregor's ability to puzzle out his situation. There is an implied agency, as if Gregor truly possesses the ability to snap out of his state and return to his old self. Whatever his decision, he can't help but fail. His escape is ultimately doomed by his utter devotion to his family, which never diminishes. The guilt brought on by Gregor's newfound inability to provide for his family—financially and emotionally—prevents him from attaining any sort of liberation. Perhaps recognizing this conundrum, Gregor chooses to remain an insect.

Though both conditions are unlivable, he prefers vermin life to human; it's the lesser of two tortures.

Kafka's story "The Burrow" concerns a character who inhabits the space *between* human and vermin. Though the narrator differentiates himself from the "field mice" (*Complete Stories*, p. 326) and "all sorts of small fry" (*Complete Stories*, p. 327) that occupy his burrow, he uses his unspecified but presumably human body in an animal fashion. He pounds the tunnel walls firm with his forehead (*Complete Stories*, p. 328); he fights and kills rats with his jaws (*Complete Stories*, p. 329). Yet the burrow itself, which the narrator dubs "Castle Keep," is the result of deliberate, extensive planning and constant maintenance. Further, the burrow's effectiveness and impregnability inspire the narrator's dreams: "tears of joy and deliverance still glisten on my beard when I awaken" (*Complete Stories*, p. 333).

The logic that gives rise to Castle Keep is one twisted by absolute isolation. It is the logic of both fantasy and ignorance, a child's uninformed rationale. In fact, the burrow is much like a child's fort—but one inhabited by someone driven insane with fear. The narrator's incessant calculations and preparations become increasingly insular, until his mind is saturated with a baseless paranoia. This compulsively cogitative yet ultimately ignorant perspective is much like the psychology of Dostoevsky's underground man. By the end of "The Burrow" the narrator's mind no longer resembles human consciousness at all, but instead a fight-or-flight, animal mentality.

The rift between child and adult roles is at the heart of "The Metamorphosis." Gregor, like the narrator of "The Burrow," possesses the mentality of a child. In Kafka's universe the child is the least authorial figure, and therefore can be likened to vermin. It is natural for Gregor's parents and the head clerk to speak to Gregor condescendingly through the door. It's almost as if they regard Gregor as throwing a childish fit. Later, the family, led ferociously by the father, forces Gregor into his room like a naughty child. And Gregor, for his part, has no interest in adult matters. He loathes his profession. He has no intention of finding a companion; the only woman in his life, besides his sister and mother, is the pin-up girl in the gilt frame. When Gregor looks around his room, Kafka, again with excruciating humor, describes it as "a regular human bedroom" (p. 7)—as if Gregor's room would be decorated to the tastes of a monstrous vermin. But the precise phrase in the original German, *kleines Menschenzimmer*, implies that it resembles a child's room.

Gregor, like Georg Bendemann of "The Judgment," is typified by his familial relationships. (The other "son," Karl Rossmann of "The Stoker," differs because we meet him on his trip to America—he's on his own.) Both Gregor and Georg are confined to their parents' homes as adults. Adult children regularly slip into childhood roles when visiting their parents. But for Kafka's characters, this stunting is not temporary. Kafka himself lived with his parents until a year before his death, and right before he died he was forced to return because of his tuberculosis. Living for so long in proximity to his parents made Kafka feel like a child—the same child he was prior to his physical and literary development. These developments vanished before his parents, who remained relatively unchanged—they even outlived him!—and whose authorial position over him was total. Walter Benjamin once described a photograph of Kafka in which Kafka's "immensely sad eyes dominate the landscape" ("Franz Kafka: On the Tenth Anniversary of His Death"). Thomas Mann wrote about Kafka in much the same way—painting a man with "large dark eyes, at once dreamy and penetrating" and an "expression at once childlike and wise" (commentary in *The Castle: The Definitive Edition*). The only difference is that Mann was talking about Kafka's final portrait, and Benjamin was looking at a picture of Franz taken when he was six years old. Kafka never grew up.

Kafka's suffocation as an adult child leaves its trace on Gregor and Georg, who each suffers a child's frustration at having no say, yet finds himself in a caretaker's role fraught with responsibility and guilt. Each is sentenced to death by his parents. Gregor's devotion to his parents and his sister forces him to interpret the family's grievances as a condemnation, whereas Georg's judgment is about as direct as you can get. And, hauntingly, Gregor and Georg each carries out his own sentence. The adult child—another of Kafka's fusions of different states—is little prepared for the world. Even Eduard Raban's fantasy of splitting into two selves in "Wedding Preparations" is a child's attempt at evasion: "Can't I do it the way I always used to as a child in matters that were dangerous?" (*Complete Stories*, p. 55). The answer to Raban's question is no. Kafka's characters, regardless of how much agency they possess, are doomed to fail. As Kafka writes in "A Message from the Emperor," the messenger's arrival "could never, ever happen" (p. 3).

If we think of Gregor as having a child's mentality, it is natural to sympathize with him—especially if we see him as trapped in the role of family provider. This sympathy is not altogether different from what we feel toward Dickens's Oliver Twist, that supreme victim of child labor. Yet this sympathy does not hold, for it is always followed by a repulsion toward Gregor's physicality: "A brown fluid had come from his mouth, oozed over the key, and dripped onto the floor" (p. 16). Kafka further complicates matters by writing "The Metamorphosis" in the third person. This mode of narration allows for Gregor's death at the end, which confirms definitively that the metamorphosis was not a hallucination or a dream. But though the narrative follows Gregor's awareness, we always have enough room to reevaluate how we feel about him.

Some of our sympathy falls to the sister, and even to the feeble parents—none of whom are fit to work. But ultimately we remain loyal to Gregor, especially because his family forsakes him. His sister stops tending to him (p. 40) and locks him in his room (p. 48); his mother faints upon seeing an enormous insect clinging to the wall (p. 33); the father, in brief, subjects him to every abuse imaginable. At the expense of Gregor's sacrifice, the sister, at the end of the story, stretches her arrogant body and gets the liberation Gregor longed for. Under Gregor's care first, and then her parents', the sister enjoys a healthy childhood, one leading to physical and mental development, and one in which she isn't trapped. Yet our loyalty to Gregor extends even beyond his death, and his sister's cheery success story offers but a bitter pill.

In the pivotal scene of "The Metamorphosis," Gregor's sister begins to play her violin. Listening to her music, Gregor "felt as though the path to his unknown hungers was being cleared" (p. 44). We have no indication that Gregor Samsa enjoyed music while he was human; his intention to send his sister to the Conservatory was to him a financial endeavor, an investment in her future. Yet to be moved by music is essentially human; it reflects sensitivity. The life Gregor led as a human being left no room for this kind of appreciation. But, by regressing into an animal, his sensibility has become refined rather than coarsened. As vermin he comes closer to a spiritual liberation, of which human beings at their best are capable. Perhaps in death Gregor attains salvation, the ultimate metamorphosis. But regardless, he's started down that path in life, through humility and contemplation. The Samsa family, which does not comprehend this less visual transformation in Gregor, interrupts it. Instead of liberation Gregor attains only confinement—both spatial and metaphysical.

In "The Metamorphosis" the physical transformation, rather than its dénouement, is merely a premise. By contrast, Ovid's classic, *Metamorphoses*, focuses on the process and novelty of transformation. Ovid consistently establishes an explicit causal, if not moral, relationship between a character's actions and the consequence of metamorphosis. In the tale of Arachne, another story of a human transformed into a bug, haughty Arachne refuses to admit that her spinning skills derive from any teacher or divine source. The spinster goes so far as to challenge Minerva (the Roman correlate of the Greek goddess Athena) to a spinning contest. After Arachne defeats Minerva, the latter strikes her with a wooden shuttle—an action much like a spanking or a public caning. Out of despair Arachne tries to hang herself, but Minerva simultaneously spares and punishes the weaver by changing her into a spider.

This metamorphosis is not mysterious. Arachne's transformation is the direct result of Minerva's anger, caused by Arachne's own impudence. For Ovid, Minerva and the rest of the deities represent the highest authority; the gods are not to be challenged or regarded as equals. Even though Minerva is defeated, her authority is absolute. As Arachne attempts suicide—again, to make the final transformation—her agency is stripped by Minerva, who has other transformative plans in mind.

It is easy to decipher the story of Arachne, whether you take her side or Minerva's, but Kafka's moral, if there is one, is not obvious or logical. The abandonment a reader feels at the end of any text is especially acute with Kafka. The few clues he leaves us are not only incomplete, they are contradictory. Kafka is notoriously incapable of completion. His three novels—*The Trial*, *The Castle*, and *Amerika*, all of them unfinished—were assembled by Max Brod, whom we have to thank for exhuming a Franz Kafka who seems to come very close, one might guess, to saying what he means. But whenever Kafka reached so deeply within himself—whether in the guise of Joseph K., simply K., or Karl Rossmann—he eventually abandoned the work. His one pride was the torrential composition of "The Judgment," which he wrote in a single night. Perhaps any project that took more than eight hours to finish lost its luster; perhaps an "opening out of the body and the soul" (*Diaries, 1910–1913*, p. 276) was too painful for an extended period; and perhaps this explains why Kafka went years at a time without writing a word of fiction.

Kafka regarded the end of "The Metamorphosis"—its composition interrupted by a business trip—as "unreadable." He also wrote in his diary that he found it "bad," but of course Kafka relished his failure. Failure is precisely what he expected and resolved to accomplish—and he hid behind it. Kafka's literature has no end, no borders like those that frame Escher's artworks. He does not write in black and white. And unlike Escher, Kafka was unable to manage the subject of liberation with any success. Yet it is "The Metamorphosis," and not necessarily "The Judgment," that is remembered by readers and that will be taught in schools forever. Kafka, it seems, is at his best when he fails.

His failure puts the burden of meaning on readers. We must reconstruct Kafka, as we do Gregor Samsa. That is what critics have been trying to do for generations—indeed, Kafka's reputation wasn't made until after his death. He is locked in time and cannot be questioned. In the end, Kafka and his fiction are inextricable. The only way out is to metamorphose Kafka into something we can parse. We have to insinuate ourselves into his universe, his allegory. Only in this way can we see our own reality for the puzzle it is. As the disconnect between author and reader dissolves, Kafka's language becomes a metaphor for the greater disconnection between ourselves and our environment. Though we lose in parable, perhaps in reading Kafka we can finish what he himself could not complete and, in so doing, nourish our own unknown hungers.

Jason Baker is a writer of short stories living in Brooklyn, New York.

*A Message from the Emperor**

*Originally published in 1919 under the German title "Eine kaiserliche Botschaft."

THE EMPEROR, OR SO they say, has sent you—his single most contemptible subject, the minuscule shadow that has fled the farthest distance from the imperial sun—only to you has the Emperor sent a message from his deathbed. He has had the messenger kneel beside his bed and he has whispered the message to him; so important was this message that he has made him repeat it in his ear. He has confirmed the accuracy of the words with a nod of his head. And then, before all the spectators assembled to witness his death—every wall obstructing the view had been knocked down and on the free-standing, vaulted staircases, all the dignitaries of the empire were gathered in a circle— before them all, he has dispatched the messenger. The messenger sets off at once, a strong and tireless man; sometimes thrusting ahead with one arm, sometimes with the other, he beats a path through the crowd; where he meets resistance, he points to the sign of the sun on his breast, and he forges ahead with an ease that could be matched by no other. But the throng is so thick, there's no end to their dwellings. If only there were an open field before him, how fast he would fly; soon you would surely hear the glorious rapping of his knock on your door. But instead, how vain his efforts are; he is still only forcing his way through the chambers of the innermost palace; he will never reach the end of them, and even if he did he'd be no closer; he would have to fight his way down the steps, and even if he did he'd be no closer; he would still have to cross the courtyards, and after the courtyards the second, outer palace, and still more stairs and courtyards, and still another palace, and so on for thousands of years, and even if he did finally burst through the outermost gate—but that could never, ever happen—the empire's capital, the center of the world, flooded with the dregs of humanity, would still lie before him. There is no one who could force his way through here, least of all with a message from a dead man.— But you sit at your window and dream it up as evening falls.

The Metamorphosis[*]

*Originally published in 1915 under the German title "Die Verwandlung."

I

As Gregor Samsa awoke from unsettling dreams one morning, he found himself transformed in his bed into a monstrous vermin.[1] He lay on his hard armorlike back and when he raised his head a little he saw his vaulted brown belly divided into sections by stiff arches from whose height the coverlet had already slipped and was about to slide off completely. His many legs, which were pathetically thin compared to the rest of his bulk, flickered helplessly before his eyes.

"What has happened to me?" he thought. It was no dream. His room, a regular human bedroom, if a little small, lay quiet between the four familiar walls. Above the desk, on which a collection of fabric samples was unpacked and spread out—Samsa was a traveling salesman—hung the picture that he had recently cut out of an illustrated magazine and put in a pretty gilt frame. It showed a lady, sitting upright, dressed in a fur hat and fur boa; her entire forearm had vanished into a thick fur muff which she held out to the viewer.[2]

Gregor's gaze then shifted to the window, and the dreary weather—raindrops could be heard beating against the metal ledge of the window—made him quite melancholy. "What if I went back to sleep for a while and forgot all this foolishness," he thought. However, this was totally impracticable, as he habitually slept on his right side, a position he could not get into in his present state; no matter how forcefully he heaved himself to the right, he rocked onto his back again. He must have tried it a hundred times, closing his eyes so as not to see his twitching legs, and stopped only when he felt a faint, dull ache start in his side, a pain which he had never experienced before.

"Oh God," he thought, "what a grueling profession I picked! Traveling day in, day out. It is much more aggravating work than the actual business done at the home office, and then with the strain of constant travel as well: the worry over train connections, the bad and irregular meals, the steady stream of faces who never become

7

anything closer than acquaintances. The Devil take it all!" He felt a slight itching up on his belly and inched on his back closer to the bedpost to better lift his head. He located the itching spot, which was surrounded by many tiny white dots that were incomprehensible to him, and tried to probe the area with one of his legs but immediately drew it back, for the touch sent an icy shiver through him.

He slid back into his former position. "This getting up so early," he thought, "makes you totally stupid. A man needs sleep. Other traveling salesmen live like harem women. For example, when I come back to the hotel late in the morning to write up the new orders, these men are still sitting at breakfast. I should try that with my boss. I would be thrown out on the spot. Who knows, however, if that wouldn't be for the best. If I were not holding back because of my parents, I would have quit long ago. I would go up to the boss and tell him my heartfelt opinion. He would be knocked off the desk. This too is a strange way to do things: He sits on top of the desk and from this height addresses the employees, who must step up very close because of the boss's deafness. Well, I have not entirely given up hope, and as soon as I have saved the money to pay off the debt my parents owe him—it might still be another five or six years—I'll definitely do it. Then I'll cut myself free. For the time being, however, I must get up because my train leaves at five."

And he looked at the alarm clock ticking on the bureau. "God Almighty!" he thought. It was half past six and the hands were steadily advancing, actually past the half hour and already closer to three quarters past. Did the alarm not ring? One could see from the bed that it was correctly set for four o'clock and so it must have gone off. Yes, but was it possible to sleep through that furniture-rattling ringing? Well, he hadn't slept peacefully but probably all the sounder for it. But what should he do now? The next train left at seven o'clock, and in order to catch it he would have to rush around like mad, and the sample collection was still unpacked and he was not feeling particularly fresh and energetic. And even if he caught the train, a bawling out from the boss was inescapable, because the office messenger had arrived by the five o'clock train and reported his absence long ago; he was the boss's creature, mindless and spineless. What if Gregor reported in sick? This would be extremely painful and suspicious, as he had not once been ill during his five-year employment. The boss would certainly come over with the health insurance doctor, reproach the parents for their lazy son, and cut off all excuses by referring to the health insurance doctor, for whom there were only healthy but work-shy people. And would he be so wrong in this case? Actually Gregor felt perfectly well, apart from a drowsiness that was superfluous after so long a sleep; in fact he even had a great appetite.

As he urgently considered all this, without being able to decide to get out of bed—the alarm clock struck a quarter to seven— there was a timid knock at the door by his head. "Gregor," a voice called—it was the mother—"it's a quarter to seven. Didn't you want to get going?" That sweet voice! Gregor was shocked when he heard his voice answering, unmistakably his own, true, but a voice in which, as if from below, a persistent chirping intruded, so that the words remained clearly shaped only for a moment and then were destroyed to such an extent that one could not be sure one had heard them right. Gregor wanted to answer thoroughly and explain everything, but restricted himself, given the circumstances, to saying: "Yes, yes, thank you, Mother, I'm just getting up." Due to the wooden door, the change in Gregor's voice was probably not apparent on the other side, for the mother contented herself with this explanation and shuffled away. However, this short conversation brought to the attention of the other family members that Gregor, quite unexpectedly, was still at home, and the father was already knocking, gently, but with his fist, on one of the side doors. "Gregor, Gregor," he called, "what is the matter?" And after a little while he called again, in a louder, warning voice: "Gregor, Gregor!" At the other side door the sister softly pleaded: "Gregor? Aren't you feeling well? Do you need anything?" To both doors Gregor answered: "I'm all ready," and strove, through enunciating most carefully and inserting long pauses between each word, to keep anything conspicuous out of his voice. The father went back to his breakfast, but the sister whispered: "Gregor, open up, I beg you." Gregor, however, had no intention whatsoever of opening the door and instead congratulated himself on the precaution he picked up while traveling of locking the doors at night, even at home.

All he wanted to do now was to get up quietly and undisturbed, get dressed, and, most important, eat breakfast, and only then consider what to do next, because, as he was well aware, in bed he could never think anything through to a reasonable conclusion. He recalled how he had often felt slight pains in bed, perhaps due to lying in an awkward position, pains that proved imaginary when he got up, and he was eager to see how today's illusion would gradually dissolve. He had no doubt that the change in his voice was nothing more than the presentiment of a severe cold, an ailment common among traveling salesmen. The coverlet was easy to throw off; he needed only to puff himself up and it fell off by itself. But then things became much more difficult, especially since he was excessively wide. He would have needed arms and hands to prop himself up, instead of which he had only the many little legs that continually waved every which way and which he could not control at all. If he wanted to bend one, it was the first to stretch itself out, and if he finally succeeded in getting this leg to do what he wanted, the others in the meantime, as if set free, waved all the more wildly in painful and frenzied agitation. "There's no use staying in bed," Gregor said to himself.

First he attempted to get the lower part of his body out of bed, but this lower part, which he had not yet seen and about which he could form no clear picture, proved too onerous to move. It shifted so slowly, and when he had finally become nearly frantic, he gathered his energy and lunged forward, without restraint, in the wrong direction and so slammed against the lower bedpost; the searing pain that shot through his body informed him that the lower part of his body was perhaps the most sensitive at present.

He then tried to get the top part of his body out first, and cautiously moved his head toward the edge of the bed. This went smoothly enough, and despite its girth and mass the bulk of his body slowly followed the direction of his head. But when he finally got his head free over the bedside, he became leery of continuing in this vein, because if he fell it would be a miracle if he did not hurt his head. And he must not, especially now, lose consciousness at any price; better to stay in bed.

But when he had repeated his former efforts and once more lay sighing and watching his puny legs struggle against each other, possibly even more viciously, and had found no way to bring peace and order to this random motion, he again told himself that he could not possibly stay in bed and that the logical recourse was to risk everything in the mere hope of freeing himself from the bed. But at the same time he did not forget to remind himself periodically that better than rash decisions was cool, indeed the very coolest, deliberation. In these moments, he fixed his gaze as firmly as possible on the window, but unfortunately the sight of the morning fog, which had even obscured the other side of the narrow street, offered little in the way of cheer or encouragement. "Seven o'clock already," he said to himself at the new chiming of the alarm clock, "seven o'clock already and still such thick fog." And for a little while he lay still, breathing lightly as if he expected total repose would restore everything to its normal and unquestionable state.

But then he said to himself: "Before a quarter past seven I absolutely must be out of bed. Besides, by that time someone from the office will have come to ask about me, because the office opens before seven o'clock." And now he began rocking the whole length of his body in a steady rhythm in order to pitch it out of the bed. If he dropped from the bed in this way, he could probably protect his head by lifting it sharply as he fell. His back seemed to be hard, so it would not be harmed by the fall to the carpet. His greatest concern was for the loud crash he was likely to make, provoking fear if not terror behind all the doors. Still, it must be risked.

When Gregor was sticking halfway out of the bed—the new method was less a struggle than a game, he had only to inch along by rocking back and forth—it struck him how much easier it would be if someone came to help. Two strong people—he thought of his father and the maid—would surely suffice: They would only have to slip their arms under his curved back to lift him from the bed, bend down with their burden, and be patient and watchful while he engineered his swing over to the floor, where he hoped his tiny legs would find some purpose. Now, putting aside the fact that all the doors were locked, should he really call for help? Despite his predicament, he could not suppress a smile at these thoughts.

He was already out so far that he could barely keep his balance while vigorously rocking, and very soon he would have to decide one way or the other, because in five minutes it would be a quarter past seven—then the doorbell rang. "That's someone from the office," he said to himself, and slightly stiffened although his legs only danced more wildly. Everything was still for a moment. "They're not going to answer," Gregor said to himself, clinging to some absurd hope. But then of course the maid marched sharply to the door as usual and opened it. Gregor needed only to hear the visitor's first words of greeting to know who it was—the head clerk himself. Why was Gregor condemned to serve at a firm where the smallest infraction was seized upon with the gravest suspicion; was each and every employee a scoundrel; was there no loyal and dedicated man serving them who, having spent several hours of the morning not devoted to the firm, might become so overcome by pangs of remorse as to be actually unable to get out of bed? Would it not have been enough to send an apprentice to inquire—if any inquiry were actually necessary; did the head clerk himself have to come, and did the whole innocent family have to be shown that only the head clerk could be entrusted to investigate this suspicious matter? And owing more to the anxiety these thoughts caused Gregor than to any real decision, he swung himself with all his might out of the bed. There was a loud thud but not really a crash. The fall was broken somewhat by the carpet, and his back was more flexible than Gregor had thought, so there resulted only a relatively unobtrusive thump. However, he had not been careful enough about raising his head and had banged it; he twisted it and rubbed it against the carpet in pain and aggravation.

"Something fell in there," said the head clerk in the adjoining room to the left. Gregor tried to imagine whether something similar to what had happened to him today might one day befall the head clerk; the possibility really had to be granted. But as if in rude reply to the question, the head clerk now took a few decisive steps in the next room, which caused his patent leather boots to creak. From the room to the right the sister informed Gregor in a whisper: "The head clerk is here." "I know," Gregor said to himself, not daring to raise his voice loud enough for his sister to hear.

"Gregor," the father said, now from the room on the left, "the head clerk has come and wants to know why you did not catch the early train. We don't know what to tell him. Besides, he wants to speak to you personally, so please open the door. He would surely be so kind as to excuse the untidiness of the room." "Good morning, Mr. Samsa," the head clerk was calling out amiably. "He is not well," said the mother to the head clerk while the father was still speaking through the door, "he's not well, sir, believe me. Why else would Gregor miss a train! All that the boy thinks about is work. It almost makes me mad the way he never goes out in the evening; he's been in the city eight days now, but he's been at home every night. He sits with us at the table quietly reading the paper or studying train schedules. His only amuse-

ment is busying himself with his fretsaw.* For example, he spent
two or three evenings carving a small frame, you'd be amazed
how pretty it is, he hung it in his room, you'll see it as soon as
Gregor opens up. I'm glad, sir, that you are here; we would never
have gotten Gregor to open the door ourselves, he's so stubborn
and he's certainly not well even though he denied it this morning." "I'm just coming," said Gregor slowly and carefully, not
moving so as not to miss one word of the conversation. "I can't
think of any other explanation, madam," said the head clerk; "I
hope it's nothing serious. On the other hand I must say we busi-
nessmen—fortunately or unfortunately, as you will—are often
obliged to simply overcome a slight indisposition to tend to business." "So can the head clerk come in now?" asked the impatient
father, knocking on the door again. "No," said Gregor. The room
on the left fell into an uncomfortable silence, the sister began
sobbing in the room on the right.

Why did the sister not join the others? She had probably just
gotten out of bed and had not yet begun to dress. And why was
she crying? Because he would not get up and let the head clerk
in, because he was in danger of losing his job, because the boss
would again start hounding Gregor's parents for their old debts?
These were surely unnecessary worries at the moment. Gregor
was still here and would not think of deserting his family. Of
course, he was currently lying on the carpet and no one who
knew of his condition could seriously expect that he would admit
the head clerk. This petty discourtesy, for which a suitable explanation could easily be found later, could hardly be grounds
for Gregor's immediate dismissal. And it seemed to Gregor that
it would be more reasonable if they were now to leave him in
peace instead of bothering him with their crying and pleading.
But the others were obviously distressed by the uncertainty, and
this excused their behavior.

"Mr. Samsa," the head clerk now called, raising his voice, "what
is the matter? You are barricading yourself in your room, giving
only yes and no answers, causing your parents serious and unnecessary concern, and neglecting—I just mention this in passing—
your professional responsibilities in an outrageous manner. I am

*Long, narrow-bladed saw used to cut ornamental work from thin wood.

speaking here in the name of your parents and your boss, and I seriously beg you to give a clear and immediate explanation. I am astonished, just astonished. I have always known you to be a quiet, reasonable man and now you suddenly seem to be indulging in rash eccentricities. The Chief did point out a possible explanation for your absence early today—concerning the cash payments that were recently entrusted to you—but in fact I practically gave him my word of honor that this could not be the true explanation. Now, however, I see your incredible obstinacy and have completely lost any desire to intercede on your behalf. And your position is by no means unassailable. I originally intended to speak with you privately, but since you are pointlessly wasting my time, I see no reason why your good parents shouldn't also hear. Your recent performance has been highly unsatisfactory; it is admittedly not a heavy business season, but a season of no business at all, I assure you, Mr. Samsa, does not exist, cannot exist."

"But, sir," cried Gregor, beside himself and forgetting all else in his agitation, "I'll open the door immediately, this instant. A slight indisposition, a spell of dizziness prevented me from getting up. I'm still lying in bed. But now I am feeling completely refreshed. I'm just getting out of bed. Please be patient a moment! I'm not as well as I thought. But really I'm all right. These things can just wipe you out so suddenly. Only last night I felt fine, my parents can tell you, or actually last night I already had some sign of it. They must have noticed it. Oh, why did I not report it at the office! But one always thinks that one will overcome an illness without staying home. Sir, please spare my parents! There are no grounds to the accusations you've just made against me, no one has said so much as a word about them to me. Perhaps you haven't seen the latest orders I sent in. In any event, I will be on the eight o'clock train. I've been invigorated by these few hours of rest. Don't let me keep you further, sir, I'll be in the office myself immediately. Please be good enough to tell them and convey my respects to the Chief!"

And while Gregor blurted all this out, hardly knowing what he said, he had easily, probably due to the exercise he had had in bed, reached the bureau and was now trying to pull himself upright against it. He actually wanted to open the door, to actually show himself and speak to the head clerk; he was eager to find out what the others, who so desired to see him now, would say at the sight of him. If they were shocked, then Gregor was no longer responsible and could be calm. But if they accepted everything calmly, then he too had no reason to get worked up and could, if he rushed, actually be at the train station by eight o'clock. At first he kept sliding off the smooth bureau but finally gave himself a last powerful push and stood upright; he no longer paid attention to the pains in his lower abdomen, however burning. He then let himself fall against the back of a nearby chair, his little legs clinging to the edges. In this way he also managed to gain control of himself and fell silent, as he could now listen to the head clerk.

"Did you understand even a word?" the head clerk asked the parents. "He isn't making fools of us?" "For God's sake," cried the mother, already weeping, "maybe he is seriously ill and we're tormenting him. Grete! Grete!" she then screamed. "Mother?" called the sister from the other side. They were communicating across Gregor's room. "You must go for the doctor immediately. Gregor is sick. Run for the doctor. Did you just hear Gregor speak?" "That was the voice of an animal," said the head clerk, in a noticeably low tone compared to the mother's shrieking. "Anna! Anna!" yelled the father through the foyer to the kitchen, clapping his hands, "go get a locksmith at once!" And already the two girls were running through the foyer with a rustling of skirts—how had the sister dressed so quickly?—and throwing open the house door. The door could not be heard closing; they must have left it open as is usual in houses visited by great misfortune.[3]

Gregor had become much calmer however. Apparently his words were no longer understandable even though they were clear enough to him, clearer than before, perhaps because his ear had become accustomed to their sound. But at least it was now believed that all was not right with him and they were ready to help him. He felt cheered by the confidence and surety with which the first orders were met. He felt encircled by humanity again and he expected great and miraculous results from both the doctor and the locksmith, without truly distinguishing between them. In order to have the clearest voice possible for the decisive conversations to come, he coughed a little, taking pains to stifle the sound, as it may not have sounded like a human cough and he could no longer trust his own judgment about it. Meanwhile in the adjoining room it had become completely still. Maybe the parents were sitting at the table whispering with the head clerk, or maybe they were all leaning against the door, listening.

With the aid of the chair, Gregor slowly pushed himself to the door, then let go and threw himself against it and held himself upright—the pads of his little legs were slightly sticky—and rested there for a moment from his exertions. He then attempted to unlock it by taking the key into his mouth. Unfortunately he appeared to have no teeth—how then should he grasp the key?— but on the other hand his jaws were certainly very powerful, and with their help he got the key to move, ignoring the fact that he was somehow harming himself, because a brown fluid had come from his mouth, oozed over the key, and dripped onto the floor. "Do you hear that," said the head clerk in the next room, "he's turning the key." This was a great encouragement to Gregor, but they should all, the mother and father too, have shouted: "Go, Gregor," they should have shouted: "Keep going, keep going with that lock!" And imagining that they were intently following his every move, he obliviously clenched the key in his jaws with all the strength he could muster. In accordance with the progress of the key, he danced around the lock, holding himself up only by his mouth, and as needed he either hung on to the key or pressed his whole weight down against it. It was the sharp click of the lock finally snapping back that abruptly roused him. Breathing a sigh of relief, he said to himself: "So I didn't need the locksmith after all," and pressed his head against the handle in order to completely open the door.

Since he had to pull the door open in this way, it was opened quite wide while he himself still could not be seen. He first had to slowly circumnavigate one of the double doors and do it very carefully so as not to flop onto his back before entering the room. He was still busy with this involved maneuver and had no time to be distracted by anything else when he heard the head clerk burst out with a loud "Oh!"—it sounded like a gust of wind— and now he also saw the head clerk, standing closest to the door, pressing his hand against his open mouth and backing away slowly as if repelled by an invisible and relentless force.[4] The mother— standing there, despite the presence of the head clerk, with her hair still undone and bristling all over—first looked at the father with clasped hands, then took two steps toward Gregor and fell down amid her billowing skirts, her face sinking out of sight onto her breast. The father, furiously shaking his fists as if willing Gregor to go back in his room, looked uncertainly around the living room, covered his eyes in his hands, and sobbed with great heaves of his powerful chest.

Gregor did not now enter the room but instead leaned against the other, firmly locked wing of the door so that only half of his body could be seen and his head above it, tilting as he peered out at the others. In the meantime it had grown much brighter; a section of the endless dark gray building across the street was clearly visible—it was a hospital, with regular windows breaking through the matte façade; the rain was still falling but now only in large individually formed and visible drops that struck the ground one at a time. The many breakfast dishes lay on the table, as breakfast was the most important meal of the day for the father, the time when he would pore over the different newspapers for hours. On the wall just opposite hung a photograph of Gregor from the time of his military service, showing him as a lieutenant and, with a carefree smile and his hand on his sword, demanding respect for his bearing and uniform. The door to the foyer was open, and since the apartment door was also open, one could see out to the landing and the top of the stairs leading down.

"Well now," said Gregor, well aware that he alone had remained calm, "I will get dressed immediately, pack my samples, and be on my way. Will you all, will you let me go catch my train? Now you see, sir, I'm not stubborn and I'm happy to work; traveling is difficult but I couldn't live without it. Where are you going, sir? To the office? Yes? Will you report on everything truthfully? A man can suddenly be incapable of working, but this is the precise moment to remember his past performance and to consider that later, after resolving his difficulties, he would work all the harder and more diligently. I am so deeply obligated to the Chief, as you well know. And besides, I am responsible for my parents and sister. I am in a tough bind but I'll work myself back out of it. Please do not make it more difficult than it already is. I beg you to speak up for me in the office! No one likes traveling salesmen, I know. They think we make a slew of money and lead charmed lives. There's no particular reason for them to further examine this prejudice. But you, sir, you have a better perspective than the rest of the office, an even better perspective, in all confidence, than the Chief himself, who, in his capacity as employer, allows his opinion to be easily swayed against an employee. You know very well that a traveling salesman, out of the office for almost the entire year, can easily fall prey to gossip, coincidences, and unfounded grievances against which he cannot possibly defend himself because he almost never hears about them except when returning home from an exhausting trip; he personally suffers the grim consequences, the causes of which he can no longer determine. Sir, do not leave without giving me a word to show that you think me at least partially right!"

But with Gregor's first words the head clerk had already turned away and with gaping lips simply looked back over his twitching shoulder at Gregor. And during Gregor's speech he did not stand still for a moment but crept step-by-step to the door, his eyes never leaving Gregor, as if obeying some secret injunction to leave the room. He was already in the foyer, and from the sudden movement with which he took his last step from the living room, one might believe he had just burned the sole of his foot. In the foyer, however, he stretched his right hand far out toward the stairs as if some supernatural deliverance were awaiting him there.

Gregor realized that he must on no account let the head clerk leave in this frame of mind or his position in the firm would be seriously jeopardized. The parents did not understand this so well; they had convinced themselves over the years that Gregor was set for life at this firm, and besides, they were so preoccupied with the current problem that they had lost all sense of the future. But Gregor did have this foresight. The head clerk had to be detained, calmed, persuaded, and ultimately won over; the very future of Gregor and his family depended on it. If only the sister had been there! She was perceptive; she had already begun to cry when Gregor was still lying quietly on his back. And the head clerk, that ladies' man, would certainly have let her guide him; she would have closed the apartment door and assuaged his fears in the foyer. But the sister was not there and Gregor would have to handle the situation himself. And without stopping to think that he still had no idea what powers of movement he had or even to think that very possibly—indeed probably—his words would once again be unintelligible, he let go of the wing of the door and flung himself through the opening; desiring to go toward the head clerk, who was already on the landing and ludicrously clutching the banister with both hands, Gregor instead, while groping for support, fell with a little cry onto his numerous little legs. This had barely happened when, for the first time that morning, he felt a sense of physical well-being: The little legs had firm ground beneath them, he was delighted to note that they were completely under his command, they even strained to carry him off wherever he might desire, and he already believed that the final alleviation of all his grief was imminent. But at that same moment, as he lay there rocking from his restrained movement not far from his mother—in fact just in front of her—she, who had seemed so self-absorbed, suddenly sprang up with arms wide and fingers outstretched, shouting: "Help, for God's sake, help!" She bent her head down as if to see Gregor better but instead ran contradictorily and madly backward and, having forgotten that the laden table stood behind her, sat down on it thoughtlessly and hastily, seemingly oblivious to the large overturned coffee pot next to her from which coffee was pouring in a steady stream onto the carpet.

"Mother, Mother," Gregor said softly, and looked up at her. The head clerk had momentarily slipped his mind and he could not help snapping his jaws in the air at the sight of the flowing coffee. This caused the mother to scream again; she fled from the table and fell into the father's arms as he rushed to her. But Gregor now had no time to waste on his parents; the head clerk was already on the stairs, with his chin on the banister he was looking back one last time. Gregor broke into a run to be sure to catch him; the head clerk must have suspected this because he leaped down several steps and disappeared; he was still yelling, "Aaahh!" which rang throughout the whole staircase. Unfortunately the head clerk's flight seemed to totally confuse the father, who until now had remained relatively calm, for instead of going after the head clerk or at least not hindering Gregor's pursuit, he seized in his right hand the head clerk's walking stick (which along with his hat and overcoat had been left behind on a chair) and with his left hand grabbed a large newspaper from the table and, stamping his feet, proceeded to brandish the walking stick and newspaper in order to drive Gregor back into his room. No plea of Gregor's helped, nor indeed was any plea understood; however humbly he turned his head, the father merely stamped his feet all the more forcefully. Across the room the mother, despite the cool weather, had thrown open a window and was leaning far out of it with her face buried in her hands. A strong draft swept in from the street to the staircase, the window curtains swelled, the newspapers on the table rustled, stray pages fluttered over the floor. The father drove Gregor back relentlessly, hissing like a savage.[5] As Gregor was as yet unpracticed in moving backward, it was very slow going. If only Gregor had been permitted to turn around, he would have been in his room at once, but he was afraid to make the father impatient by this time-consuming rotation, and at any moment the stick in the father's hand threatened to deal a fatal blow to the back or the head. In the end, however, there remained no other choice, for Gregor observed to his horror that he could not control his direction when moving backward, and so he began as quickly as possible, which was actually very slowly, to turn himself around. Perhaps the father recognized his good intentions because he did not interfere; instead he occasionally even directed the movement from a distance with the tip of his stick. If only the father would quit that infernal hissing! It made Gregor completely lose his head. He was almost turned all the way around when, distracted by the hissing, he made a mistake and turned back the other way for a stretch. When he successfully ended up headfirst in front of the doorway, it was obvious that his body was too wide to get through as it was. Naturally it did not occur to the father in his present mood to open the other wing of the door to give Gregor a wide enough passage. He was fixed on the idea of getting Gregor back in his room as quickly as possible. And he would never have allowed the elaborate preparations that Gregor needed to pull himself upright and perhaps attempt to go through the door that way. Rather, he drove Gregor forward, as if there were no obstacle, with a considerable amount of noise; it no longer sounded like just one father behind him and now it was really no longer a joke, and Gregor—come what may—thrust himself into the doorway. One side of his body rose up and he lay at an angle in the doorway, one of his flanks was scraped raw and the white door was stained with ugly blotches, he was soon stuck fast and could not move on his own, the little legs on one side hung trembling in midair and on the other side they were pinned painfully to the floor—when his father gave him a terrific shove from behind and he flew, bleeding profusely, far into the room. The door was slammed shut with the stick, then all was still.

II

IT WAS TWILIGHT WHEN Gregor awoke from his deep slumber. Even without being disturbed he doubted he would have slept much later, as he felt so well rested, but it seemed to him that a furtive step and a cautious shutting of the foyer door had roused him. The glow of the electric street lamps shone in pale patches on the ceiling and upper parts of the furniture, but where Gregor slept it was dark. Slowly, still groping awkwardly with his antennas, which he was only now learning to appreciate, he pushed himself over to the door to see what had been happening. His left side felt like a single long unpleasantly taut scar and he actually had to limp on his two rows of legs. One little leg, moreover, had been seriously injured during the course of the morning's events—it was nearly a miracle that only one had been hurt—and dragged behind him lifelessly.

Only when he reached the door did Gregor discover what had actually tempted him there: the smell of something edible. For there stood a bowl filled with fresh milk in which small slices of white bread were floating. He could have almost laughed for joy, as he was even hungrier than in the morning, and immediately plunged his head, almost up to the eyes, into the milk. But he quickly withdrew it in disappointment; not only was eating difficult on account of his tender left side—and eating had to be a collaboration of the whole heaving body—but he did not care at all for the milk, which was otherwise his favorite drink and surely the reason his sister had set it out for him. In fact, it was almost in revulsion that he turned away from the bowl and crawled back to the middle of the room.

In the living room, as Gregor could see through the crack in the door, the gas was lit; although the father usually liked to read the afternoon paper at this hour in a loud voice to the mother and sometimes to the sister as well, not a sound was heard. Well, perhaps this custom of reading that the sister had told him about

and wrote of in her letters had been recently discontinued. But
it was so silent everywhere, even though the apartment was certainly not empty. "What a quiet life the family has led," Gregor
said to himself, and felt, as he stared pointedly into the darkness,
a great surge of pride that he had been able to provide his parents
and his sister such a life and in such a beautiful apartment. But
what if all the tranquillity, all the comfort, all the contentment
were now to come to a horrifying end? So as not to dwell on
such thoughts, Gregor started to move and began crawling up
and down the room.

Once during the long evening, one of the side doors and then
the other was opened a small crack and quickly shut again; someone had apparently had the urge to come in but had then thought
better of it. Gregor now stationed himself directly before the
living room door, determined to persuade the hesitant visitor to
come in or at least discover who it might be, but the door was
not opened again and Gregor waited in vain. That morning, when
the doors had been locked, they all wanted to come in; now after
he had opened the one door and the others had been opened
during the day, no one came and the keys were now on the other
side.

It was late into the night before the light went out in the living
room, and it was now obvious that the parents and the sister had
stayed awake until then, because he could clearly discern that all
three were tiptoeing away. Certainly no one would come in to
Gregor until morning, therefore he had a long undisturbed time
to ponder how best to reorder his life. But the high-ceilinged,
spacious room in which he was forced to lie flat on the floor filled
him with an unaccountable dread; it was, after all, his own room
which he had inhabited for five years, and with an almost invol-
untary movement—and not without a faint feeling of shame—
he scurried under the sofa, where, despite his back being slightly
squashed and being unable to raise his head, he felt immediately
cozy and only regretted that his body was too wide to fit completely underneath the sofa.

There he stayed the whole night, sometimes dozing but then
waking up with a start from hunger pains; sometimes he worried
and entertained vague hopes, but it all led him to the same conclusion: For now he must lie low and try, through patience and

the greatest consideration, to help his family bear the inconven-
ience he was bound to cause them in his present condition.

So early in the morning that it was almost still night, Gregor
had an opportunity to test the strength of his new resolutions,
because the sister, nearly fully dressed, opened the door from
the foyer and eagerly peered in. She did not immediately find
him, but when she noticed him underneath the sofa—well, he
had to be somewhere, he couldn't have just flown away—she was
so startled that, unable to control herself, she slammed the door
shut from the outside. But, as if regretting her behavior, she
instantly reopened it and tiptoed in as though she were visiting
someone seriously ill or even a stranger. Gregor had pushed his
head forward to the edge of the sofa and was watching her.
Would she notice that he had left the milk untouched not from
any lack of hunger and bring something he liked better? If she
did not do so on her own, he would rather starve than bring it
to her attention, although he was extremely hard-pressed not to
dart out from under the sofa and throw himself at her feet to
beg for something good to eat. But the sister immediately and
with surprise noticed the bowl, still full except for a little milk
that had spilled around it, and promptly picked it up, not with
bare hands of course but with a rag, and carried it out. Gregor
was exceedingly curious as to what she would bring instead, and
he advanced all sorts of theories. But he could never have
guessed what in the goodness of her heart the sister actually did.
To find out his likes and dislikes, she brought him a wide selec-
tion all spread out on an old newspaper. There were old, half-
rotten vegetables, bones covered with congealed white sauce
from supper the night before, some raisins and almonds, a cheese
that Gregor had declared inedible two days before, dry bread,
bread with butter, and bread with butter and salt. Beside this she
set down the bowl, now presumably reserved for Gregor's exclu-
sive use, which she had filled with water. And it was out of delicacy, knowing Gregor would not eat in her presence, that she
hurriedly removed herself and even turned the key in the lock
to indicate to Gregor that he was free to indulge himself as comfortably as he pleased. Gregor's little legs whizzed toward the
food. His wounds must have already been fully healed, he felt
no more injury; he marveled at this and thought about when he
had cut his finger with a knife over a month ago and how this

wound had still bothered him just the day before yesterday. "Have I become less sensitive?" he thought, sucking greedily at the cheese, to which he was initially and primarily drawn before all the other food. With tears of gratitude he quickly devoured, one after the other, the cheese, the vegetables, and the sauce; the fresh food on the other hand did not appeal to him and he even dragged what he did want to eat a bit farther away. He had long finished with everything and lay drowsily on the same spot when the sister, to signify her return, slowly turned the key in the lock. This jerked him into action, as he was dozing, and he rushed back under the sofa. But he truly had to force himself, even for the short time that the sister was in the room, to stay beneath the sofa, because he had bloated slightly from the large meal and he could barely breathe in such strict confinement. In between minor bouts of suffocation, he watched with bulging eyes as the unsuspecting sister swept up not only the remaining scraps but even what Gregor had not touched, as if they now had no more use, and dumped it all quickly into a bucket that she covered with a wooden lid and carried away. Hardly had she turned her back when Gregor came out from under the sofa, stretched, and puffed himself out.

Gregor was fed twice daily in this way, once in the morning while the parents and the maid still slept, and once after dinner was eaten while the parents napped for a short time and the sister could send the maid on some errand. The parents certainly did not want Gregor to starve, but perhaps it was as much as they could bear to hear about it, perhaps the sister wanted to save them from even the smallest possible discomfort, as they surely had enough to bear.

Gregor had no idea what excuse was used that first morning to put off the doctor and locksmith, because as no one could understand him, no one thought, including the sister, that he could understand them, and so he had to content himself, whenever his sister was in the room, with hearing a sigh now and then or an appeal to the saints. A little time later, when she was a bit more at ease—of course it was never a question of being completely at ease—Gregor sometimes caught a remark that was meant kindly or at least could be so considered. "Oh, he enjoyed it today," she said when Gregor had eaten well, or when he had not, which was more frequently the case, she would say almost sadly, "It's all been left again."

Although Gregor could get no news directly, he overheard a great deal from the neighboring rooms, and as soon as he heard voices he would run over to the corresponding door and press his entire body against it. There was no conversation, especially early on, that did not concern him even if only indirectly. At every meal for two whole days there were discussions about what should be done, but this same theme was also debated between meals, because there were always at least two family members home since no one wanted to be alone in the apartment and it certainly could not be left empty under the circumstances. Furthermore, on the very first day, the cook—it was not entirely clear what and how much she knew of the situation—begged the mother on her knees to be discharged immediately, and when she took her leave a quarter of an hour later, she was tearfully thankful for the dismissal, as if it were the greatest service they had ever conferred upon her, and with no prompting swore a dreadful oath never to breathe to anyone a word of what had happened.

Now the sister also had to cook, as did the mother, but this was not much trouble, as the family ate almost nothing. Again and again Gregor heard one encouraging another in vain to eat and receiving no answer but: "Thank you, I've had enough," or something very similar. Perhaps they did not drink either. The sister often asked the father whether he would have some beer and kindly offered to procure it herself, and when the father did not reply she suggested that she could send the janitor's wife to fetch it to offset any hesitation, but then in the end the father answered with a firm "No," and it was discussed no further.

In the course of the very first day, the father explained the family's financial position and prospects to both the mother and the sister. Now and then he rose from the table to get some receipt or notebook from the small safe he had managed to rescue from the collapse of his business five years earlier. He could be heard opening the complicated lock, removing the desired document, and closing it again. The father's explanations were the first encouraging news Gregor had heard since his captivity. He had been of the opinion that nothing had been salvaged from the father's business; at least the father had said nothing to the contrary, although Gregor had also never asked him. Gregor's only concern at that time had been to do whatever he could to have the family forget as quickly as possible the financial misfortune that had plunged them into total despair. And so he began to work with consuming energy and was promoted, almost overnight, from a minor clerk to a traveling salesman with much greater potential to earn money, and his success was soon transformed, by way of commission, into cash that he could then lay on the table before the astonished and delighted family. Those had been happy times and they had never returned, at least not with the same brilliance, even though Gregor later earned enough to meet the expenses of the entire family and did so. They had simply grown used to it, both the family and Gregor; the money was gratefully accepted and gladly given but it no longer brought any particular warmth. Only the sister remained close to Gregor, and it was his secret plan that she, who unlike Gregor greatly loved music and played the violin movingly, should be sent to the Conservatory next year despite the considerable expense it was sure to incur, which would just have to be met in some other way. During Gregor's short stays in the city, the Conservatory would often come up in conversation with the sister but always as a beautiful dream that could never be realized. The parents were displeased to hear even these innocent allusions, but Gregor had very definite ideas about it and intended to announce his plan on Christmas Eve.

Such were the thoughts, utterly useless in his present condition, that went through his head as he stood listening, glued to the door. Sometimes, from general weariness he could listen no longer and carelessly let his head slump against the door, but he promptly recovered because even the small noise he had made had been heard in the next room and had silenced them all. "What's he up to now?" the father said after a while, obviously turning toward the door, and only then did the interrupted conversation resume.

Gregor was now very thoroughly informed—because the father tended to repeat his explanations, partly because he had not dealt with these matters himself in a long time and partly because the mother did not always understand the first time—and discovered that despite the disaster a sum, admittedly very small, remained from the old days and had increased slightly in the meantime due to the untouched interest. And besides that, the money Gregor brought home every month—he had kept only a few guilder for himself—had not been entirely depleted and had now accumulated into a small capital sum. Behind the door Gregor nodded his head emphatically, delighted to learn of this unexpected frugality and foresight. Of course he actually could have used this extra money to further pay off the father's debt to the Chief, thus bringing much closer the day he could have rid himself of this job, but doubtless things were better this way, the way his father had arranged them.

However, this money was by no means sufficient to support the family on the interest; the principal might support the family for a year, or two at the most. So it was just a sum that should not be touched, put aside for emergencies, and the money to live on would still need to be earned. Now the father was certainly healthy but an old man who had not worked in five years and could not be expected to do much; during these years, the first leisure time in his laborious albeit unsuccessful life, he had gained a lot of weight and become quite sluggish as a result. And how should the elderly mother earn a living, when she suffered from asthma and even a walk through the apartment was trying, leaving her gasping for breath every other day on the sofa by an open window? And should the sister work, still a child of seventeen whose life had been so pleasant until now—dressing nicely, sleeping late, helping with the housework, enjoying a few modest amusements, and above all playing the violin? At first, whenever the conversation turned to the need to earn money, Gregor let go of the door and threw himself onto the cool leather sofa nearby, he felt so flushed with shame and grief.

He often lay there through the whole night, not sleeping a wink, just scrabbling on the leather for hours. Or, not shying from the great effort, he would push a chair over to the window, climb up to the sill, and lean, propped up on the chair, against the windowpanes, evidently in some vague remembrance of the freedom he had once found in gazing out. For actually he now saw things just a short distance away becoming dimmer each day; he could no longer make out the hospital opposite, whose sight he used to curse for having seen it all too often, and if he were not so certain that he lived on the quiet but decidedly urban Charlotte Street, he could have believed that he was gazing out the window at a barren wasteland where the ashen sky merged indistinguishably with the gray earth. The observant sister had needed to notice the chair standing by the window only twice; whenever she straightened the room after that, she carefully replaced the chair at the window and now even left the inner casements open.

If only Gregor had been able to speak with the sister and thank her for everything she was obliged to do for him, he could have borne her ministrations more easily; as it was they oppressed him. The sister certainly tried to lessen the general awkwardness of the situation as much as possible, and as time went by she naturally succeeded more and more, however with the passing time Gregor too saw everything more clearly. Her very entrance was terrible for him. Hardly had she entered when she rushed directly to the window without taking the time to close the door— although she was usually so careful to shield everyone from the sight of Gregor's room—tore the window open with hasty hands as if almost suffocating, and stayed there awhile, even when it was bitterly cold, breathing deeply. This bustle and racket of hers tortured Gregor twice a day, and he lay the entire time quaking under the sofa, knowing very well that she would have spared him this if it were at all possible to remain in a room with Gregor with the window shut.

Once, approximately a month after Gregor's transformation, when there was no reason for the sister to be especially alarmed at his appearance, she came a little earlier than usual and caught Gregor perfectly still, gazing out the window, thus giving him a particularly frightful aspect. It would not have surprised Gregor if she had not come in, as his position prevented her from immediately opening the window, but not only did she not enter, she actually jumped back and shut the door; a stranger could easily have thought Gregor had been lying in wait for her and meant to bite her. Gregor naturally hid himself at once under the sofa but had to wait until noon for the sister's return, and then she seemed much more uneasy than usual. He concluded that the sight of him was still repulsive to her and was bound to remain repulsive, and that she must have exercised great self-control not to take flight at the sight of even the smallest portion of his body protruding from under the couch. To spare her from even these glimpses, he dragged the sheet to the sofa on his back one day—this required four hours' work—and laid it in such a way as to conceal himself entirely, so the sister could not see him even if she stooped down. If she did not find the sheet necessary, she certainly could have removed it, because it was clear enough that Gregor could not possibly be pleased by his total confinement, but she left the sheet as it was, and Gregor imagined he caught a grateful look once when he cautiously raised the sheet a little with his head to see how the sister was taking the new arrangement.

During the first two weeks, the parents could not bring themselves to enter his room and he often heard them praising the efforts of the sister, whereas earlier they had frequently been annoyed with her because she appeared to them to be a somewhat useless girl. Now, however, both the father and the mother often waited outside Gregor's room while the sister cleaned up inside, and as soon as she stepped out she had to report fully to them on exactly how the room looked, what Gregor had eaten, how he had behaved this time, and whether perhaps some slight improvement was noticeable. Incidentally, the mother wanted to visit Gregor relatively soon but the father and the sister put her off with logical arguments that Gregor listened to very attentively and approved of wholeheartedly. But later she had to be held back by force, and when she cried out: "Let me go to Gregor, he's my unfortunate son! Can't you understand that I must go to him?" Gregor then thought that it would perhaps be beneficial if the mother did come in, not every day of course, but maybe once a week; she understood everything much better than the sister, who for all her pluck was still just a child and may have ultimately undertaken such a difficult task out of childish recklessness.

Gregor's desire to see the mother was soon fulfilled. During the daytime Gregor did not want to show himself at the window, if only out of consideration for his parents, but he could not crawl around very far in the few square meters of floor, nor could he bear to lie still even at night, and eating gave him scant pleasure, so as a distraction he acquired the habit of crawling crisscross over the walls and ceiling. He especially liked hanging from the ceiling; it was entirely different from lying on the floor, he could breathe more freely and a mild tingling ran through his body, and in the near joyful oblivion in which Gregor found himself up there he could, to his own surprise, lose hold and plunge to the floor. But naturally he now had much more control over his body than before and was not harmed by even so great a fall. The sister immediately noticed Gregor's newfound entertainment—after all he did leave behind the sticky traces of his crawling here and there—and she got it into her head to allow Gregor the widest crawling space possible by the removal of the furniture that hindered him, namely the bureau and the desk. She was not, however, able to do this alone; she did not dare ask for the father's help and the maid would certainly not help her because, although she, a girl of about sixteen, had had the courage to stay on after the cook's departure, she had asked for the privilege of keeping the kitchen door locked at all times and opening it only upon specific requests. This left the sister no choice but to ask the mother at a time when the father was out. The mother did come with exclamations of excited delight but fell silent outside the door to Gregor's room. Naturally the sister first checked to see that everything was in order in the room and only then admitted the mother. Gregor had very hastily pulled the sheet down lower in tighter folds so that it really looked like a sheet casually thrown over the couch. He refrained from peeking out from under the sheet this time, renouncing this very first sight of his mother, and was only glad she had come at all. "Come in, you can't see him," said the sister, evidently leading the mother by the hand. Gregor now heard the two frail women pushing the extremely heavy old bureau from its place and the sister taking on most of the work, not heeding the warnings of the mother, who feared she might overexert herself. It took a very long time. After struggling for a good quarter of an hour, the mother declared that they had better leave the bureau where it was; first, it was just too heavy, they would not be finished before the father's arrival, and Gregor's every movement would be hindered with the bureau in the middle of the room, and second, it was not at all certain that removing the furniture was doing Gregor any great service. It seemed to her that the opposite was true: The look of the empty wall was heartrending, and wouldn't Gregor feel that same way since he had been used to the furniture for so long and might feel bereft in the empty room. "And doesn't it look," concluded the mother very softly, in fact she practically whispered the whole time as if, not knowing Gregor's precise whereabouts, she did not want him to hear even the sound of her voice, as she was convinced that he could not understand the words, "and doesn't it look, by removing all the furniture, like we've abandoned all hope of his recovery and are callously leaving him completely on his own? I think it would be best if we tried to keep the room exactly as it was before, so that when Gregor comes back to us he can find everything unchanged and forget that much more easily what happened in the meantime."

Upon hearing the mother's words, Gregor realized that the lack of any direct human exchange, coupled with the monotony of the family's life, must have confused his mind; he could not otherwise explain to himself how he could have seriously wished to have his room cleared out. Did he really wish his warm room, comfortably furnished with old family heirlooms, to be transformed into a lair in which he would certainly be able to crawl freely in any direction, but at the price of rapidly and completely forgetting his human past? He had indeed been so close to forgetting that only the voice of the mother, so long unheard, brought him to his senses. Nothing should be removed, everything must stay as it was, he could not do without the beneficial influence of the furniture on his state of mind, and if the furniture impeded his senseless crawling about, it was not a loss but a great boon.

Unfortunately, however, the sister thought differently; she had grown accustomed, not entirely without reason, to being especially expert in any discussion with her parents concerning Gregor, and so now the mother's advice was grounds enough for her to insist on removing not only the bureau and desk, as she had originally planned, but also the rest of the furniture, with the exception of the indispensable sofa. This determination of course did not arise only from childish defiance and the self-confidence she had recently and so unexpectedly developed at such a cost; she had in fact observed that Gregor needed more room to crawl, and as far as one could see, he never used the furniture. Her determination may also have arisen from the romantic enthusiasm of girls her age that seeks expression at every opportunity and tempted Grete to overplay the horror of Gregor's predicament in order that she might perform even more heroically on his behalf than previously. For in a room where Gregor alone ruled over the bare walls, no one other than Grete was likely to dare set foot.

And so she refused to be shaken from her resolve by the mother, who seemed extremely anxious and unsure of herself in this room and soon quieted and helped the sister, to the best of her abilities, to push the bureau outside. Now, in a pinch Gregor could do without the bureau but the desk must absolutely stay. And no sooner had the women left the room, grunting and heaving with the bureau, than Gregor poked his head out from under the sofa to ascertain how he could cautiously and tactfully intervene. But as luck would have it, it was the mother who returned first while Grete was still in the next room with her arms around the bureau, rocking it and trying to shift it on her own but naturally not budging it an inch. The mother, however, was unaccustomed to Gregor's appearance and it might have sickened her; so Gregor panicked and scuttled back to the other end of the sofa, but he could not prevent the sheet from stirring a little in front. This was enough to catch the mother's eye. She froze, stood still for a beat, then retreated to Grete.

Although Gregor said over and over to himself that nothing out of the ordinary was happening, that some furniture was just being moved around, he soon had to concede that the coming and going of the women, their soft exclamations, the scraping of the furniture along the floor were all like a roaring rising up and pressing in around him, and no matter how he tucked in his head and legs and flattened his body to the floor, he was forced to admit that he could not stand the ruckus much longer. They were clearing out his room, taking from him everything that he loved; they had already dragged out the bureau, which contained the fretsaw and other tools, and now they were prying loose the firmly entrenched desk, at which he had done his assignments during business school, high school, and even as far back as elementary school—there was now no longer any time to contemplate the finer intentions of the two women, whose existence he had actually almost forgotten, because from sheer exhaustion they were struggling in silence and only the heavy shuffling of their feet could be heard.

And so he broke out—the women were in the next room, leaning on the desk to catch their breath—and ran in four different directions, not knowing what to save first; then he saw on the otherwise barren wall opposite him the picture of the lady swathed in furs and quickly scrambled up and pressed himself against the glass, a surface he could stick to and that soothed his heated belly. At the very least this picture, which Gregor now completely concealed, would be removed by no one. He twisted his head around to the living room door to observe the women's return.

They had not taken much of a break and were already headed back; Grete had put an arm around the mother and was almost carrying her. "So what should we take now?" said Grete, looking around. And then her eyes met Gregor's gaze from the wall. It was probably due only to the presence of the mother that she maintained her composure, bent her head down to the mother to keep her from looking up, and said, rather shakily and without thinking: "Come, why don't we go back to the living room for a moment?" It was clear to Gregor that she intended to get the mother to safety and then chase him down from the wall. Well, just let her try! He cleaved to his picture and would not relinquish it. He would rather fly in Grete's face.

But Grete's words had quite unnerved the mother; she took a step to the side, took in the huge brown splotch on the flowered wallpaper, and, before realizing what she saw was actually Gregor, screamed in a loud, harsh voice: "Oh God! Oh God!" and collapsed, arms, outflung in total abandon, onto the sofa and did not move. "Gregor, you!" yelled the sister, glaring fiercely and raising her fist. These were her first direct words to him since the metamorphosis. She ran to the next room for some kind of aromatic spirits to revive the mother from her faint; Gregor wanted to help too—there was time enough to save the picture— but he was stuck fast to the glass and had to wrench himself free, then he also ran into the next room, as if to offer advice as he used to, but had to stand idly behind her once there while she was rummaging among the various bottles; she was freshly shocked when she turned around, one of the vials fell to the floor and shattered, a splinter of glass sliced Gregor's face and a corrosive medicine splashed around him; Grete, without further delay, grabbed as many vials as she could hold, ran with them to her mother, and kicked shut the door. Gregor was now cut off from the mother, who might be near death because of him; he could not open the door for fear of frightening away the sister,

who had to stay with the mother; there was nothing to do but
wait, and plagued with worry and self-reproach he began to crawl,
to crawl all over, over everything, walls, furniture, ceiling, and
finally fell in despair, when the whole room was spinning, onto
the middle of the large table.

A little while passed, Gregor still lay prostrate and everything
was quiet; perhaps this was a good sign. Then the doorbell rang;
the maid was naturally locked in the kitchen so Grete had to
answer it. It was the father. "What's happened?" were his first
words; Grete's appearance must have told all. Grete answered in
a muffled voice, her face obviously thrust against the father's
chest: "Mother fainted, but she's better now; Gregor's broken
out." "Just as I expected," said the father. "I keep telling you, but
you women won't listen." It was clear to Gregor that the father
had misinterpreted Grete's all too brief statement and assumed
Gregor was guilty of some kind of violence. Gregor now had to
try to placate the father, for he had neither the time nor the
means for an explanation. And so Gregor flew to the door of his
room, crouching against it, to show his father as soon as he came
in from the foyer that he had every intention of returning at once
to his room and that it was not necessary to drive him back; if
only someone would open the door, he would immediately disappear.

But the father was in no mood to make such fine distinctions.
"Ah!" he cried as soon as he entered, in a tone both furious and
exultant. Gregor drew his head back from the door and raised it
toward the father. He had not at all pictured his father like this
as he was standing there now; admittedly he had been too preoccupied of late with his newly discovered crawling to concern
himself about what was going on in the household, and he really
should have been prepared for some changes. And yet, and yet
could this indeed still be the father? The same man who used to
lie wearily buried in bed when Gregor left for a business trip;
who welcomed his return in the evening by merely raising his
arms to show his joy, not being quite able to get up, and reclining
in an armchair in his robe; who, during the rare family walks a
few Sundays a year and on the highest holidays, shuffled labori-
ously between Gregor and the mother, always moving a bit slower
than their already slowed pace, bundled in his old overcoat and
carefully plodding forward by meticulously placing his cane; and

who, when he wanted to say something, nearly always stood still and gathered everyone around him?[6] Now, however, he held himself erect, dressed in a tight blue uniform with gold buttons, like that of a bank messenger; his heavy double chin bulged over the high stiff collar of his jacket; from under the bushy eyebrows his alert black eyes flashed penetratingly; his previously disheveled white hair was combed flat, exactingly parted and gleaming. He tossed his cap, on which there was a gold monogram, very possibly a bank's, clear across the room in an arc and onto the sofa, and with his hands in his pockets and the tails of his long uniform jacket thrown back, he went after Gregor with a grimly set face. He probably did not know what he himself intended to do, nevertheless he lifted his feet unusually high and Gregor was astonished at the gigantic size of his boot soles. But Gregor did not dwell on this; he had known from the very first day of his new life that the father considered only the strictest measures appropriate when dealing with him. And so he ran from the father, stopping only when the father stood still, and scurried away again as soon as the father moved. In this way they circled the room several times without anything decisive happening; in fact they proceeded so slowly it did not look like a chase. With this in mind Gregor kept to the floor for the moment, especially since he feared the father might view an escape to the walls or ceiling as a particularly malevolent act. At the same time Gregor had to admit that he could not keep up with this running for long, because for every step the father took Gregor had to execute a countless number of maneuvers. He was already short of breath, as his lungs had never been all that reliable in his previous life. He staggered along, his eyes barely open, trying to focus all his energy on running; in this daze he could not think of anything to do but run, and had already almost forgotten that the walls were available to him, although in this room they were blocked by elaborately carved furniture, thorny with points and notches— suddenly something that had been lightly tossed almost hit him, but landed next to him and rolled in front of him. It was an apple,[7] and a second instantly flew in his direction. Gregor froze in terror; further running was useless, for the father was determined to bombard him. He had filled his pockets from the bowl on the sideboard and was now throwing apple after apple, taking no more than general momentary aim. These small red apples rolled around the floor as if electrified and collided with each other. One weakly lobbed apple grazed Gregor's back and harmlessly slid off. But another, pitched directly after it, actually lodged itself in Gregor's back; Gregor tried to drag himself away, as if this shockingly unbelievable pain would ease with a change in position, but he felt nailed to the spot and stretched out, all his senses in complete confusion. And it was with his last conscious sight that he saw the door of his room burst open and in front of the screaming sister the mother tearing out in her chemise, because when she fainted the sister had undressed her to let her breathe more freely. He saw the mother run to the father, stumbling over her loosened petticoats as they slipped to the floor one by one, and press herself against him, uniting them in her embrace—now Gregor's vision failed him—and with her arms flung around his neck, she begged the father to spare Gregor's life.

III

GREGOR'S SERIOUS INJURY, FROM which he suffered for almost a month—the apple remained embedded in his flesh as a visible souvenir because no one had the courage to remove it—served to remind even the father that Gregor, despite his now pathetic and repulsive shape, was a member of the family who could not be treated as an enemy; on the contrary, in accordance with family duty they were required to quell their aversion and tolerate him, but only tolerate.

And now, although Gregor had lost some mobility, most likely permanently due to his injury, and traversing his room now took many long minutes like an old invalid—crawling above floor level was out of the question—he was granted, in his mind, entirely satisfactory compensation for this deterioration of his condition: toward evening every day the living room door, which he got used to watching intently for an hour or two beforehand, was opened, so that lying in the darkness of his room and unseen from the living room, he could view the whole family at the brightly lit table and could listen to their conversation more or less with their consent, completely unlike his prior eavesdropping.

Of course there no longer were the lively conversations of earlier times that Gregor would wistfully recall whenever he'd had to sink down into the damp bedding of some small hotel room. Now it was mostly very subdued. The father fell asleep in his armchair soon after supper, and the mother and the sister would caution each other to keep still; the mother, bent over toward the light, sewed delicate lingerie for an apparel shop; the sister, who had taken a job as a salesgirl, was studying shorthand and French in the hope of attaining a better position in the future. The father sometimes woke up and, as if he were not aware he had been sleeping, would say to the mother: "How long you're sewing again today!" and instantly fall back asleep while mother and sister exchanged a tired smile.

Out of some absurd obstinacy, the father refused to take off his messenger's uniform even in the house, and while the dressing gown hung uselessly on the clothes hook, the father sat fully dressed in his chair, as if he were ever ready for duty and awaited, even here, his superior's call. As a result the uniform, which was not new to begin with, became more and more seedy despite all the efforts of the mother and sister, and Gregor often spent whole evenings staring at this garment, covered with greasy stains and gleaming, constantly polished gold buttons, in which the father slept awkwardly but very peacefully.

As soon as the clock struck ten, the mother tried to rouse the father with gentle words and then persuade him to go to bed, for he simply was not getting any proper rest where he was, something he sorely needed since he had to go on duty at six. But, with this stubbornness that he had acquired since becoming a bank messenger, he always insisted on staying longer at the table even though he nodded off regularly, and it was then a monumental task to coax him into exchanging the chair for the bed. However much the mother and sister prodded him with admonishments, he would go on shaking his head slowly with his eyes closed for another quarter of an hour and refuse to get up. The mother plucked at his sleeve, cajoling softly in his ear, and the sister left her lessons to help the mother, all to no avail. The father only ensconced himself farther in the chair. Not until the two women pulled him up under the arms would he open his eyes and look back and forth from the mother to the sister, with the customary remark: "What a life. This is the rest of my old age." And supported by the two women, he rose haltingly to his feet as if he himself were his greatest burden and allowed the women to steer him to the door, where he shrugged them off and labored on alone, while the mother dropped her sewing and the sister her pen to run after him and aid him further.

Who in this overworked and exhausted family had time to fuss over Gregor more than was absolutely necessary? The household was even further reduced; the maid was dismissed after all and a huge bony charwoman with white hair flapping around her head came mornings and evenings to see to the heaviest chores; the mother took care of everything else on top of her copious sewing. Even various pieces of family jewelry, which the mother and sister used to joyously display at parties and celebrations, had to be sold, as Gregor learned from a discussion of the obtained prices one evening. However, their most persistent lament was that they could not leave this apartment, much too large for their present needs, because it was inconceivable how Gregor was to be moved. But Gregor fully comprehended that it was not only consideration for him that prevented a move, for he could easily have been transported in a suitable crate with a few airholes; what truly hindered them was an utter hopelessness and the belief that a plight had befallen them unlike any other that had been visited upon their friends or relatives. They carried out the world's demands on poor people to the extreme: The father fetched breakfast for the minor bank clerks, the mother sacrificed herself to the underwear of strangers, the sister ran to and fro behind the counter at customers' beck and call, but beyond this the family had no more strength. And the wound in Gregor's back began to hurt anew whenever the mother and sister, after putting the father to bed, returned to the table, left their work idle, drew close to each other, and sat cheek to cheek, and whenever the mother, pointing toward Gregor's room, now said: "Go shut that door, Grete," and Gregor was in darkness again while next door the women mingled their tears or stared dry-eyed at the table.

Gregor spent the days and nights almost entirely without sleep. Sometimes he mulled over the idea that the next time the door opened he would take control of the family affairs as he had done in the past; these musings led him once more after such a long interval to conjure up the figures of the boss, the head clerk, the salesmen, the apprentices, the dullard of an office messenger, two or three friends from other firms, a sweet and fleeting memory of a chambermaid in one of the rural hotels, a cashier in a milliner's shop whom he had wooed earnestly but too slowly— they all appeared mixed up with strangers or nearly forgotten people, but instead of helping him and his family they were each and every one unapproachable, and he was relieved when they evaporated. Then other times he could not be bothered to worry about his family, he was filled with rage at their miserable treatment of him, and even though he could not imagine anything that might spark his appetite he still devised plans to raid the pantry and, even if he was not hungry, get the food due him. No longer concerning herself about what Gregor might particularly care for, the sister hastily shoved any old food through the door to Gregor's room with her foot, both morning and noon before she raced to work, and in the evening cleared it all out with one sweep of the broom, indifferent to whether the food had only been tasted or—as was most frequently the case—left completely untouched. The cleaning of his room, which she now always did in the evening, could not have been more cursory. Grimy dirt streaked the walls, layers of dust and filth had settled everywhere. At first, whenever the sister came in, he would station himself in corners particularly offensive in this respect as if to impart some reproach. But he could have waited there for weeks without the sister showing any improvement; she could see the dirt just as well as he, but she had simply made up her mind to leave it there. At the same time, with a testiness that was new to her and had in fact overtaken the whole family, she made certain that this tidying remained in her sole domain. The mother once subjected Gregor's room to thorough cleaning that was effected only after many buckets of water—all this dampness sickened Gregor of course, and he lay sprawled on the sofa, embittered and immobile—but the mother's punishment was not far off. Because as soon as the sister noticed the change in Gregor's room that evening, she ran into the living room deeply insulted and despite the mother's hands, raised imploringly, burst into a fit of tears while the astonished parents—the father was naturally shocked out of his chair—looked on helplessly. Then they quickly started in; the father admonished the mother to his right for not having left the cleaning of Gregor's room to the sister and shouted at the sister to his left that she was never again allowed to clean Gregor's room; meanwhile the mother tried to drag the overexcited father to the bedroom, the sister shaking with sobs beat her small fists on the table, and Gregor hissed furiously because no one had thought to close his door and spare him this racket and spectacle.

But even if the sister, worn out by her job, ceased to tend to him as she used to, there was no need for the mother's intervention or for Gregor to be at all neglected. For now there was the charwoman. This old widow, who must have weathered the worst in her long life with the help of her sturdy bone structure, was not particularly disgusted by Gregor. Without being truly nosy, she happened to open the door to Gregor's room one day and, at the sight of Gregor—who was completely caught off guard and, although no one chased him, began running back and forth—she merely stood still, her arms folded over her middle, in amazement. Since then she never failed to briefly open the door a crack every morning and evening to look in on Gregor. Initially she would also call him over to her with words she probably considered friendly, like "Come on over, you old dung beetle!"[8] or "Just look at the old dung beetle!" Gregor did not respond to these overtures but remained in his place as if the door had never been opened. If only they had ordered this charwoman to clean his room every day instead of allowing her to uselessly barge in on him whenever the whim seized her! Early one morning—a heavy rain, maybe a sign of the coming spring, was pelting the windowpanes—Gregor was so exasperated when the charwoman started up again with her sayings that he turned toward her as if to attack, albeit decrepitly and slowly. Instead of being frightened, however, the charwoman simply raised a chair that was close to the door and stood there with her mouth wide open; it was clearly her intention to shut her mouth only when the chair was smashed on Gregor's back. "So you're not coming any closer?" she inquired when Gregor turned back around, and calmly put the chair back down in the corner.

Gregor now ate next to nothing. Only when by chance he passed the food set out for him would he take a bite just for fun, hold it in his mouth for hours, and mostly spit it back out. At first he thought he was mourning the state of his room and that this kept him from eating, but he soon grew accustomed to precisely these changes. It had become habit to put anything that had no other place in the house in this room, and these things now amounted to a lot because a room in the house had been let to three gentlemen boarders.[9] These dour men—all three had full beards, as Gregor ascertained once through a crack in the door—were passionate about order, not only in their room but, since they were boarding there, throughout the whole household, especially the kitchen. They could not abide useless, let alone dirty, junk. Besides, they had for the most part brought their own household goods with them. For this reason many things had become superfluous, and while they had no commercial worth they also could not be thrown away. All these things ended up in Gregor's room. This included the ash can and the rubbish bin from the kitchen. Anything deemed useless for now was hastily hurled into Gregor's room by the charwoman; Gregor was usually lucky enough to see just the object in question and the hand that held it. Perhaps the charwoman intended to collect these things as time and opportunity afforded, or to throw everything out together, but in fact they lay wherever they happened to land unless Gregor waded through the junk pile and set it in motion, at first out of necessity because there was no other free space to crawl but later with increasing pleasure, though after these forays he lay still for hours, achingly tired and miserable.

Since the boarders sometimes took their evening meal in the common living room as well, the living room door stayed shut certain evenings, yet Gregor was easily reconciled to the door's closing: On many evenings it was opened he had not taken advantage of it but, without the family noticing it, had lain in the darkest corner of his room. One time, however, the charwoman had left the living room door slightly ajar and it stayed open, even when the boarders entered in the evening and the lamp was lit. They sat at the head of the table where the father, mother, and Gregor had sat in the old days; they unfolded their napkins and took knife and fork in hand. The mother at once appeared in the doorway with a platter of meat and directly behind her was the sister with a heaping dish of potatoes. Thick plumes of steam rose from the food. The boarders bent over the dishes as if to examine them before eating; in fact the one in the middle, seemingly regarded as an authority by the other two, cut into a piece of meat still on the platter, evidently to determine whether it was tender enough or needed to be sent back to the kitchen. He was satisfied and mother and sister, who were anxiously watching, released their breath and began to smile.

The family itself ate in the kitchen. Nevertheless the father came into the living room before retiring to the kitchen, bowed deeply, hat in hand, and made the rounds of the table. The boarders stood up as one and mumbled something into their beards. When they were alone again they ate in virtual silence. It seemed odd to Gregor that out of the myriad noises from the meal, he could always distinguish the mashing teeth, as if to indicate to Gregor that teeth were needed in order to eat and even the best of toothless jaws could do nothing. "I'm hungry enough," said Gregor to himself mournfully, "but not for these things. How these boarders stuff themselves and here I am starving to death!"

On this very evening—Gregor could not remember having heard the violin all this time—the sound of the violin came from the kitchen. The boarders had already finished their supper, the middle one had taken out a newspaper and distributed a sheet each to the two others, and they were now leaning back, reading and smoking. When the violin began playing they all looked up, got to their feet, and tiptoed to the foyer door, where they huddled together. They must have been heard from the kitchen because the father called out: "Are the gentlemen disturbed by the violin playing? It can be stopped at once." "On the contrary," said the middle gentleman, "wouldn't the young lady care to come in here with us and play where it is more spacious and comfortable?" "Oh, certainly," cried the father, as though he were the violinist. The boarders retreated to the room and waited. Soon the father entered with the music stand, the mother with the music, and the sister with the violin. The sister calmly prepared everything to start playing; the parents, who had never before let a room and were consequently excessively polite to the boarders, did not dare to sit in their own chairs; the father leaned against the door with his right hand tucked between two buttons of his fastened uniform jacket; the mother, however, was offered a chair by one of the gentlemen and sat down where he had chanced to put it, off in a corner.

The sister began to play; the mother and father on either side of her attentively followed the movement of her hands. Gregor, seduced by the playing, had ventured farther forward and his head was already in the living room. His growing lack of concern for the others hardly surprised him, whereas previously he had prided himself on being considerate. And yet now he had more reason than ever to stay hidden: He was coated with the dust that blanketed his room and blew around at the slightest movement, bits of fluff, hair, and food stuck to his back and trailed from his sides; he was so deeply indifferent that he would not turn over and scrape his back clean against the carpet as he once did several times a day. And despite his condition, he was not ashamed to inch farther onto the immaculate living room floor.

No one, to be sure, paid him any mind. The family was completely absorbed by the violin playing; the boarders on the other hand had at first stood with their hands in their pockets so close behind the sister that they could all have read the music, which must have irritated her, but they soon withdrew to the window and stayed there with lowered heads and half-heard grumblings while the father eyed them nervously. Indeed it was more than obvious that their hopes of hearing the violin played well or entertainingly were disappointed, that they had had enough of the recital and were only suffering through this disturbance of their peace out of politeness. In particular, the manner in which they blew their clouds of cigar smoke to the ceiling through their mouths and noses displayed severe aggravation. And yet the sister played so beautifully. Her face was tilted to one side and she followed the notes with soulful and probing eyes. Gregor advanced a little, keeping his eyes low so that they might possibly meet hers. Was he a beast if music could move him so? He felt as though the path to his unknown hungers was being cleared. He was grimly determined to reach the sister and tug on her skirt to suggest that she take her violin and come into his room, for no one here was as worthy of her playing as he would be. He would never let her leave his room, at least as long as he lived; for the first time, his horrifying appearance would work to his advantage: He would stand guard at all the doors simultaneously, hissing at the attackers; the sister, however, would not be forcibly detained but would stay with him of her own free will. She would sit beside him on the sofa, she would lean down and listen as he confided how he had intended to send her to the Conservatory and how, if misfortune had not interfered, he would have announced this plan to everyone last Christmas—had Christmas really passed already?—and brooked no argument. After this declaration the sister would burst into emotional tears and Gregor would raise himself to her shoulder and kiss her neck, which she kept bare since she started working, wearing no ribbon or collar.

"Herr Samsa!" yelled the middle man to the father, and without wasting another word pointed his index finger at Gregor, who was slowly crawling forward. The violin stopped abruptly, and the middle boarder first smiled at his friends, shaking his head, and then looked at Gregor again. Rather than drive Gregor out, the father seemed to consider it more urgent to pacify the boarders, although they were not upset in the least and appeared to be more entertained by Gregor than the violin playing. The father rushed to them and tried to herd them back to their room with his outstretched arms while at the same time blocking their view of Gregor with his body. They now became a bit annoyed, but it was not clear whether the father's behavior was to blame or whether the realization was dawning on them that they had unwittingly had a neighbor like Gregor. They demanded explanations from the father, they raised their arms at him and nervously yanked their beards, then they very reluctantly backed away toward their room. In the meantime the sister woke up from the bewildered state she had fallen into after the sudden interruption of her music; after she listlessly dangled the violin and bow awhile in her slack hands and gazed at the music as though she were still playing, she pulled herself together, put the instrument in the mother's lap (the mother was still seated, gasping asthmatically for breath), and ran into the next room, which the boarders were rapidly nearing under the father's pressure. One could see blankets and pillows fly in the air around the bed and arrange themselves under the sister's practiced hands. Before the men even reached the room she had finished making the beds and skipped out. Once again the father seemed so overpowered by his own obstinacy that he had forgotten the very least courtesy due his tenants. He just kept pushing and pushing them up to the very door of the room, where the middle boarder brought him to a halt by thunderously stamping down his foot. "I hereby declare," he said, raising his hand and looking around for the mother and sister, "that in view of the revolting conditions prevailing in this household and family"—here he promptly spat on the floor—"I give immediate notice. Naturally I will not pay a cent for the days I have already spent here; on the contrary I shall seriously consider pursuing some legal claim against you that—believe me—will be quite easy to substantiate." He stopped and stared directly before him as though awaiting something. Sure enough, his two friends jumped in with the words: "We too give our notice." Thereupon he grabbed the door handle and banged shut the door.

The father staggered and groped for his chair, which he collapsed into; it looked like he was stretching out for his usual evening nap, but the seemingly uncontrollable bobbing of his head revealed that he was anything but asleep. All this time Gregor had lain quietly where the boarders had first spied him. The disappointment at his plan's failure and perhaps also the weakness caused by his persistent hunger kept him firmly rooted to the spot. He feared, with a fair degree of certainty, that in the next moment he would bare the brunt of the whole disaster, and so he waited. He did not stir, even when the violin slipped from the mother's shaky fingers and fell from her lap with a reverberating twang.

"My dear parents," said the sister, pounding the table with her hand by way of introduction, "things can't go on like this. Maybe you don't realize it, but I do. I refuse to pronounce my brother's name in front of this monstrosity, and so I say: We have to try to get rid of it. We've done everything humanly possible to care for it and tolerate it; I don't believe anyone could reproach us."

"She's absolutely right," the father said to himself. The mother, who was still struggling to catch her breath and had a wild look in her eyes, began to cough hollowly into her hand.

The sister rushed to the mother and cradled her forehead. The father's thoughts seemed to have cleared in the aftermath of the sister's words; he sat up straight, played with the cap of his uniform among the dishes that still lay on the table from the boarders' supper, and from time to time glanced over at Gregor's inert form.

"We have to try to get rid of it," said the sister, addressing only the father because the mother could hear nothing over her coughing. "It'll kill you both, I can see that coming. We all work too hard to come home to this interminable torture. And I can't stand it anymore." And she began sobbing so violently that her tears coursed down onto the mother's face, where she mechanically wiped them away.

"Oh, child," said the father compassionately and with apparent understanding, "what can we do?"

The sister just shrugged her shoulders, displaying the helplessness that had overtaken her during her crying jag in stark contrast to her former self-confidence.

"If only he could understand us," the father said, almost as a question; the sister, still sobbing, vehemently waved her hand to show how unthinkable it was.

"If only he could understand us," repeated the father, closing his eyes to absorb the sister's conviction that this was impossible, "then we might be able to come to some sort of agreement with him. But as it is—"

"It has to go," the sister cried, "that's the only way, Father.

You have to try to stop thinking that this is Gregor. Our true misfortune is that we've believed it so long. But how can it be Gregor? Because Gregor would have understood long ago that people can't possibly live with such a creature, and he would have gone away of his own accord. Then we would have no brother, but we could go on living and honor his memory. But instead this creature persecutes us and drives out the boarders; it obviously wants to take over the whole apartment and throw us out into the gutter. Just look, Father," she suddenly screamed, "he's at it again!" And in a state of panic that was totally incomprehensible to Gregor—she even abandoned the mother, she literally bolted from the chair as if she would rather sacrifice the mother than stay in the vicinity of Gregor—she rushed behind the father, who got to his feet only out of agitation from her behavior and half-raised his arms as if to protect her.

But Gregor had no intention of frightening anyone, least of all his sister. He had merely begun to turn around to start the journey back to his room, although it was an alarming operation to watch, since his enfeebled condition forced him to use his head to achieve the complex rotations by alternately lifting it and then banging it down. He paused and looked around him. His good intentions appeared to have been recognized; it had only been a momentary alarm. Now they all watched him in glum silence. The mother lay back in her chair, her legs outstretched but squeezed together and her eyes almost shut from exhaustion; the father and sister sat side by side—her hand around his neck.

"Now maybe I can turn around," Gregor thought, and resumed his labor. He could not help panting from the effort and had to rest every once in a while. At least he left on his own with no one harassing him. As soon as he had finished turning, he started to crawl straight back. He was astonished by how far away the room was and could not understand how he had recently and in his pathetic condition so unknowingly traveled that great a distance. He was so intent on crawling rapidly that he barely noticed that not a single word or any interference came from his family. Only when he was already in the doorway did he turn his head—not all the way, for he felt his neck stiffening—and saw that nothing had changed behind him except that the sister had risen. His final gaze fell on the mother, who was now deeply asleep.

He was hardly in his room when the door was shut hastily, then bolted and locked. The sudden noise behind him rattled Gregor so much that the little legs gave way beneath him. It was the sister who had been in such a rush. She had been standing by ready and waiting and had lightly leapt forward before Gregor even heard her coming; "Finally!" she cried to the parents as she turned the key in the lock.

"What now?" Gregor wondered, peering around in the darkness. He soon discovered that he could no longer move at all. This did not particularly puzzle him, rather it seemed unnatural to him that he had actually been able to walk on these skinny little legs. Otherwise he felt relatively comfortable. Of course his whole body ached, but it seemed to him that the pain was gradually fading and would eventually disappear altogether. He could hardly feel the rotten apple in his back and the enflamed area around it, which were covered over by soft dust. His thoughts, full of tenderness and love, went back to his family. He was even more firmly convinced than his sister, if possible, that he should disappear. He remained in this state of empty and peaceful reflection until the tower clock struck three in the morning. He hung on to see the growing light outside the window. Then his head sank involuntarily to the floor and his last feeble breath streamed from his nostrils.

When the charwoman came early in the morning—from sheer energy and impatience she always slammed all the doors, no matter how many times she had been asked not to, so it was impossible for anyone to sleep peacefully after her arrival—she found nothing unusual during her brief customary visit to Gregor's room. She thought he was lying motionless on purpose, pretending to sulk; she imbued him with all manner of intelligence. Since she happened to be holding the long broom, she tried to tickle him from the doorway. When this produced no response she became annoyed and began to jab at Gregor; it was only when her shoves were met with no resistance and moved him from his place that she became alerted. She soon grasped the truth of the matter; her eyes went wide and she gave a low whistle but did not hesitate to tear open the Samsas' bedroom door and yell into the dark: "Come and look at this, it's croaked; it's lying there, dead as a doornail!"

Herr and Frau Samsa[10] sat up in their matrimonial bed, struggling to overcome the shock of the charwoman's announcement before realizing its full import. Then they each clambered quickly out of bed from either side, Herr Samsa wrapped the blanket around his shoulders and Frau Samsa came out in her nightgown, and so attired they stepped into Gregor's room. Meanwhile the living room door also opened, where Grete had slept since the advent of the boarders; she was fully dressed as though she had not slept all night and her wan face seemed to confirm this. "Dead?" said Frau Samsa, and looked up inquiringly at the charwoman, although she could have investigated herself and it was plain enough without examination. "I'd say so," said the charwoman, and to prove it she pushed Gregor's corpse well to one side with the broom. Frau Samsa made a move to stop her, but checked it. "Well," said Herr Samsa, "thanks be to God." He crossed himself and the three women followed suit. Grete, her eyes never leaving the corpse, said: "Look how thin he was. It's so long since he's eaten anything. The food came out just as it was brought in." Indeed, Gregor's body was completely flat and dry; this could be truly appreciated for the first time, since it was no longer supported by the little legs and nothing else distracted their gaze.

"Grete, come in with us for a while," said Frau Samsa, with a sad smile, and Grete traipsed after her parents into their bedroom without looking back at the corpse. The charwoman shut Gregor's door and opened the window wide. Although it was very early in the morning, there was a mildness in the fresh air. It was, after all, already the end of March.

The three boarders emerged from their room and looked around in astonishment for their breakfast; they had been forgotten. "Where is breakfast?" the middle gentleman gruffly demanded of the charwoman. But she just shushed the men with a finger to the mouth and silently ushered them into Gregor's room. They filed into the now fully lit room and circled around Gregor's corpse, with their hands in the pockets of their rather shabby coats.

Just then the bedroom door opened and Herr Samsa appeared in his uniform with his wife on one arm and his daughter on the other. They were all a little teary-eyed, and from time to time Grete pressed her face against her father's sleeve.

"Leave my house at once!" pronounced Herr Samsa, and

pointed to the door without releasing the women. "Whatever do you mean?" said the mildly disconcerted middle boarder, with a sugary smile. The two other gentlemen stood with their hands held behind their backs, incessantly rubbing them together as if in gleeful anticipation of a terrific row that they were bound to win. "I mean exactly what I said," answered Herr Samsa, making a beeline for the boarders with his two companions in tow. The middle boarder quietly stood his ground at first, eyeing the floor as if reordering things in his head. "Well then, we'll be going," he said, and looked up at Herr Samsa as though in a sudden fit of humility he were seeking fresh approval for this decision. Herr Samsa just nodded briefly several times with his eyes bulging. Thereupon the gentleman immediately strode into the foyer; his two friends had been standing at attention for a while and now positively chased after him, seemingly fearful that Herr Samsa might reach the foyer before them and cut them off from their leader. In the foyer, all three took their hats from the coatrack, their canes from the umbrella stand, silently bowed, and then left the apartment. In what proved to be unfounded mistrust, Herr Samsa and the two women stepped out onto the landing and, leaning on the banisters, they watched the gentlemen slowly but surely descend the long staircase, disappearing on each floor at a certain turn and then reappearing a moment later; as they dwindled down, the family's interest in them waned, and when a butcher's boy cockily carrying a tray on his head swung past them and on up the stairs, Herr Samsa and the women quit the banister and, as if relieved, returned to the apartment.

They decided to spend the day resting and going for a walk; they not only deserved this respite from work, they desperately needed it. So they sat down at the table to write three letters of excuse,[11] Herr Samsa to the bank director, Frau Samsa to her client, and Grete to the shopkeeper. While they were writing, the charwoman came in to announce that she was off, as her morning chores were done. The three scribes merely nodded at first without looking up, but when the charwoman kept hovering they eyed her irritably. "Well?" asked Herr Samsa. The charwoman stood grinning in the doorway as if about to report some great news for the family but would only do so after being properly questioned. The little ostrich feather sitting almost erect on top of her hat, which had annoyed Herr Samsa throughout the whole of her employ, fluttered about in all directions. "Well, what is it then?" queried Frau Samsa, for whom the charwoman had the most respect. "Well," answered the charwoman, interrupting herself with good-natured chuckling, "well, you don't have to worry about getting rid of the thing next door. It's already been taken care of." Frau Samsa and Grete bowed their heads to the letters as if to resume writing; Herr Samsa, who realized that she was eager to begin describing the details, cut her short with a definitive gesture of his hand. But since she could not tell her story, she remembered that she was in a great hurry, and, obviously insulted, she called out: "So long, everyone," then furiously whirled around and slammed out of the apartment with a terrific bang of the door.

"She'll be dismissed tonight," said Herr Samsa, receiving no reply from either his wife or daughter, for the charwoman had dismantled their barely maintained composure. They got up, went to the window, and stayed there hugging each other. Herr Samsa turned in his chair and quietly watched them a little while. Then he called: "Come now, come over here. Put the past to rest. And have a little consideration for me too." The women promptly obeyed him, caressed him, and hurriedly finished their letters.

Then all three left the apartment together, which they had not done in months, and took a trolley to the countryside on the outskirts of town. Their trolley car had no other passengers and was flooded with warm sunshine. Leaning back comfortably in their seats, they discussed their prospects for the future and concluded, on closer inspection, that these were not at all bad; for all three had jobs which, although they had never really questioned each other about this, were entirely satisfactory and seemed to be particularly promising. The greatest immediate amelioration of their circumstances would easily come to fruition with a change of residence: They wanted to take some place smaller and less expensive but better situated and more efficiently designed than the apartment they had, which had been Gregor's choice. It occurred almost simultaneously to both Herr and Frau Samsa, while they were conversing and looking at their increasingly vivacious daughter, that despite the recent sorrows that had paled her cheeks, she had blossomed into a pretty and voluptuous young woman. Growing quieter and almost unconsciously communicating through exchanged glances, they thought it was time to find her a good husband. And it was like a confirmation of their new dreams and good intentions that at their journey's end their daughter jumped to her feet and stretched her young body.

The Judgment[*]

---

[*]Originally published in 1913 under the German title "Das Urteil. Ein Geschichte."

IT WAS A SUNDAY morning at the peak of spring. Georg Bendemann, a young businessman, sat in his own room on the second floor of one of the low, shabbily constructed houses that stretched alongside the river in an extensive row, almost indistinguishable from each other except in height and color. He had just finished writing a letter to a childhood friend who now lived abroad, he fiddled with the letter as he languidly sealed it, and then, with his elbow propped up on the writing desk, gazed out the window at the river, the bridge, and the faintly green hills on the far bank.

He recalled how his friend, disgruntled by his prospects at home, had more or less fled to Russia. Now he ran a business in St. Petersburg that started off very well but had long since faltered, as the friend bitterly complained during his increasingly rare visits. And so he was pointlessly grinding himself down in a foreign country, an unfamiliar full beard barely hiding the face Georg had known so well since childhood and a sallow complexion indicating an advancing disease. By his own account he had no real contact with the local colony of his countrymen and virtually no social intercourse with the Russian families and so resigned himself to becoming an incurable bachelor.

What could one write to such a man, a man who had obviously gone astray and who was certainly to be pitied but could not be helped? Should he be advised to come home, to transplant his life and resume all the old friendships—nothing prevented this— and generally rely on the help of friends? But all this would mean to him, and the more tactfully it was put the more offensive it would be, was that his every effort had been for naught, and he should finally abandon them, that he should return home and suffer being viewed by everyone as the prodigal returned forever, that only his friends had any understanding of things, and that he was a big child who must simply listen to those friends who had remained home and been successful. And after all, could one be assured that there would be any purpose to all this certain pain inflicted upon him? Perhaps it would be impossible to coax him home at all—he himself said that he no longer understood the goings-on here at home—and so he would remain banished despite everything, embittered by his friends' advice and further alienated from them. But if he did actually follow their advice and then could not get along at home—not out of malice but through force of circumstance—either with his friends or without them, suffering the humiliation of becoming truly friendless and homeless, would it not be better for him to stay abroad, just as he was? Could one really imagine, considering the circumstances, that he could make a successful go of it back here?

For these reasons it was impossible to send any of the real news, if one wanted to keep up a correspondence at all, that one would nonchalantly reveal to the most casual acquaintance. It was more than three years since the friend's last visit, a circumstance he ineffectually blamed on Russia's uncertain political situation, which apparently would not permit even the shortest trip of a small business man while hundreds of thousands of Russians peacefully traveled the world over. In the course of these three years, however, much had changed in Georg's own life. The news of his mother's death—she died two years ago and Georg had since been living with his elderly father—had reached the friend, who sent a letter expressing his condolences so dryly that it could be concluded that the grief over such an event could not be felt from such a distance. But since that time Georg had tackled his business, as well as everything else, with more fervor. Perhaps his father had insisted on running the business his own way during the mother's lifetime and prevented Georg from making his own mark; perhaps his father, while still working, had become less active since her death; perhaps—and indeed this was most probable—accidental good fortune had played a far more important role, but whatever the cause, the business had grown quite dramatically during these two years: The personnel had been doubled, the profits had increased fivefold, and there was undoubtedly further prosperity just around the corner.

But Georg's friend had no inkling of this change. Earlier, perhaps the letter of condolence was the last time, he had tried to lure Georg into emigrating to Russia and expounded upon the prospects that St. Petersburg offered in precisely Georg's line of business. The figures he quoted were minuscule compared to the scale Georg's business had assumed. But Georg was not inclined to write of his commercial success to his friend, and were he to do so now, it would appear especially peculiar.

So Georg always confined himself to relating the trivial matters that randomly arise from a disorganized memory on a reflective Sunday. His sole desire was to leave intact the picture of the hometown the friend must have constructed over the years and had come to accept. Thus it happened that Georg had informed his friend in three fairly widely spaced letters about the engagement of an inconsequential person to an equally inconsequential girl until, quite contrary to his intentions, the friend became interested in this noteworthy event.

Yet Georg preferred writing about these sorts of things rather than admit that he himself had gotten engaged a month ago to a Fraulein Frieda Brandenfeld, a girl from a well-to-do family. He often spoke of his friend to his fiancée and the strange relationship that had developed from their correspondence. "So he won't be coming to our wedding," she said, "and yet I have the right to meet all your friends." "I don't want to trouble him," Georg replied; "please understand me, he would probably come, at least I think so, but he would feel obligated and hurt and he might even envy me; at any rate he'd feel dejected and, with no other recourse, he'd have to go back alone. Alone—do you know what that is?" "Yes, but might he not learn of our marriage some other way?" "I can't help that of course, but it's unlikely considering his circumstances." "If you have such friends, Georg, you should never have even gotten engaged." "Well, we both have that cross to bear, but now I wouldn't have it any other way." And when, breathing quickly under his kisses, she still protested with: "It really does offend me," he decided there wouldn't be much harm in telling his friend everything. "This is how I am and so this is how he must take me," he said to himself. "I can't fashion myself into a different person who might be better suited to be his friend."

And in the long letter he had written that Sunday morning, he did in fact announce to his friend his engagement with the following words: "I have saved the best news for last. I have become engaged to a Fraulein Frieda Brandenfeld, a girl from a well-to-do family that only settled here long after your departure, so that you most likely don't know them. There will be time to tell you more about my fiancée later, but for today suffice it to say that I am very happy and that, insofar as our own relationship is concerned, the only difference is that you have exchanged a quite ordinary friend for a happy one. Furthermore, in my fiancée, who sends her warm regards and who will shortly be writing to you personally, you will acquire a sincere friend, a not wholly unimportant thing for a bachelor. I know there is much to keep you from visiting us, but wouldn't my wedding be precisely the right occasion for overcoming these obstacles? Be that as it may, do as you see fit, all other considerations aside."

Georg had been sitting at his writing desk with this letter in his hand for a long time, his face turned to the window. With a vacant smile, he had barely acknowledged the greeting of an acquaintance passing in the street below.

He finally tucked the letter into his pocket, left his room, crossed a little passageway, and entered his father's room, which he had not set foot in for months. Indeed, there was usually no cause for him to do so, since he saw his father regularly at the office; middays they always dined together at a restaurant, and although they fended for themselves in the evening, they usually—unless Georg, as was most often the case, went out with friends or, more recently, visited his fiancée—sat for a while, each with his own newspaper, in their common living room.

Georg was shocked to see how dark his father's room was even on this sunny morning. The high wall towering on the other side of the narrow courtyard really cast quite a shadow. His father was sitting by the window in a corner elaborately decorated with mementos of Georg's late mother, reading a newspaper held up at an angle from his eyes to compensate for some deficiency in his vision. The remains of his breakfast, not much of which seemed to have been eaten, stood on the table.

"Ah, Georg!" said his father, and promptly rose to meet him. His heavy dressing gown swung open as he walked and the skirts flapped around him.—"My father is still such a giant," Georg remarked to himself.

"It's unbearbly dark in here," he then said.

"Yes, it certainly is dark," his father agreed.

"And you've shut the window too?"

"I prefer it like this."

"Well, it's quite warm outside," said Georg, almost as an addendum to his previous comment, and sat down.

His father cleared away the breakfast dishes and put them on a chest.

"I only wanted to tell you," continued Georg, blankly mesmerized by the old man's movements, "that I've written to St. Petersburg of my engagement." He drew the letter out of his pocket a little, then let it drop back down.

"To St. Petersburg?" the father asked.

"To my friend there," said Georg, seeking his father's eye.— "He's so different at the office," he thought, "sitting here so expansively with his arms crossed over his chest."

"Yes. To your friend," the father emphasized.

"Well, you know, Father, that I didn't want to tell him about my engagement at first. Out of consideration for him, no other reason. You know yourself he's a difficult man. I said to myself that, however unlikely, considering his solitary life, he might hear of my engagement some other way. I can't stop that, but he wasn't going to hear it from me."

"And now you've reconsidered?" asked his father, placing the huge newspaper on the windowsill and his spectacles on top of it, then covering them with his hand.

"Yes, now I've reconsidered. If he is a good friend of mine, I said to myself, then my happy engagement should also make him happy. And so then I didn't hesitate any longer to tell him. But before I posted it, I did want to let you know."

"Georg," said his father, opening wide his toothless mouth, "listen to me! You've come to me with this matter to consult me. No doubt that's to your credit. But it is nothing, less than nothing, if you do not tell me the whole truth. I don't want to stir up inappropriate matters here. Since the death of our dear mother, certain unpleasant things have occurred. Perhaps the time to speak of them will come too and perhaps it will come sooner than we think. At the office there is much that escapes me, perhaps things aren't exactly being kept from me—I won't assume they are being kept from me—but I'm not up to it any longer: My memory's failing and I can't keep track of so many things anymore. First of all, that's the course of nature, and second, I was hit harder than you by the death of our precious mother.—

But since we're just talking about this, this letter, I beg of you, Georg, don't lie to me. It's a trivial matter, barely worth one's breath, so don't lie to me. Do you really have this friend in St. Petersburg?"

Georg stood up, embarrassed. "Never mind my friends. A thousand friends cannot replace my father. Do you know what I think? You're not taking good enough care of yourself. But your age demands it. You know very well that you are indispensable to me at the office, but if the business is going to endanger your health, then tomorrow I'll shut it down for good. But that won't do. We have to make changes in your daily routine. From the ground up. You sit here in the dark while the living room is streaming with light. You pick at your breakfast instead of nourishing yourself properly. You sit by a closed window when the air would do you so much good. No, Father! I will fetch the doctor and we will follow his instructions. We'll switch rooms, you'll take the front room and I'll take this one. It won't be any different for you, we'll move all your things in there. But all in due time, just lie down in bed for a bit now, you really need to rest. Come, I'll help you undress, you'll see, I know how. Or would you rather go straight to the front room and lie down in my bed for now? That would be the most sensible thing."

Georg stood close to his father, whose head, with its fleecy white hair, had sunk onto his chest.

"Georg," his father said softly, without moving.

Georg immediately knelt down by his father, he saw the enormous pupils fixing him from the corners of the eyes in his father's worn face.

"You have no friend in St. Petersburg. You have always been a prankster and you've also never spared me from your pranks. How could you possibly have a friend there! I simply can't believe it."

"Just think back a bit, Father," said Georg, lifting his father out of the chair and slipping off the dressing gown as soon as he rather feebly stood there, "it'll soon be three years since my friend came to visit us. I still remember that you didn't especially like him. At least twice I pretended to you that he wasn't here, even though he was sitting in my room. I could understand your aversion to him perfectly well, my friend has his quirks. But then you got along with him quite well later on. At the time I felt very proud that you were listening to him, nodding and asking him questions. If you think about it, you're bound to remember. He used to tell us the most incredible stories of the Russian Revolution. Like the time he was on a business trip to Kiev, and during a riot he saw a priest on a balcony who had cut a broad bloody cross into his palm and raised it, appealing to the mob. You've even repeated this story once or twice."

Meanwhile Georg had successfully eased his father back into the chair and carefully removed the socks and the long woolen underclothes he wore over his linen underwear. At the sight of these rather soiled undergarments he reproached himself for neglecting his father. It would certainly have been his duty to ensure that his father had clean clothes. So far he had not explicitly discussed his father's future with his fiancée, for they had both tacitly assumed that he would remain on in the old house by himself. But Georg now resolved, with swift and firm determination, to move his father into his new household with him. It almost seemed, on closer inspection, that the care his father would get there might come too late.

He carried his father to bed in his arms. During the few steps to the bed he noticed, with an awful feeling, that his father was playing with his watch chain as he curled against Georg's chest. He could not lay him down right away because he clutched the watch chain so fiercely.

But no sooner was he in bed than all seemed well. He covered himself up and then drew the blankets especially high over his shoulders. He looked up at Georg with a not unfriendly gaze.

"You are beginning to remember him, aren't you?" asked Georg, giving him an encouraging nod.

"Am I well covered now?" his father asked, as if he could not check to see whether his feet were covered or not.

"So you're already quite snug in bed," remarked Georg, and he tucked the blankets more closely around him.

"Am I well covered?" his father repeated, and seemed to be keenly interested in the answer.

"Don't worry, you're all covered up."

"No!" shouted his father, so loudly that the answer slammed back into the question, throwing off the blankets with such force that they unfurled completely for a moment in the air, and then springing to his feet in bed. He had only one hand on the ceiling to steady himself. "You wanted to cover me up, I know it, you little cretin, but I'm not covered up yet. And even if I'm at the end of my strength, it's still enough for you, more than enough for you. Yes, I know your friend. He would have been the son after my own heart. That's why you've been cheating him all these years. Why else? Do you think I haven't wept for him? And that's why you lock yourself up in your office, the chief is busy, mustn't be disturbed—so you can write your deceitful little letters to Russia. But fortunately no one has to teach a father to see through his son. And just when you thought you had him down, all the way down, so far down you can sit your backside on him and he won't move, then my fine son decides to get himself married!"

Georg stared up at the monstrous specter of his father.[12] His friend in St. Petersburg, whom his father suddenly knew so well, wrenched his heart as never before. He imagined him lost in the vastness of Russia. He pictured him standing in the doorway of his empty, plundered warehouse. He could barely stand amid the wreck of his showcases, his ruined wares, and the falling gas brackets. Why did he have to move so far away?

"Now listen to me!" his father cried, and Georg, nearly half frantic, ran to the bed to absorb everything, but stopped midway there.

"Because she lifted her skirts," his father started simpering, "because she pulled up her skirts like this, the nasty little goose," and demonstrated by hiking his shirt high enough to reveal the scar on his thigh from his war days, "because she lifted her skirts like this and like that, you threw yourself on her, and in order to have your way with her undisturbed, you disgraced your mother's memory, betrayed your friend, and shoved your father into bed so that he can't move. But can he move, or can't he?"

And he stood up, independent of any support, and kicked out his legs. He was radiant with insight.

Georg stood in a corner, as far from his father as possible. He had already made up his mind years ago to guard his every move so as to be on the lookout for a surprise attack from above, behind, or below. He recalled this long-forgotten resolve just now and as quickly forgot it, like a short length of thread drawn through the eye of a needle.

"But your friend has not been betrayed after all!" cried his father, punctuating his words with a pointed finger. "I've been representing him locally."

"What a comedian!" burst from Georg, but he realized just as soon the damage that had been done, and only too late bit down—his eyes bulging—so hard on his tongue that he recoiled in pain.

"Yes, I have been acting out a play! A play! Great word! What other comfort was left for an old widowed father? Tell me—and when you answer, still be my living son—what was left for me, in my back room, plagued by a disloyal staff, and old to the very marrow? And my son saunters exultantly through the world, closing deals I had prepared, falling all over himself with joy, and slinking away from his father with the stiff mug of an honorable man! Do you think I didn't love you, I who fathered you?"

"Now he's going to lean forward," thought Georg; "what if he fell and shattered to pieces!" These words buzzed through his brain.

His father did lean forward but did not tumble. Since Georg had not come any nearer, as expected, his father righted himself again.

"Stay where you are, I don't need you! You think you still have the power to come over here and only hold back of your own free will. Don't fool yourself! I am still stronger by far. Alone I may have had to yield, but Mother left her strength to me, your friend has joined me in a splendid alliance, and I have your clientele here in my pocket!"

"He even has pockets in his nightshirt!" Georg said to himself, and believed that this remark could render his father ridiculous before the whole world. But this thought stayed with him only a moment, because he always forgot everything.

"Just bring your fiancée around here on your arm! I'll sweep her from your side, you don't know how quick!"

Georg grimaced in disbelief. His father merely nodded at Georg's corner, assuring the truth of his words.

"How you amused me today, coming to ask me if you should tell your friend about your engagement. He already knows it, you stupid boy, he knows everything! I've been writing because you forgot to take away my writing things. That's why he hasn't come here for years, he knows everything a hundred times better than you; he crumples your unread letters in his left hand while he holds up his right hand to read my letters!"

He flung his arms over his head in his enthusiasm. "He knows everything a thousand times better!" he cried.

"Ten thousand times!" said Georg, to ridicule his father, but the words came out of his mouth deadly earnest.

"For years I've been waiting for you to come to me with this question! Do you think I've been interested in anything else? Do you believe I read newspapers? Look!" and he threw at Georg a sheet of newspaper that had somehow been swept into the bed. It was an old newspaper whose name was entirely unfamiliar to him.

"How long you fought off your adulthood! Your mother had to die, she couldn't witness the joyous day; your friend is rotting in Russia, three years ago he was already yellow enough to toss out, and as for me, you can see how I'm faring. You can see that much!"

"So you've been waiting to pounce on me!" cried Georg.

In a pitying tone, his father casually remarked: "You probably meant to say that earlier. Now it's beside the point."

And then louder: "So now you know what else existed in the world outside of you, before you knew only about yourself! Yes, you were a truly innocent child, but you were even more truly an evil man!—And for that reason, I hereby sentence you to death by drowning!"

Georg felt forcibly driven from the room, the crash of his father falling to the bed still rained down on him as he fled. On the stairs, which he slipped down as he would a hill, he ran into the cleaning woman, who was on her way up to do the morning tidying. "Jesus!" she yelped, and covered her face with her apron, but he was already gone. He leapt from the door and across the road, driven toward the water. Already he clung to the railing like a starving man to food. He swung himself over, like the outstanding gymnast he had been in his youth, the pride of his parents. He was still clinging with a weakening grip when he spied an approaching motor bus through the railings that would easily dampen the sound of his fall; he softly called out: "Dear parents, I have always loved you," and let himself drop.

At that moment an unending stream of traffic crossed over the bridge.

The Stoker: A Fragment*

*Originally published in 1913 under the German title "Der Heizer. Ein Fragment"; the story eventually became the first chapter of Kafka's novel *Amerika*.

AS SIXTEEN-YEAR-OLD KARL ROSSMANN, whose poor parents had sent him off to America because a maid had seduced him and then had his child, sailed into New York harbor on the now slowly moving ship, he saw the Statue of Liberty, which he had already been watching from far off, stand out as if shining in suddenly brighter sunlight. The arm with the sword[13] reached up as if freshly thrust out, and the free breezes blew around the figure.

"So high!" he said to himself, and without any thought of disembarking, he was pushed farther and farther along, all the way to the railing, by the constantly swelling throng of porters pressing past him.

On his way by, a young man with whom he had been briefly acquainted during the voyage said to him: "Well, don't you feel like going ashore yet?" "Oh yes, I'm ready," said Karl, laughing, and out of sheer joy and youthful strength, he hoisted his trunk onto his shoulder. But as he looked beyond his acquaintance, who was already moving off and lightly swinging his stick, he remembered with dismay that he had left his own umbrella below deck. He hastily begged his acquaintance, who seemed none too pleased, to be kind enough to watch his trunk a moment; he surveyed his surroundings to regain his bearings and hurried off. Down below he was disappointed to find that a passageway that would have shortened his route considerably was barred now for the first time, probably because of all the disembarking passengers, and he had to arduously make his way through a long series of small rooms, down countless short staircases, one after another, through continually winding corridors, past a room with a deserted desk, until finally, as he had only gone this way once or twice before and always in a large group, he was utterly lost. In his bewilderment he came to a stop by a small door, and because he encountered no one and could hear only the endless trampling

of thousands of human feet overhead, and from a distance like a
sigh the final whine of the engines shutting down, he began,
without consideration, to pound on the door.

"It's open," a voice called from inside, and Karl opened the
door with a genuine sigh of relief. "Why are you pounding on
the door like a madman?" asked a huge man, barely glancing at
Karl. Through some kind of overhead hatch murky light, long
stale from its use on the decks above, seeped into the miserable
cabin, where a bed, a closet, a chair, and the man were crowded
together side by side as if stowed there. "I've lost my way," said
Karl. "I never really noticed it during the voyage, but this is an
awfully large ship." "Yes, you're right about that," the man said
with a certain degree of pride but did not stop fiddling with the
lock of a small footlocker that he kept pressing shut with both
hands to hear the catch snap home. "But come on in!" the man
continued. "You don't want to stand around outside!" "Am I intruding?" asked Karl. "No, how would you be intruding!" "Are
you German?" Karl tried to reassure himself further because he
had heard a lot about the dangers that threatened newcomers to
America, from the Irish especially.[14] "That I am, yes indeed," said
the man. Karl still hesitated. Then the man unexpectedly seized
the door handle and swiftly shut the door, sweeping Karl into the
cabin. "I can't stand being peered at from the corridor," he said,
fiddling with the chest again; "they all run by and peer in, who
can put up with it!" "But the corridor is totally empty now," said
Karl, who was pressed uncomfortably against the bedpost. "Yes,
now," said the man. "But we're talking about now," thought Karl;
"this is a difficult man to talk to." "Why don't you lie down on
the bed, you'll have more room," said the man. Karl crawled in
as best he could and chuckled loudly at his first unsuccessful
attempt to pitch himself across the bed. But as soon as he was
in the bed he exclaimed: "Good God, I've completely forgotten
my trunk!" "Well, where is it?" "Up on deck, someone I met is
watching it. Now what was his name?" And from a secret pocket
that his mother had sewn into his jacket lining specially for this
voyage, he fished out a visiting card. "Butterbaum, Franz Butterbaum." "Is your trunk really necessary?" "Of course." "Well
then, why did you give it to a complete stranger?" "I had forgotten my umbrella down below and ran to get it, but I didn't
want to lug my trunk along. And then I got lost too." "Are you

alone? No one accompanying you?" "Yes, I'm alone."—"Maybe I should stick with this man," went through Karl's mind, "where could I find a better friend?" "And now you've also lost your trunk. Not to mention the umbrella." And the man sat down on the chair as if he had developed some interest in Karl's problem. "But I don't believe the trunk is really lost yet." "Believe what you want," said the man, vigorously scratching his short, dark thatch of hair, "on a ship the morals change as often as the ports. In Hamburg, your Butterbaum might have guarded your trunk; here there's most likely no trace left of either of them." "Then I must go look for it immediately," said Karl, looking around to see how he could leave. "Stay where you are," the man said, and thrust a hand against Karl's chest, pushing him roughly back onto the bed. "But why?" Karl asked peevishly. "Because it makes no sense," said the man; "in a little while I'm going and then we can go together. Either the trunk is stolen and there's no help for it, or the man has left it there and we'll find it all the more easily when the ship is empty. The same goes for your umbrella." "Do you know your way around the ship?" asked Karl warily, as it seemed to him that there must be some catch in the otherwise convincing notion that his things would be best found on an empty ship. "Well, I'm a stoker,"* the man said. "You're a stoker!" Karl cried happily, as if this exceeded all expectation and, propping himself up on his elbows, he inspected the man more closely. "Just outside the cabin where I slept with the Slovak there was a porthole through which you could see into the engine room." "Yes, that's where I worked," said the stoker. "I have always been interested in technology," said Karl, pursuing his own train of thought, "and would surely have become an engineer later on if I hadn't had to leave for America." "Why did you have to leave, then?" "Oh, that!" said Karl, waving away the whole business with his hand. At the same time he looked at the stoker with a smile as if asking his indulgence for what he hadn't even admitted. "I'm sure there was some reason," said the stoker, and it was hard to tell whether he was demanding or dismissing the story behind that reason. "Now I could become a stoker too,"

---

*Laborer employed to tend and fuel a furnace used to generate steam on a steamship.

said Karl, "my parents don't care what becomes of me." "My job
will be free," said the stoker, and as a show of this he put his
hands in the pockets of his creased and leathery, iron gray trousers and flung his legs across the bed in order to stretch them
out. Karl had to move over closer to the wall. "Are you leaving
the ship?" "Yes, we're moving out today." "But why? Don't you
like it?" "Well, that's the way things go, it's not always a matter
of what pleases you or not. But as a matter of fact you're right,
I don't like it. You're probably not seriously thinking of becoming
a stoker, but that's exactly when it's easiest to become one. So,
I strongly advise you against it. If you wanted to study in Europe,
why don't you want to study here? The American universities are
incomparably better than the European ones." "It's certainly possible," said Karl, "but I have almost no money for a university. I
did read about someone who worked all day and studied at night
until he got a doctorate and became a mayor, I believe, but that
requires a lot of perseverance, doesn't it? I'm afraid that's something I lack. Anyway, I was never a very good student, and leaving
school was not particularly hard on me. And perhaps the schools
here will be even more stringent. I speak almost no English. And
besides, I think people here are prejudiced against foreigners."
"So you've found that out already? Well, that's good. Then you're
my man. Look, we're on a German ship, it belongs to the
Hamburg-America line, so why aren't we all Germans here? Why
is the chief engineer a Romanian? His name is Schubal. It's beyond belief. And that villain makes us slave away on a German
ship! Don't go thinking"—he was out of breath and flailing his
hand—"that I'm complaining just to complain. I know you have
no influence and are just a poor young lad yourself. But it's a
shame!" And he beat the table repeatedly, his eyes fixed on his
fist as he banged. "I've served on so many ships"—and he fired
off twenty names as if they were one word, making Karl dizzy—
"and I've always excelled, I was praised, the captains always liked
my work, I even worked for several years on the same merchant
ship"—he stood up as if this had been the high point of his life—
"and here on this tub, where everything is done by the book and
no brains are required, here I'm no good, here I'm always in
Schubal's way, I'm a lazybones who deserves to be thrown out
and only get his pay out of mercy. Can you understand that? I
can't." "You shouldn't put up with that," said Karl heatedly. He

felt so at home here on the stoker's bed that he had almost lost
any sense of being on the unsteady ground of a ship off the coast
of an unknown continent. "Have you been to see the captain?
Have you asked him to see to your rights?" "Oh, go away, just
go away. I don't want you here. You don't listen to what I say
and then you give me advice. How am I supposed to go to the
captain?" And the stoker wearily sat down again and buried his
face in both hands.

"I can't give him any better advice," Karl said to himself. And
the overwhelming thought occurred to him that he would have
been better off going after his trunk instead of staying here and
offering advice that was only considered stupid. When his father
had handed over the trunk to him for good he had jokingly asked:
"How long will you keep it?" and now this precious trunk might
already be well and truly lost. His sole consolation was that his
father, even if he did make inquiries, could hardly find out about
his present situation. The shipping company could only say that
he had gotten as far as New York. But Karl was sorry that he
had hardly used the items in the trunk, though he ought to have,
for instance, long since changed his shirt. So he had economized
in the wrong place, and now, at the very start of his career, when
it was necessary to arrive neatly dressed, he would have to appear
in a dirty shirt. Otherwise the loss of the trunk would not have
been so bad, as the suit he was wearing was actually better than
the one in the trunk, which was only an emergency suit that his
mother had had to mend just before his departure. Now he also
remembered that a piece of Verona salami was still in his trunk;
his mother had packed this as a special treat, but he had eaten
only the tiniest bit of it because he had had no appetite during
the voyage and the soup served in steerage* amply sufficed. But
he would gladly have that sausage in hand now, so that he could
present it to the stoker. For people such as this are easily won
over if one slips them any old trifle; Karl had learned that from
his father, who by distributing cigars won over all the underlings
with whom he had to do business. At present all Karl had to give
away was his money, and he did not want to touch that for the

---

*Part or division of a ship that formerly contained the steering apparatus and is
allotted to passengers who travel at the cheapest rate.

moment, considering he might have already lost his trunk. Again his thoughts returned to the trunk, and now he could not understand why he had kept watch over it so vigilantly during the voyage that it had almost cost him his sleep, when he had later allowed the same trunk to be taken from him so easily. He remembered the five nights during which he had incessantly suspected a little Slovak, lying two berths to his left, of having designs on the trunk. This Slovak had merely been waiting for Karl to be overcome by fatigue and nod off for a moment so that he could hook the trunk and pull it over to him with a long pole that he played or practiced with all day long. During the day the Slovak seemed innocent enough, but as soon as night fell he would periodically rise from his berth and mournfully eye Karl's trunk. Karl could see him quite clearly, for there was always someone lighting a lamp here or there, even though this was forbidden by the ship's regulations, with the restless anxiety of an emigrant trying to decipher the incomprehensible brochures from the emigration agencies. If such a light was nearby, Karl could doze off for a while; but if the light was far away or it was totally dark, then he had to keep his eyes open. This strain had thoroughly exhausted him and now it may have all been in vain. Oh, that Butterbaum, if he ever saw him again somewhere!

At that instant the absolute silence was broken by brief little thuds in the distance like children's footsteps; they came nearer and grew louder until it was the steady tread of men marching. They were evidently walking single file as was natural in the narrow passage, and a clattering sound like weapons could be heard. Karl, who had been on the verge of stretching out on the bed and sleeping, free from worry over trunks and Slovaks, started up and nudged the stoker to fully alert him, as the head of the procession seemed to have just reached the door. "That's the ship's band," said the stoker, "they've been playing on deck and now they're going to pack up. It's all clear now and we can go. Come on!" He seized Karl by the hand, took a framed picture of the Madonna off the wall at the last moment and stuffed it in his breast pocket, grabbed his footlocker, and hastily left the cabin with Karl.

"Now I'm going to the office and giving those gentlemen a piece of my mind. There are no more passengers, so I don't have to mince words." The stoker kept repeating variations of this, and as he went along he kicked out sideways, attempting to stomp on a rat that scurried across their path but only driving it faster into a hole that it reached in the nick of time. The stoker was generally slow in his movements, for while his legs were long they were just too heavy.

They passed through a section of the kitchen where some girls in dirty aprons—they were deliberately splashing themselves—were washing dishes in large tubs. The stoker called over a girl named Line, put his arm around her waist, and led her a ways away while she pressed herself coquettishly against his arm. "It's time to get our pay, do you want to come along?" he asked. "Why should I bother; bring the money back here," she replied, and slipped under his arm and ran away. "Where did you pick up that beautiful boy?" she called back, but did not wait for an answer. There was laughter from all of the girls, who had stopped their work.

But Karl and the stoker kept walking until they came to a door with a small pediment over it supported by little gilded caryatids. It looked quite extravagant for a ship's decor. Karl realized that he had never been in this area of the ship, which had probably been reserved for first- and second-class passengers during the voyage, whereas now all the partitions had been removed for the scouring of the ship. In fact, they had already run into some men with brooms on their shoulders, who had greeted the stoker. Karl marveled at the intense flurry of activity; he knew little of it, of course, in steerage. Running along the passageways there were also wires from electrical lines, and a little bell could be heard ringing constantly.

The stoker respectfully knocked at the door, and when a voice called, "Come in," he motioned at Karl with a wave of his hand to be brave and enter. This he did, but then remained standing by the door. Beyond the three windows of the room he saw the waves of the ocean, and his heart soared as he took in their buoyant motion, as if he had not been looking incessantly at the ocean for five long days. Immense ships were crossing in front of one another, yielding to the swell of the waves only as much as their tonnage allowed. Through narrowed eyes the ships appeared to be staggering under their own massive weight. Their masts bore slim but elongated flags which were drawn taut by the ships' movement yet kept fluttering to and fro. Salvos, probably fired from warships, rang out; one such ship was passing fairly nearby and its gun barrels were glinting in the sunlight, seemingly enveloped by the sure, smooth, but rippling glide of the ship through the water. The smaller ships and boats, from the doorway at least, could only be seen in the distance as swarms of them darted through the gaps between the larger ships. But beyond all this towered New York, examining Karl with the hundred thousand windows of its skyscrapers. Yes, in this room one knew where one was.

Three gentlemen were sitting at a round table, one a ship's officer in a blue naval uniform and the other two, officials of the harbor authority, in black American uniforms. On the table lay a mountainous stack of different documents, which the first officer skimmed through with pen in hand, then turned over to the other two, who read them, made excerpts, then filed them away in their briefcases, except when one of the two officials, who was almost constantly clacking his teeth, dictated something for his colleague to record.

A small man sat at a desk by one window with his back to the door and fussed over weighty ledgers, which were arranged side by side on a solid bookcase just in front of him. Beside him lay an open cash box, which appeared empty at first glance.

The second window was clear and provided the best view. But two gentlemen stood by the third window, conversing in low tones. One of them, who was leaning against the window, also wore a naval uniform and was toying with the hilt of a sword. The man with whom he was speaking was facing the window, and every so often his movements partially revealed a row of medals on the other man's chest. He was dressed in civilian clothes and held a thin bamboo cane which, since he stood with his hands on his hips, also jutted out like a sword.

Karl did not have much time to ingest all this, for an attendant quickly stepped up to them and asked the stoker, with a purposeful look conveying that he had no business here, what it was he wanted. Responding as softly as he had been asked, the stoker replied that he wished to speak to the chief purser.* The attendant, for his part, dismissed this request with a wave of his hand

---

*Officer on a ship who handles financial accounts.

but nevertheless tiptoed, giving the round table a wide berth, over to the man with the ledgers. This gentleman—as was obvious—abruptly stiffened at the attendant's words but eventually turned to face the man who wanted to speak to him and proceeded to gesticulate furiously at the stoker to ward him off and then, as a further precaution, at the attendant too. The attendant returned to the stoker and said in a confidential manner: "Get out of this room at once!"

Upon receiving this response, the stoker looked down at Karl as if Karl were his heart to which he was silently bemoaning his sorrows. Without further thought Karl charged forward and ran straight across the room, brushing the officer's chair on his way past; the attendant also set off running, crouching low with arms spread wide and ready to scoop, as if he were hunting some sort of vermin, but Karl was the first to reach the chief purser's desk, which he held on to tightly in case the attendant should try to drag him away.

Naturally the whole room came immediately to life. The ship's officer at the table sprang to his feet; the men from the harbor authority looked on calmly but attentively; the two gentlemen by the window had moved side by side; the attendant, feeling out of place now that his superiors were interested, stepped back. The stoker waited anxiously by the door for the moment when his help would be needed. The purser finally swung his armchair forcefully around to the right.

Karl, rummaging in his secret pocket, which he had no qualms about revealing to these people, pulled out his passport, which he opened and laid on the desk in lieu of further introduction. The purser seemed to consider the passport irrelevant, for he flicked it aside with two fingers, whereupon Karl, as if this formality had been concluded to his satisfaction, put it back in his pocket.

"Please allow me to say," he then began, "that in my opinion the stoker has been done an injustice. There is a certain Schubal on board who's on his case. The stoker has worked on many ships, all of which he can name and all of which were very satisfactorily served; he is industrious and serious about his work, and it's difficult to comprehend why his performance would not be up to standard on this ship, where the duties are not nearly so taxing as they are, for example, on a merchant ship. Therefore it can only be slander that prevents his advancement and robs him of the reward that would otherwise assuredly be his. I have only outlined this matter in general terms, he can enumerate his specific grievances for you himself." Karl had directed his remarks to all the gentlemen present because they were all in fact listening, and it seemed much more likely that a just man could be found among all of them than that this just man should be the purser. Karl had also been clever enough to conceal the fact that he had known the stoker only a short time. But he would have spoken more effectively if he had not been disconcerted by the red face of the man with the bamboo cane as he first viewed it from his current position.

"Every single word is true," said the stoker before anyone asked him anything or even looked in his direction. This over-zealousness would have been a gross error if the gentleman with the medals, who, it suddenly dawned on Karl, was obviously the captain, had not clearly made up his mind already to hear the stoker out. For he extended a hand and called to the stoker: "Come here!" with a voice firm enough to be hit with a hammer. Now everything hinged upon the stoker's conduct, for Karl did not doubt the justness of his cause.

Fortunately it became evident at this point that the stoker was an experienced man of the world. With perfect calm he reached into his little chest and unerringly pulled out a small bundle of papers and a notebook, and then, as if it were the most natural thing to do, he completely ignored the purser, walked directly to the captain, and spread out his evidence on the windowsill. Having no choice, the purser was forced to make his own way across. "The man is a known whiner," he said by way of explanation. "He spends more time in my office than the engine room. He has driven that poor, calm Schubal to distraction. Now listen for once!" He turned to the stoker. "This time you're really taking your obtrusiveness too far. How many times have you already been thrown out of pay rooms, and it served you right with your demands, which are without exception totally and completely unjustified! How many times have you then come running to the purser's office! How many times have you been told nicely that Schubal is your immediate superior, with whom you have to come to terms yourself! And now you even have the gall to come in here when the captain's present and you have no shame about pestering him; you even have the effrontery to go so far as to bring this boy along, whom you've trained as the mouthpiece for your ridiculous accusations, and yet this is the first time I have ever seen him on this ship!"

Karl had to forcibly restrain himself from jumping forward. But the captain had already intervened, saying: "Let's listen to what the man has to say. In any case Schubal is becoming much too independent for my liking, by which, however, I don't mean to imply anything in your favor." These last words were directed to the stoker; it was only natural that the captain could not immediately take his side, but everything appeared to be moving in the right direction. The stoker began his explanations and was in control of himself enough at the start to give Schubal the title of "Mister." How Karl rejoiced, standing at the purser's abandoned desk, where he took great pleasure in pressing down on a postal scale again and again.—Mr. Schubal is unfair! Mr. Schubal prefers foreigners! Mr. Schubal had ordered the stoker out of the engine room and made him clean toilets, which was certainly not the stoker's job!—At one point, Mr. Schubal's competence was challenged as being more apparent than actual. At that moment Karl eyed the captain very closely and openly, as if they were colleagues, to ensure that the captain would not be unfavorably influenced by the stoker's somewhat awkward manner of expression. Still, nothing tangible emerged from the stream of words, and even though the captain's gaze was still fixed ahead of him as a sign of his resolve to hear the stoker through to the end this time, the other gentlemen were growing impatient and soon the stoker's voice no longer dominated the room unquestionably, which was disturbing to Karl. First, the gentleman in civilian clothes started playing with his bamboo cane, tapping it, albeit softly, against the parquet floor, and the other gentlemen naturally looked his way from time to time. The harbor officials, who were obviously in a hurry, took up their documents again and began, if somewhat distractedly, to look through them; the ship's officer edged closer to his table, and the chief purser, believing he had won this round, heaved a deep and ironic sigh. Only the attendant seemed exempt from the gathering lack of interest; sympathetic to the sufferings of a poor man surrounded by the great, he nodded earnestly at Karl as if he wanted to explain something.

Meanwhile, outside the windows, life in the harbor continued: A flat barge with a mountain of barrels, which must have been ingeniously stowed because none of them rolled around, tugged past and almost completely darkened the room; small motorboats, which Karl could have minutely examined if he had had the time, roared by in straight lines, each obeying the jerking hands of a man standing upright at the wheel; here and there peculiar bobbing objects surfaced on their own from the restless waves and were submerged just as quickly, sinking before Karl's astonished eyes; boats from the ocean liners surged past, rowed by furiously working sailors and full of still, expectant passengers sitting exactly as they had been squeezed in, although some of them could not resist turning their heads to look at the shifting scenery. An endless movement, a restlessness passed from the element of restlessness to the helpless human beings and their works!

But everything called for haste, for clarity, for accurate description, and what was the stoker doing? He was certainly talking up a storm, his trembling hands were long past being able to hold the papers on the windowsill, complaints about Schubal came flooding into his mind from all directions, and in his opinion, each and every one would have sufficed to bury Schubal forever, but all he could present to the captain was a pitiful tangle of everything jumbled together. For a long time the gentleman with the bamboo cane had been whistling up at the ceiling, the harbor officials had already detained the ship's officer at their table and showed no signs of releasing him, the chief purser was visibly held back from an outburst only by the calmness of the captain, and the attendant was standing at the ready, awaiting at any moment the captain's orders concerning the stoker.

Karl could remain idle no longer. Therefore he approached the group slowly, considering all the quicker how to tackle the situation as cleverly as possible. It was now or never, it could not be long before they were both thrown out of the office. The captain might well be a good man and in addition he might, or so it seemed to Karl, have some special reason for demonstrating that he was a fair superior at present, but in the end he was not an instrument that one could play into the ground—and that was just how the stoker was treating him, although it was only out of his profound sense of indignation.

So Karl said to the stoker: "You must tell the story more simply, more clearly; the captain can't fully appreciate it the way you're telling it now. Does he know all the engineers and cabin boys by their last names, let alone by their first names, so that you just mention such a name and he instantly knows who it is? Sort out your complaints and tell him the most important first and then the others in descending order; perhaps then you won't even have to voice most of them. You've always explained it to me so clearly!" "If one could steal trunks in America, one could also lie now and again," he thought to justify himself.

If only it would help! Might it not be too late already? The stoker did fall silent upon hearing the familiar voice, but his eyes were so blinded by tears of wounded pride, awful memories, and the extreme distress of the moment that he could barely recognize Karl anymore. How could he now—and Karl privately realized this upon seeing his silent friend—how could he suddenly change his tack now when he felt that he had already said all there was to say without receiving the slightest acknowledgment, and yet on the other hand he had really not said anything at all and could hardly expect these gentlemen to listen to everything again. And at this particular point Karl, his sole supporter, steps in wanting to give good advice but instead shows him that everything, absolutely everything is lost.

"If only I'd come forward sooner instead of staring out the window," Karl said to himself, bowing his head before the stoker and slapping his hands on his thighs to signal that all hope had vanished.

But the stoker misinterpreted this, probably sensing that Karl was secretly reproaching him, and with the honest intention of convincing him otherwise, he superseded all his previous deeds by starting to argue with Karl. Now of all times—when the gentlemen at the round table had long since grown aggravated by the pointless barrage that was disrupting their important work, when the chief purser had gradually found the captain's patience incomprehensible and was on the verge of exploding, when the attendant, by now fully reestablished within the sphere of his superiors, was measuring the stoker with menacing looks, and when the gentleman with the bamboo cane, to whom even the captain was sending friendly glances now and then, was completely inured to and even disgusted by the stoker and pulled out a small notebook and, evidently preoccupied with other matters, let his eyes wander back and forth between the notebook and Karl.

"Yes, I know, I know," said Karl, who was having difficulty fighting off the stoker's tirade yet still managed to keep up a friendly smile throughout the quarreling, "you're right, quite right, I've never once doubted it." He would have liked to restrain the stoker's flailing hands for fear of being struck, or better yet, he would have liked to press him into a corner and whisper a few calm, soothing words that no one else need hear. But the stoker was beyond the pale. Karl began to take some comfort in the thought that, if necessary, the stoker could overpower all seven men present with the strength of his despair. However, on the desk, as a peek in that direction informed him, there lay a panel crammed with push buttons connected to electrical wires: One hand simply pressing them down could turn the entire ship rebellious, its passages full of hostile men.

Here, the seriously indifferent gentleman with the bamboo cane stepped up to Karl and asked, not too loudly but audibly enough to be heard above all the stoker's racket: "So what is your name?" At that moment, as if someone behind the door were awaiting this remark, there came a knock. The attendant looked over to the captain, who nodded. At this the attendant went to the door and opened it. Outside, in an old imperial coat, stood a man of medium build who, judging by his appearance, did not seem suited to engine work but was nevertheless—Schubal. If Karl had not inferred this from the look in everyone's eyes, which exuded a certain satisfaction that even the captain was not immune to, then he would have been horrified to realize it by looking at the stoker, who clenched his fists at the end of his stiffened arms as if this concentration of force were the most important thing to him, something for which he was willing to sacrifice the very life in his body. All his strength, even the power to keep himself upright, was concentrated in his fists.

And so here was the enemy, jaunty and fresh in his festive dress, a ledger under one arm—probably records of the stoker's work and pay—making it unabashedly clear by scanning each face in turn that it was his intention to ascertain the mood of each individual. All seven were already friends of his, for even if the captain had had reservations about him, or perhaps had only pretended to, he could probably not find fault with Schubal after all the pain he had just been subjected to by the stoker. A man like the stoker could not be dealt with severely enough, and if Schubal were to be reproached for anything at all it was for failing to succinctly and sufficiently subdue the stoker's recalcitrance and thus prevent him from having the audacity to appear before the captain today.

Now one might still assume that the confrontation between the stoker and Schubal could not fail to have the same effect upon men as it would certainly have before a higher tribunal; for even if Schubal could disguise himself well, he might not be able to keep up this ruse to the very end. A single flash of his wicked temperament would be enough to enlighten these gentlemen, and Karl wanted to make sure of that. He already had some insight into the acumen, the weaknesses, the moods of these men individually, and from that standpoint the time he had already spent here had not been wasted. If only the stoker were in better shape, but he seemed entirely incapable of fighting. If Schubal were held in front of him, he would probably have battered that hated skull with his fists. But even the few steps separating them were most likely more than the stoker could manage. Why had Karl not foreseen the so easily foreseeable: That Schubal was bound to turn up in the end, if not of his own accord, then summoned by the captain? Why had he not discussed a plan of action with the stoker on the way here instead of simply marching, hopelessly unprepared, through a random door, which in fact is what they did? Was the stoker still capable of speech, of saying yes and no as would be necessary during the cross-examination, which, however, would only happen in the most hopeful scenario? The stoker stood there, his legs spread apart, his knees slightly bent, his head half raised, and the air flowing through his open mouth as if he had no lungs within to process it.

Karl on the other hand felt more vigorous and alert than he had perhaps ever been at home. If only his parents could see him now: fighting the good fight in a foreign country before highly respected persons, and although not yet triumphant, entirely prepared for the ultimate conquest! Would they revise their opinion of him? Sit him down between them and praise him? Look once, just once, into his devoted eyes? Uncertain questions, and the most inappropriate moment to ask them!

"I have come here because I believe the stoker is accusing me of some sort of dishonesty. A girl from the kitchen told me she'd seen him on his way here. Captain, sir, and the rest of you gentlemen, I am ready to refute any charge with my own documents and, if necessary, with statements by impartial and unbiased witnesses who are waiting outside the door." So spoke Schubal. This was indeed the clear speech of a man, and from the change in the listeners' faces one might have thought that these were the first human sounds they had heard in a long time. They failed to notice, of course, that even this eloquent speech had holes in it. Why was the first word that occurred to him "dishonesty"? Should the accusations have started here, rather than with his national prejudices? A girl from the kitchen had seen the stoker on his way to the office and had understood immediately? Was it not a sense of guilt that sharpened his mind? And he had automatically brought witnesses along with him and then called them impartial and unbiased? A fraud, nothing but a fraud! And these gentlemen tolerated it and even acknowledged it as proper conduct? Why had he apparently let so much time elapse between the kitchen girl's message and his arrival here? Evidently it was for the purpose of allowing the stoker to weary the men to the point where they would gradually lose their capacity for clear judgment, which Schubal had most to fear. Had he not, obviously having stood behind the door for a long time, only knocked after the gentleman asked his casual question and when he had reason to hope that the matter of the stoker was disposed of?

It was all very clear and that was how it was unwittingly presented by Schubal, but it had to be clarified for these gentlemen in a different, more tangible manner. They needed to be jolted awake. So Karl, quick, at least take advantage of what time is left to you before the witnesses arrive and take over everything.

At that moment, however, the captain waved off Schubal, who—since his affair appeared to be momentarily postponed—immediately stepped aside and was joined in quiet conversation by the attendant; the two men kept leering at the stoker and gesturing emphatically, and it seemed to Karl that Schubal was rehearsing his next grand speech.

"Didn't you wish to ask the young man something, Mr. Jakob?" the captain said to the gentleman with the bamboo cane amid general silence.

"Indeed," he said, acknowledging this courtesy with a slight bow. And then he asked Karl once more: "So what is your name?"

Karl, who believed the main issue would best be served by dispensing with the stubborn inquisitor quickly, answered tersely and without his usual custom of presenting his passport, which he would have had to hunt for first: "Karl Rossmann."

"Well," said the man addressed as Mr. Jakob, taking a step backward at first with an almost incredulous smile. The captain too, the chief purser, the ship's officer, and even the attendant were all extremely astonished upon hearing Karl's name. Only the men from the harbor authority and Schubal remained indifferent.

"Well," repeated Mr. Jakob, approaching Karl somewhat stiffly, "then I am your Uncle Jakob and you are my dear nephew. I suspected it all along!" he said to the captain before he embraced and then kissed Karl, who suffered all this in silence.

"And what is your name?" Karl asked very politely, yet wholly unmoved after he felt himself released; he struggled to foresee the consequences this latest development might have for the stoker. For the moment, there was no indication that Schubal could derive any benefit from it.

"You don't seem to understand your luck," said the captain, believing that Karl's question had wounded Mr. Jakob's personal dignity, since he had withdrawn to the window, evidently to conceal his agitated face, which he kept dabbing at with a handkerchief. "That's Senator Edward Jakob who has just introduced himself to you as your uncle. Now a brilliant career awaits you, no doubt completely contrary to your previous expectations. Try to grasp this as best you can right now and pull yourself together!"

"Indeed I do have an Uncle Jakob in America," said Karl, turning to the captain, "but if I understood correctly, Jakob is merely the Senator's surname."

"So it is," said the captain expectantly.

"Well, my Uncle Jakob, who is my mother's brother, has Jakob for his Christian name, but his surname would naturally be the same as my mother's, whose maiden name is Bendelmayer."

"Gentlemen!" exclaimed the Senator, reacting to Karl's statement as he cheerfully returned from his recuperative break at the window. Everyone present, except for the harbor officials, burst out laughing, some as if moved to do so, others for no apparent reason.

"But what I said was by no means ridiculous," thought Karl.

"Gentlemen," repeated the Senator, "you are taking part, contrary to both my intentions and yours, in a little family scene, and therefore I cannot avoid providing you with an explanation, since I believe only the captain"—at this mention they exchanged bows—"is completely informed of the circumstances."

"Now I must really pay attention to every word," Karl told himself, and was delighted to note, from a sideways glance, that life was beginning to return to the stoker.

"During all the long years of my sojourn in America—although the word 'sojourn' is hardly fitting for an American citizen, which I am heart and soul—well, during all these long years, I have been living entirely without contact with my European relatives for reasons that, in the first place, have no business here, and secondly, would truly be too painful to discuss. I actually dread the moment when I may be forced to explain them to my dear nephew, and unfortunately it will be impossible to avoid frank references to his parents and their nearest and dearest."

"He is my uncle, no question," Karl told himself as he listened; "he's probably changed his name."

"My dear nephew is now—let us use the proper word—quite simply cut off by his parents, the same as a cat tossed out the door when it has become annoying. I wish by no means to gloss over what my nephew did to be so punished, but his fault was such that its mere mention is absolution enough."

"That sounds fair enough," thought Karl, "but I don't want him to tell everyone the story. Besides, he can't possibly know about it. Who could have told him?"

"He was, in fact," his uncle continued, occasionally rocking forward on his bamboo cane, whereby he did indeed successfully avoid the unnecessary solemnity the situation was otherwise bound to assume, "in fact, he was seduced by a maidservant, Johanna Brummer, a woman of thirty-five. I do not mean to offend my nephew by using the word 'seduced,' but it is difficult to find another word equally suitable."

Karl, who had moved much closer to his uncle, turned around at this point to gauge the reactions on the faces of those present. No one was laughing, they were all listening patiently and earnestly. After all, one does not laugh at a senator's nephew at the first opportunity that presents itself. The most that could be said was that the stoker was smiling at Karl, albeit faintly, which was encouraging in the first place as a sign of renewed life and pardonable in the second as Karl, in the stoker's cabin, had tried to keep secret this very same affair that was now being made public.

"Now, this Brummer woman," his uncle went on, "had a child by my nephew, a healthy boy who was christened Jakob, no doubt after my humble self, who I'm sure was casually mentioned by my nephew but made a great impression on the girl. Fortunately, I may add. For the parents, in order to avoid paying for child support or being further involved in personal scandal—I must emphasize that I am not familiar with either the laws over there or the parents' situation—therefore, so as to avoid paying for child support and their son's scandal, they shipped my dear nephew off to America miserably unprovided for, as one can see, so that he would soon, without the miracles that still happen, at least in America, in all likelihood have met his lonely end in some alley near New York harbor if that maid hadn't sent me a letter, which reached me the day before yesterday after a long odyssey and which provided me with the whole story, a personal description of my nephew, and also, very sensibly, the name of the ship. If my purpose here were to entertain you gentlemen, I could read a few passages of this letter"—he pulled out and flourished two huge, densely written pages from his pocket. "It would surely affect you, as it was written with a somewhat simple yet well-intentioned cleverness and with much love for the father of the child. But I wish neither to entertain you anymore than is necessary to enlighten you nor to potentially wound any feelings my nephew may still harbor; he can, if he so desires for his own information, read the letter in the privacy of the room that already awaits him."

Karl however had no feelings for that girl. In the rush of memories from an ever-dimming past, she sat in her kitchen, with her elbows propped up on the kitchen cupboard. She would stare at him whenever he would come into the kitchen for a glass of water for his father or to pass on some instructions from his mother. Sometimes she would be writing a letter, awkwardly sitting beside the kitchen cupboard and drawing her inspiration from Karl's face. Sometimes she would hide her eyes behind her hands, and then no words could get through to her. Sometimes she would kneel in her narrow little room next to the kitchen, praying before a wooden cross; Karl would then shyly watch her from the passage through the narrow crack of the door. Sometimes she raced around the kitchen and jumped back, laughing like a witch, if Karl got in her way. Sometimes she would shut the kitchen door after Karl came in and hold on to the latch until he demanded to leave. Sometimes she brought him things he did not at all desire and pressed them silently into his hands. But one time she said, "Karl," and led him, still shocked at the unexpected familiarity, into her little room, which she then locked with much grimacing and sighing. She almost choked him as she clung to his neck, and while asking him to undress her, she actually undressed him and put him into her bed as if she wanted no one else to have him from now on and wished to caress him and coddle him until the end of the world. "Karl, oh, my Karl!" she cried, as if by gazing at him she were confirming her possession, while Karl saw absolutely nothing and felt uncomfortable in the warm bedding that she seemed to have piled up specially for his benefit. Then she lay down next to him and wanted to extract some secrets from him, but he could tell her none and she was annoyed, either in jest or in earnest; she shook him, she listened to his heart beating, she offered her own breast for him to do the same, but she could not induce Karl to do so; she pressed her naked belly against his body, fondled him between the legs so repulsively that Karl thrust his head and neck from the pillows, then ground her belly against him a few times—it felt as if she were part of him, and perhaps this was the reason he was seized by a dreadful helplessness. He was weeping when he finally reached his own bed, after she entreated him repeatedly to visit her again. That was all it was and yet his uncle had succeeded in making a grand story out of it. And that cook[15] had evidently been thinking of him and notified his uncle of his arrival. That was very kind of her and he hoped to one day repay her.

"And now," cried the Senator, "I would like to hear loud and clear whether I am your uncle or not."

"You are my uncle," said Karl, kissing his hand and receiving a kiss on the forehead in return. "I'm very glad to have met you, but you are mistaken if you believe that my parents speak only ill of you. But aside from that, your speech contained several errors, that is to say, I mean, everything didn't really happen like that. But you can't judge things so well from here, and besides, I don't think it will cause any great harm if these gentlemen are slightly misinformed about the details of a matter that could hardly interest them very much."

"Well said," remarked the Senator, guiding Karl over to the visibly sympathetic captain and asking: "Don't I have a splendid nephew?"

"I am happy," said the captain, with a bow that only a militarily trained person can execute, "to have made your nephew's acquaintance, Mr. Senator. It is a particular honor for my ship to have provided the setting for such a meeting. But the voyage in steerage must have been less than pleasant, it's difficult to know who's traveling down there. Of course we do everything possible to make the passengers in steerage as comfortable as possible, much more, for example, than the American lines, but we have not succeeded yet in making this excursion a pleasure."

"It did me no harm," said Karl.

"It did him no harm!" the Senator repeated, laughing loudly.

"Only I'm afraid I've lost my trunk—" and with this he was reminded of everything that had happened and all that still remained to be done; he looked around him and saw all those present, still in their former positions, ogling him and struck dumb with awe and amazement. Only the harbor official, as much as their harsh complacent faces could be read, betrayed regret at having come at such an inopportune time, and the pocket watch they had now laid before them was probably more important to them than anything that was happening or might still happen in the room.

The first person to express his sympathy, after the captain, was oddly enough the stoker. "I heartily congratulate you," he said, and shook Karl's hand, trying to impart something like appreciation with this gesture. When he attempted to turn and address the same words to the Senator, the Senator pulled back as if the stoker were overstepping his bounds, and the stoker left off immediately.

But the others now understood what was expected of them and formed a huddle around Karl and the Senator at once. And so it happened that Karl received congratulations from Schubal, which he accepted and thanked him for. The last to step in, once order was somewhat restored, were the harbor officials, who said a couple of words in English that made an absurd impression.

The Senator was now well disposed to make the most of this pleasurable occasion by recalling, for his own benefit and that of the others, some of the more incidental details, which were naturally not only tolerated but greeted with interest. Thus he pointed out that he had recorded in his notebook, should he need them on short notice, Karl's most distinguishing features as listed in the cook's letter. And then, during the stoker's unbearable rambling, he had taken out the notebook for no other purpose than to distract himself and tried, for the sake of amusement, to compare Karl's appearance with the cook's observations, which were naturally not up to the standards of a detective. "And that is how one finds one's nephew!" he concluded, in a tone that seemed to invite further congratulations.

"What will happen to the stoker now?" asked Karl, ignoring his uncle's latest anecdote. He believed his new position gave him the freedom to express whatever crossed his mind.

"The stoker will get what he deserves," said the Senator, "and what the captain deems appropriate. I believe we have had enough and more than enough of the stoker, and I'm sure that every gentleman present here will agree."

"But that's not the point in a matter of justice," said Karl. He stood between his uncle and the captain and believed, perhaps because of this position, that he could influence a decision.

And yet the stoker seemed to have abandoned all hope. His hands were shoved halfway into his trouser belt, which had been exposed along with a strip of checked shirt due to his agitated movements. This did not trouble him in the least: He had vented all his woes and now they might as well see the few rags that covered his body, after which they could carry him away. He imagined that Schubal and the attendant, being the two lowest in rank of those present, should perform this final kindness. Schubal would have his peace then and no longer be driven to distraction, as the chief purser had put it. The captain would be free to hire no one but Romanians, Romanian would be spoken everywhere, and maybe everything really would run smoother that way. No stoker would be yammering away in the purser's office; only his last yammering would be fondly remembered since, as the Senator had explicitly stated, it led indirectly to the recognition of his nephew. This nephew, by the way, had previously attempted to help him a number of times and had been more than fully repaid by the stoker's aid in the recognition; it did not even occur to the stoker to ask anything further of him now. Besides, even if he were the Senator's nephew, he was still a long way from being a captain and it was from the captain's lips that the foul verdict must fall.—And in accordance with this view, the stoker did his best to avoid looking at Karl but, unfortunately, in this room full of enemies there was no other place to rest his eyes.

"Do not misunderstand the situation," the Senator said to Karl; "it may be a matter of justice, but at the same time it is a matter of discipline as well. Both matters, especially the latter, are for the captain to decide in this case."

"So it is," murmured the stoker. Those who heard and understood this smiled uneasily.

"In any event, we have kept the captain from his official duties far too long, and these undoubtedly accumulate immeasurably upon arriving in New York, so now it is high time we left the ship rather than make matters worse by turning this petty squabble between two engineers into a bigger incident through our completely unnecessary intervention. And I do understand your conduct perfectly, my dear nephew, but that is precisely what gives me the right to take you away from here posthaste."

"I will have a boat lowered for you immediately," said the captain, without, to Karl's utter amazement, raising the least objection to the uncle's words, although these could unquestionably be considered self-abasement on his uncle's part. The chief purser raced to his desk and telephoned the captain's order to the boatswain.

"Time's running out," Karl said to himself, "but I can do nothing without offending everyone. I can't desert my uncle after he's just found me again. The captain is certainly polite, but that's where it ends. When it comes to discipline, his courtesy stops, and I'm sure my uncle spoke from the captain's soul. I don't want to speak to Schubal and I regret I ever shook his hand. And all the other people here aren't worth a hill of beans."

And with these thoughts in his mind, Karl walked slowly over and drew the stoker's right hand out of his belt, gently cupping it in his own. "Why don't you say anything?" he asked. "Why do you take everything lying down?"

The stoker merely furrowed his brow, as if searching for the right words to express what he had to say. Meanwhile he gazed down at Karl's hand and his own.

"You've been wronged like no one else on this ship, that I know." And Karl ran his fingers to and fro between the fingers of the stoker, who peered around with gleaming eyes as if he were experiencing a joy that no one ought to begrudge him.

"But you must defend yourself, say yes and no; otherwise people will have no idea of the truth. You must promise me that you will do as I say, for I have every reason to fear that I will no longer be able to help you." And now Karl wept as he kissed the stoker's hand, and then took that cracked and almost lifeless hand and pressed it to his cheeks like a treasure that must be forsaken.—But his uncle the Senator was already at his side, leading him away, if only with the gentlest of pressures.

"The stoker seems to have cast a spell over you," he said, glancing knowingly at the captain over Karl's head. "You felt lost, then you found the stoker, and now you feel grateful, that's all very commendable. But don't go too far, if only for my sake, and please try to understand your position."

Noises erupted outside the door and shouts were heard, it even sounded as if someone were being brutally shoved against the door. A sailor entered in a rather disheveled state and had a girl's apron tied around his waist. "There's a crowd of people out there," he yelled, swinging his elbows as if he were still in the crowd. He finally collected himself and was about to salute the captain when he noticed the apron, ripped it off, threw it to the floor, and shouted: "This is disgusting, they've tied a girl's apron on me." Then he clicked his heels together and saluted. Someone almost laughed, but the captain said severely: "That's what I call a good mood. Just who is it outside?"

"They're my witnesses," said Schubal, stepping forward. "I humbly beg your pardon for their improper behavior. When the crew has the voyage behind them, they sometimes go a little crazy."

"Call them in immediately!" commanded the captain, and turning directly to the Senator, politely but rapidly said: "Please be so good as to take your nephew and follow this sailor, who will bring you to the boat, Mr. Senator, sir. I hardly need say what an honor and a pleasure it has been, Mr. Senator, to have met you in person. I only hope to have the opportunity soon to continue our interrupted conversation about the state of the American fleet, sir, and that it may be interrupted in as agreeable a manner as today."

"This one nephew is enough for now," said Karl's uncle, laughing. "And now please accept my deep gratitude for your kindness, and I bid you farewell. It is by no means impossible, after all, that we"—he hugged Karl closely to himself—"might be able to spend a longer time with you on our next journey to Europe."

"That would please me greatly," said the captain. The two gentlemen shook hands, Karl could only mutely grasp the captain's hand, for the captain was already preoccupied with the fifteen or so people led by Schubal, who were pouring into the room slightly cowed but still very noisy. The sailor asked the Senator if he could be permitted to lead the way, and then he cleared a path through the crowd for the Senator and Karl, who passed easily through the bowing people. It was apparent that these people, a good-natured bunch in general, regarded Schubal's quarrel with the stoker as a joke that was still amusing even in the presence of the captain. Among them, Karl noticed Line the kitchen maid, who, winking gaily at him, put on and tied the apron the sailor had thrown down, for it belonged to her.

Still following the sailor, they left the office and turned into a short pasageway, which, after a few steps, brought them to a smaller door from which a short ladder led down to the boat that had been made ready for them. The sailors in the boat, into which their guide had leapt in a single bound, stood up and saluted. The Senator was just admonishing Karl to exercise caution in climbing down when Karl, still on the topmost rung, burst into violent sobs. The Senator put his right hand under Karl's chin and held him tight, stroking him with his left hand. Clinging together in this way, they slowly descended step-by-step and landed in the boat, where the Senator selected a comfortable seat for Karl just opposite himself. At a sign from the Senator the sailors pushed off from the ship and were immediately rowing at full steam. They were hardly a few yards from the ship when Karl made the unexpected discovery that they were on the same side of the ship as the windows of the office. All three windows were filled by Schubal's witnesses, who greeted them with friendly waves; even Karl's uncle acknowledged them with a wave, and a sailor accomplished the feat of blowing them a kiss without ever breaking his even stroke. It was truly as if the stoker no longer existed. Karl more closely examined his uncle, whose knees were almost touching his, and he began to doubt whether, for him, this man could ever replace the stoker. And his uncle, avoiding his gaze, stared out at the waves jostling their boat.

In the Penal Colony*

*Originally published in 1919 under the German title "In der Strafkolonie."

"IT'S AN EXCEPTIONAL APPARATUS," the officer said to the world traveler and, with a certain admiration, surveyed the apparatus that was, after all, quite familiar to him. The traveler appeared to have accepted purely out of politeness the commandant's invitation to attend the execution of a soldier, who had been condemned for insubordination and insulting a superior officer. There did not seem to be much interest in the execution throughout the penal colony itself. In any event, the only other persons present besides the officer and the traveler in this small but deep and sandy valley, surrounded by barren slopes on all sides, were the condemned man—a dull, thick-lipped creature with a disheveled appearance—and a soldier, who held the heavy chain that controlled the smaller chains attached to the condemned man's ankles, wrists, and neck, chains that were also linked together. But the condemned man looked so submissively doglike that it seemed as if he might have been allowed to run free on the slopes and would only need to be whistled for when the execution was due to begin.

The traveler was not particularly enthralled by the apparatus and he paced back and forth behind the condemned man with almost visible indifference while the officer made the final preparations, one moment crawling beneath the apparatus that was deeply embedded in the ground, another climbing a ladder to inspect its uppermost parts. These were tasks that could really have been left to a mechanic, but the officer performed them with energetic eagerness, perhaps because he was a devoted admirer of the apparatus or because, for whatever other reasons, the work could be entrusted to no one else. "Now everything's ready!" he called out at last, and climbed down from the ladder. He had worked up a sweat and was breathing with his mouth wide open; he had also tucked two very fine ladies' handkerchiefs under the collar of his uniform. "Surely these uniforms are too heavy for the tropics," said the traveler instead of inquiring, as the officer expected, about the apparatus. "Of course," the officer said, washing the oil and grease from his hands in a nearby bucket of water, "but they represent home for us; we don't want to forget about our homeland—but now just take a look at this machine," he immediately added, drying his hands on a towel and simultaneously indicating the apparatus. "Up to this point I have to do some of the operations by hand, but from now on the apparatus works entirely by itself." The traveler nodded and followed the officer. Then the officer, seeking to prepare himself for all eventualities, said: "Naturally there are sometimes problems; I hope of course there won't be any problems today, but one must allow for the possibility. The apparatus should work continually for twelve hours, but even if anything does go wrong, it will be something minor and easy to repair at once."

"Won't you sit down?" he inquired at last, pulling out a cane chair from a whole heap of them and offering it to the traveler, who was unable to refuse. The traveler was now sitting at the edge of a pit, and he glanced cursorily in its direction. It was not very deep. On one side of the pit, the excavated earth had been piled up to form an embankment, on the other side of the pit stood the apparatus. "I don't know," said the officer, "whether the commandant has already explained the apparatus to you." The traveler made a vague gesture with his hand, and the officer could not have asked for anything better, for now he was free to explain the apparatus himself. "This apparatus," he said, grabbing hold of the crankshaft and leaning against it, "was the invention of our former commandant. I myself was involved in the very first experiments and also shared in the work all the way to its completion, but the credit for the invention belongs to him alone. Have you ever heard of our former commandant? No? Well, it wouldn't be too much to say that the organization of the whole penal colony is his work. We who were his friends knew long before his death that the organization of the colony was so perfectly self-contained that his successor, even if he had a thousand new schemes brewing in his head, would find it impossible to alter a thing from the old system, at least for many years to come. Our prediction has indeed come true, and the new commandant has had to acknowledge as much. It's too bad you never met the old commandant!—but," the officer interrupted himself, "I'm rambling, and here is his apparatus standing right in front of us. It consists, as you can see, of three parts. In the course of time each part has acquired its own nickname. The lower part is called the bed, the upper one is the designer, and this one in the middle here that hovers between them is called the harrow." "The harrow?" asked the traveler. He had not been listening very intently; the sun beat down brutally into the shadeless valley and it was difficult to collect one's thoughts. He had to admire the officer all the more: He wore his snugly fitting dress uniform, hung with braiding weighted with epaulettes; he expounded on his subject with zeal and tightened a few screws here and there with a screwdriver while he spoke. As for the soldier, he seemed to be in much the same condition as the traveler: He had wound the condemned man's chain around both his wrists and propped himself up with one hand on his rifle; his head hung down and he took no notice of anything. The traveler was not surprised by this, as the officer was speaking in French and certainly neither the soldier nor the condemned man understood French. It was therefore that much more remarkable that the condemned man nevertheless strove to follow the officer's explanations. With a drowsy sort of persistence he directed his gaze wherever the officer pointed, and when the traveler broke in with his question, he, like the officer, looked at the traveler.

"Yes, the harrow," answered the officer, "a perfect name for it. The needles are arranged similarly to the teeth of a harrow and the whole thing works something like a harrow, although it is stationary and performs with much more artistry. You'll soon understand it anyway. The condemned man is laid here on the bed—you see, first I want to explain the apparatus and then start it up, that way you'll be able to follow it better; besides, one of the gears in the designer is badly worn, it makes a horrible screeching noise when it's turning and you can hardly hear yourself speak; unfortunately spare parts are difficult to come by around here—well, so here is the bed, as I said before. It's completely covered with a layer of cotton wool, you'll find out what that's for later. The condemned man is laid facedown on the cotton wool, naked of course; here are straps for the hands, the feet, and here for the neck, in order to hold him down. So, as I was saying, here at the head of the bed, where the condemned man is at first laid facedown, is the little felt gag that can be adjusted easily to fit straight into the man's mouth. It's meant to keep him from screaming or biting his tongue. The man has to take the felt in his mouth since otherwise the neck strap would break his neck." "That's cotton wool?" asked the traveler, leaning forward. "It certainly is," the officer said with a smile, "feel for yourself." He grabbed hold of the traveler's hand and guided it over the bed's surface. "It's specially prepared cotton wool, which is why you don't recognize it; I'll come to its purpose in a minute." The traveler was starting to feel the stirrings of interest in the apparatus; he gazed up at it with one arm raised to shield his eyes from the sun. It was a large structure. The bed and the designer were the same size and looked like two dark steamer trunks. The designer hung about two meters above the bed; they were joined at the corners by four brass rods that practically gleamed in the sunlight. The harrow was suspended on a steel band between the two trunks.

The officer had barely noticed the traveler's previous indifference but definitely sensed his burgeoning interest, so he paused in his explanations in order to give the traveler time for undisturbed observation. The condemned man imitated the traveler, but since he could not shield his eyes with a hand, he blinked up into the sun.

"So, the man lies down," said the traveler, leaning back in his chair and crossing his legs.

"Yes," said the officer, pushing his cap back a little and mopping his sweaty face with his hand, "now listen! Both the bed and the designer have their own electric battery; the bed needs one for itself and the designer needs one for the harrow. As soon as the man is strapped in, the bed is set in motion. It quivers with tiny, rapid vibrations, both from side to side and up and down. You will have seen similar contraptions in sanitariums, but for our bed, all the movements are calibrated precisely, for they must correspond to movements of the harrow. But it is the harrow that actually carries out the sentence."

"And just what is the sentence?" inquired the traveler. "You don't know that either?" the officer said in astonishment, and bit his lip. "Excuse me if my explanations seem a bit incoherent, I beg your pardon. The commandant always used to take care of the explanations, but the new commandant seems to scorn this duty; but that such a distinguished visitor"—the traveler attempted to wave this distinction away with both hands, but the officer insisted on the expression—"that such a distinguished visitor should not even be made aware of the form our sentencing takes is a new development, which"—an oath was about to pass his lips but he checked himself and said only: "I was not informed of this, it's not my fault. In any case, I'm certainly the man best equipped to explain our sentencing, since I have here"—he patted his breast pocket—"the relevant drawings made by our former commandant."

"Drawings by the commandant himself?" the traveler asked. "Was he everything himself? Was he soldier, judge, engineer, chemist, draftsman?"

"Yes sir, he was," the officer answered, nodding his head with a remote, contemplative look. Then he examined his hands closely; they did not seem to be clean enough for him to handle the drawings, so he went over to the bucket and washed them again. Then he drew out a small leather folder and said: "The sentence does not sound severe. Whatever commandment the condemned man has transgressed is engraved on his body by the harrow. This man, for example"—the officer indicated the man—"will have inscribed on his body: 'Honor thy superiors!'"

The traveler briefly looked at the man, who stood, as the officer pointed him out, with bowed head, apparently straining with all his might to catch something of what was said. But the movement of his thick, closed lips clearly showed that he understood nothing. There were a number of questions the traveler wanted to ask, but at the sight of the man he asked only: "Does he know his sentence?" "No," said the officer, eager to continue his explanations, but the traveler interrupted him: "He doesn't know his own sentence?" "No," repeated the officer, and paused for a moment as if he were waiting for the traveler to elaborate on the reason for his question, then said: "It would be pointless to tell him. He'll come to know it on his body." The traveler would not have spoken further, but he felt the condemned man's gaze trained on him; it seemed to be asking if the traveler approved of all this. So after having already leaned back in his chair, he bent forward again and asked another question: "But does he at least know that he's been sentenced?" "No, not that either," the officer replied, smiling at the traveler as if expecting him to make more strange statements. "Well," said the traveler, "then you mean to tell me that the man is also unaware of the results of his defense?" "He has had no opportunity to defend himself," said the officer, looking away as if talking to himself and trying to spare the traveler the embarrassment of having such self-evident matters explained to him. "But he must have had some opportunity to defend himself," the traveler said, and got up from his seat.

The officer realized that his explanations of the apparatus were in danger of being held up for quite some time, so he approached the traveler, put his arm through his, and gestured toward the condemned man, who was standing up straight now that he was so obviously the center of attention—the soldier had also given the chain a jerk—and said: "Here's the situation. I have been appointed judge in this penal colony—despite my youth—as I was the previous commandant's assistant in all penal matters and also know the apparatus better than anyone else. The guiding principle for my decisions is this: Guilt is unquestionable. Other courts cannot follow that principle because they have more than one member and even have courts that are higher than themselves. That is not the case here, or at least it was not so during the time of the former commandant. Although the new one has shown signs of interfering with my judgments, I have succeeded in fending him off so far and shall continue to do so—you wanted to have this case explained; it's quite simple, as they all are. A captain reported to me this morning and charged this man—who is assigned to him as an orderly and sleeps in front of his door—with sleeping on duty. You see, it is his duty to get up every time the hour strikes and salute the captain's door. This is certainly not a tremendously difficult task but a necessary one, as he must be alert both to guard and wait on his master. Last night the captain wanted to find out whether the orderly was performing his duty. When the clock struck two, he opened the door and found the man curled up asleep. He took his horsewhip and lashed him across the face. Now instead of rising and begging for pardon, the man grabbed his master by the legs, shook him, and cried: 'Throw away that whip or I'll swallow you whole'—those are the facts. The captain came to me an hour ago, I wrote down his statement and immediately followed it up with the sentence. Then I had the man put in chains. That was quite simple. If I had called for this man first and interrogated him, it would only have resulted in confusion. He would have lied, and had I been successful in exposing those lies, he would just have replaced them with new ones, and so on. But as it stands now, I have him and I won't let him go—is everything clear now? But time's marching on, the execution ought to be starting and I haven't finished explaining the apparatus yet." He pressed the traveler back into his seat, returned to the apparatus, and began: "As you can see, the shape of the harrow corresponds to the human form; here is the harrow for the upper body, here are the harrows for the legs. For the head there is just this one small spike. Is that clear?" He bent forward toward the traveler amiably, eager to furnish the most comprehensive explanations.

With a furrowed brow the traveler examined the harrow. He was not satisfied with the explanation of the judicial process. Still, he had to remind himself, this was a penal colony, special measures were needed here, military procedures must be adhered to up to the very end. He also placed some hope in the new commandant, who intended to introduce, albeit slowly, new procedures that the officer's narrow mind could not conceive of. These thoughts led him to his next question: "Will the commandant attend the execution?" "It's not certain," the officer said, wincing at the direct question, and his friendly expression clouded over. "That is why we must hurry. As much as it pains me, I'll have to cut my explanations short. But of course tomorrow, after the apparatus has been cleaned—its only drawback is that it gets so messy—I can go into more detail. So for now, just the essentials: When the man is laid down on the bed and it has started vibrating, the harrow is lowered onto his body. It automatically adjusts itself so that the needles just graze the skin; once the adjustment is completed, the steel band promptly stiffens to form a rigid bar. And now the performance begins. An uninformed observer would not be able to differentiate between one punishment and another. The harrow appears to do its work in a uniform manner. As it quivers, its points pierce the body, which is itself quivering from the vibrations of the bed. So that the progress of the sentencing can be seen, the harrow is made of glass. Securing the needles in the glass presented some technical difficulties, but after many attempts we were successful. We spared no effort, you understand. And now anyone can observe the sentence being inscribed on the body. Don't you want to come closer and examine the needles?"

The traveler rose to his feet slowly, walked across, and bent over the harrow. "You see," said the officer, "there are two types of needles arranged in various patterns. Each long needle has a short one adjacent to it. The long needle does the writing, and the short one flushes away the blood with water so that the writing is always clearly legible. The bloody water is then conducted through grooves and finally flows into this main pipe, which empties into the pit." With his finger the officer outlined the exact route the bloody water had to take. When, in order to make the image as vivid as possible, he cupped his hands under the mouth of the pipe as if to catch the outflow, the traveler drew his head back and, groping behind him with one hand, tried to return to his chair. To his horror he then saw that the condemned man had also accepted the officer's invitation to examine the harrow more closely. He had tugged the sleepy soldier forward a little and was leaning over the glass. One could see that he was searching, with a puzzled expression, for what the gentlemen had been examining, but since he had not heard the explanation he was not successful. He bent this way and that; he repeatedly ran his eyes over the glass. The traveler wanted to drive him back because what he was doing was probably a criminal offense, but the officer restrained the traveler with a firm hand and with the other hand picked up a clump of dirt from the embankment and hurled it at the soldier. The soldier jerked awake and saw what the condemned man had dared to do; he dropped his rifle, dug in his heels, yanked the condemned man back so forcefully that he immediately fell, and then stood over him, watching him writhe around and rattle his chains. "Get him on his feet!" shouted the officer, for he noticed that the traveler was dangerously distracted by the condemned man. The traveler even leaned across the harrow, taking no notice of it, only concerned with what was happening to the condemned man. "Be careful with him!" the officer yelled again. He circled the apparatus and grasped the condemned man under the armpits himself; with the help of the soldier he hauled him to his feet, which kept slipping and sliding.

"Now I know all there is to know about it," the traveler said as the officer returned to his side. "All but the most important thing," he replied, seizing the traveler by the arm and pointing upward. "Up there in the designer is the machinery that controls the movements of the harrow, and this mechanism is then programmed to correspond with the drawing of the prescribed sentence. I am still using the former commandant's drawings. Here they are"—he pulled some sheets out of the leather folder— "unfortunately I can't let you touch them, they're my most prized and valuable possession. Just sit, and I'll show them to you from here, then you'll be able to see everything perfectly." He held up the first drawing. The traveler would gladly have said something complimentary, but all he saw was a labyrinth of crisscrossing lines that covered the paper so thickly that it was difficult to discern the blank spaces between them. The officer said: "Read it." "I can't," said the traveler. "Well, it's clear enough," remarked the officer. "It's very artistic," the traveler offered evasively, "but I can't make it out." "Sure," agreed the officer, with a laugh, and put away the folder, "it's not calligraphy for schoolchildren. It must be carefully studied. I'm sure you'd eventually understand it too. Of course the script can't be too simple: It's not meant to kill on first contact, but only after twelve hours, on average; but the turning point is calculated to come at the sixth hour. So the lettering itself must be surrounded by lots and lots of flourishes; the actual wording runs around the body only in a narrow strip, and the rest of the body is reserved for the ornamentation. Now do you appreciate the work of the harrow and the whole apparatus?—Just watch!" and he leaped up the ladder, rotated a wheel, and called out: "Look out, step to the side!" then everything started up. If it had not been for the screeching gear it would have been fantastic. As if he were surprised by the noisy gear, he shook his fist at it, then shrugged apologetically to the traveler and clambered down the ladder to check the working of the apparatus from below. Something that only he could detect was still not in order; he climbed up again and reached inside the designer with both hands, then, instead of using the ladder, slid down one of the rails to get down quicker and started hollering into the traveler's ear at the top of his lungs in order to be heard above the din: "Are you following the process? First, the harrow begins to write; as soon as it has finished the initial draft of the inscription on the man's back, the layer of cotton wool is set rolling and slowly turns the body onto its side, giving the harrow fresh room to write. Meanwhile, the raw flesh that has already been inscribed rests against the cotton wool, which is specially prepared to staunch the bleeding immediately and ready everything for a further deepening of the script. Then, as the body continues to turn, these teeth here at the edge of the harrow tear the cotton wool away from the wounds and toss it into the pit; now there is fresh work for the harrow. So it keeps on writing more and more deeply for all twelve hours. For the first six hours the condemned man is alive almost as before, he only suffers pain. The felt gag is removed after two hours, as he no longer has the strength to scream. This electrically heated bowl at the head of the bed is filled with warm rice gruel, and the man is welcome, should he so desire, to take as much as his tongue can reach. No one ever passes up the opportunity; I don't know of one, and my experience is vast. The man loses his pleasure in eating only around the sixth hour. At this point I usually kneel down to observe the phenomenon. The man rarely swallows the last mouthful but merely rolls it around in his mouth and spits it into the pit. I have to duck just then, otherwise he would spit it in my face. But how still the man becomes in the sixth hour! Enlightenment comes to even the dimmest. It begins around the eyes, and it spreads outward from there—a sight that might tempt one to lie down under the harrow oneself. Nothing more happens, just that the man starts to interpret the writing, he screws up his mouth as if he were listening. You've seen yourself how difficult the writing is to decipher with your eyes, but our man deciphers it with his wounds. Of course it is hard work and it takes him six hours to accomplish it, but then the harrow pierces him clean through and throws him into the pit, where he's flung down onto the cotton wool and bloody water. This concludes the sentence and we, the soldier and I, bury him."

The traveler had his ear cocked toward the officer and, with his hands in his pockets, was watching the machine at work. The condemned man watched as well but with no understanding. He was bent slightly forward, watching the moving needles intently when the soldier, at a sign from the officer, sliced through his shirt and trousers from behind with a knife so that they slipped off him; he tried to grab at the falling clothes to cover his nakedness, but the soldier lifted him up in the air and shook off the last of his rags. The officer turned off the machine, and in the ensuing silence the condemned man was placed under the harrow. The chains were removed and the straps fastened in their stead; for a moment this almost seemed a relief to the condemned man. The harrow now lowered itself a bit farther—as this was a thin man. When the needle points reached his skin, a shudder ran through him; while the soldier was busy with the condemned man's right hand, he stretched the left one out in a random direction; it was, however, in the direction of the traveler. The officer kept glancing at the traveler out of the corner of his eye as if to ascertain from his face how the execution, which had been at least nominally explained to him by now, impressed him.

The wrist strap snapped; the soldier had probably pulled it too tight. The officer's help was required; the soldier showed him the frayed piece of strap. So the officer went over to him and said, still facing the traveler: "The machine is very complex so something or other is bound to break down or tear, but one mustn't allow this to cloud one's overall judgment. Anyway, a substitute for the strap is easy to find: I will use a chain—of course the delicacy of the vibrations for the right arm will be adversely affected." And while he was arranging the chain, he remarked further: "The resources for maintaining the machine are quite limited these days. Under the old commandant I had unlimited access to a fund set aside for just this purpose. There was a store here that stocked all sorts of spare parts. I must confess I wasn't exactly frugal—I mean before, not now as the new commandant claims, but he uses everything as an excuse to attack the old ways. Now he's wrested control of the machine fund; if I request a new strap, the old one is required as evidence and the new one takes ten days to arrive and is of inferior quality, not much use at all. But in the meantime, how I'm supposed to operate the machine without a strap—no one worries about that."

The traveler reflected that it is always dicey to meddle decisively in the affairs of other people. He was neither a citizen of the penal colony nor a citizen of the state to which it belonged. If he were to condemn, to say nothing of prevent, the execution, they could say to him: "You are a foreigner, keep quiet." He could make no answer to that, he could only add that he himself didn't understand his actions, for he traveled solely as an observer and certainly had no intention of revamping other people's judicial systems. But in the present circumstances it was very tempting: The injustice of the process and the inhumanity of the execution were unquestionable. No one could assume any selfish interest on the traveler's part, as the condemned man was a complete stranger, not even a fellow countryman, and he certainly inspired no sympathy. The traveler himself had been recommended by men in high office and received here with great courtesy, and the very fact that he had been invited to attend this execution seemed to suggest that his views on the judicial process were being solicited. And this was all the more probable since the commandant, as had just been made plain, was no fan of this procedure and was nearly hostile in his attitude toward the officer.

Just then the traveler heard the officer howl in rage. He had just succeeded, and not without difficulty, in shoving the felt gag into the mouth of the condemned man who, in an uncontrollable fit of nausea, squeezed his eyes shut and vomited. The officer rushed to pull him away from the gag and turn his head toward the pit, but it was too late, the vomit was running down the machine. "It's all that commandant's fault!" he shouted, thoughtlessly shaking at the brass rods closest to him. "The machine is as filthy as a sty." With trembling hands, he showed the traveler what had happened. "Haven't I spent hours trying to explain to the commandant that no food should be given for a whole day preceding the execution? But there are other opinions in this new, permissive regime. The commandant's ladies stuff the man's gullet full of sweets before he's led away. He's lived on stinking fish his whole life and now he must dine on sweets! But that would be all right, I wouldn't object to it, but why can't they get me a new felt gag like I've been asking for the last three months? How could a man not be sickened when the felt in his mouth has been gnawed and drooled on by more than a hundred men as they lay dying?"

The condemned man had laid his head down and looked quite peaceful; the soldier was busy cleaning the machine with the condemned man's shirt. The officer approached the traveler, who stepped back a pace in some vague dread, but the officer grasped his hand and drew him aside. "I would like to speak to you confidentially," he said, "if I may." "Of course," said the traveler, and listened with his eyes cast down.

"This procedure and execution, which you now have the opportunity to admire, no longer have any open supporters in our colony. I am their sole advocate and, at the same time, the sole advocate of our former commandant's legacy. No longer can I ponder possible developments for the system, I spend all my energy preserving what's left. When the old commandant was alive, the colony was full of his supporters; I do possess some of his strength of conviction, but I have none of his power, and consequently his supporters have drifted away; there are many of them left but none will admit to it. If you went into the tea-house today, an execution day, and listened to what was being said, you'd probably hear only very ambiguous remarks. These would all be made by supporters, but considering the present commandant and his current beliefs, they're completely useless to me. And now I ask you: Is a life's work such as this"—he indicated the machine—"to be destroyed because of the commandant and the influence his women have over him? Should this be allowed to happen? Even by a stranger who has only come to our island for a few days? But there's no time to lose, plans are being made to undermine my jurisdiction. Meetings that I am excluded from are already being held in the commandant's headquarters. Even your presence here today seems significant: They are cowards and sent you ahead, you, a foreigner. Oh, how different an execution used to be in the old days! As much as a whole day before the event the valley would be packed with people: They lived just to see it. The commandant appeared early in the morning with his coterie of ladies; fanfares roused the entire camp; I reported that everything was ready; the assembly—no high official could be absent—arranged themselves around the machine. This stack of cane chairs is a pathetic leftover from that time. The machine was freshly cleaned and gleaming; for almost every execution I used new spare parts. Before hundreds of eyes—all the spectators would stand on tiptoe to the very rims of the slopes—the commandant himself installed the condemned man beneath the harrow. What today is left to a common soldier was performed by me, the presiding judge, at that time, and it was a great honor for me. And then the execution began! There were no discordant sounds to disturb the working of the machine. Many no longer watched but lay in the sand with their eyes closed; everyone knew: The wheels of justice were turning. In the silence nothing but the moaning of the condemned man could be heard, though his moans were muffled by the gag. These days the machine can induce no moan too loud for the gag to stifle; of course back then an acid that we're no longer allowed to use dripped from the writing needles. Well, anyway—then came the sixth hour! It was not possible to grant every request to watch from close-up. In his wisdom, the commandant decreed that children should be given first priority. By virtue of my office, of course, I was always nearby; often I was squatting there with a small child in either arm. How we drank in the transfigured look on the sufferer's face, how we bathed our cheeks in the warmth of that justice—achieved at long last and fading quickly. What times those were, my comrade!" The officer had evidently forgotten whom he was addressing; he had embraced the traveler and laid his head on his shoulder. The traveler was deeply embarrassed and stared impatiently past the officer's head. The soldier had finished cleaning by now and was pouring rice gruel into the bowl from a can. As soon as the condemned man, who seemed to be fully recovered, saw this, he began to lap after the gruel with his tongue. The soldier continually pushed him away, since it was certainly meant for another time, but it was equally unfair of the soldier to stick his dirty hands into the basin and eat in the condemned man's ravenous face.

The officer quickly recovered, "I did not want to upset you," he said. "I know it's impossible to make you understand what it was like then. In any event, the machine still works and is effective in and of itself. It is effective even though it stands alone in this valley. And in the end the corpse still slips unbelievably smoothly into the pit, even if there aren't, as there once were, hundreds gathered like flies all around it. At that time, we had to erect a sturdy fence around the pit. It was torn down long ago."

The traveler wanted to avert his face from the officer and looked about aimlessly. The officer assumed that he was marking the desolation of the valley, so he seized his hands and turned him around to meet his gaze and asked: "Can't you just see the shame of it?"

But the traveler said nothing. The officer left him alone for a little while and stood absolutely still, his legs apart, hands on his hips, staring at the ground, then he smiled encouragingly at the traveler and said: "I was right beside you yesterday when the commandant invited you. I heard him, I know the commandant,

I immediately understood what his intentions were. Although he's powerful enough to move against me, he doesn't yet dare do it, but he certainly intends to subject me to your judgment, the judgment of a respected foreigner. He has calculated carefully: This is your second day on the island, you didn't know the old commandant and his ways, you're conditioned by European mores, perhaps on principle you object to the death penalty in general and such a mechanical method as this one in particular; besides, you can see that executions are pathetic and have no public support here, even the machine is badly worn—now, taking all this into consideration (so thinks the commandant), isn't it quite possible that you would disapprove of my methods? And if you do disapprove (I am still speaking as the commandant), you wouldn't conceal this fact, for certainly you have confidence in your own tried and true convictions. Of course you have seen and learned to respect the peculiarities of many other peoples, and you probably wouldn't condemn our proceedings as forcefully as you would in your own land. But the commandant has no need for all that. Just letting slip a casual little remark will suffice. It may not even reflect your true opinions, so long as it serves his purpose. He will be very clever in his interrogation, of that I am sure, and his ladies will circle around you and prick up their ears. You might just say: 'Our judicial system is quite different,' or, 'The defendant is questioned before he is sentenced in our country,' or, 'In our country the condemned man is informed of his sentence,' or 'We haven't used torture since the Middle Ages'—all of which are statements that are as true as they seem self-evident to you, innocent enough remarks that don't malign my methods in any way. But how will the commandant take them? I can picture him, the good commandant, hastily shoving his chair aside and rushing onto the balcony, I can see his ladies streaming out after him, I can hear his voice—the ladies call it a booming, thunderous voice—and so now he speaks: 'A renowned scholar from the West, charged with investigating the judicial systems of all the countries in the world, has just pronounced our traditional system of administering justice inhumane. After receiving the verdict of such a distinguished person, I can naturally no longer tolerate this procedure. Effective immediately I therefore ordain . . . ,' and so on and so forth. You would like to recant: You never said what he is asserting; you never called my methods inhumane, on the contrary you regard them, in keeping with your deep insight, as the most humane and worthy of humanity; you also admire this machinery—but it's too late; you'll never get to the balcony, which is already crowded with ladies; you'll try to draw attention to yourself; you'll want to shout but your mouth will be covered by a lady's hand— and both I and the work of the old commandant will be finished."

The traveler had to suppress a smile; the task that he thought would be so difficult was now so easy. He evasively said: "You overestimate my influence; the commandant has read my letters of recommendation and knows that I am no expert in legal matters. If I were to express an opinion, it would be the opinion of a private individual, with no more weight than anyone else's and in any case far less influential than the opinion of the commandant, who, as I understand it, has very extensive powers in this penal colony. If he is as decidedly against you as you believe, then I fear that the end of your procedure is indeed near— without any modest assistance on my part."

Did the officer finally understand? No, he still didn't understand. He shook his head firmly, glanced at the condemned man and the soldier, who both flinched and abruptly abandoned their rice, came right up to the traveler, and instead of looking him in the eye, addressed some spot of his coat and said in a lower voice: "You don't know the commandant, you believe your position in regard to him and the rest of us is somewhat—please pardon the expression—ineffectual, but trust me, your influence cannot be rated too highly. I was overjoyed when I heard that you would attend the execution alone. This decision of the commandant's was intended as a blow to me, but I shall now turn it to my advantage. Without the distraction of whispered lies and scornful glances—which would have been unavoidable with a large crowd of spectators—you have heard my explanations, seen the machine, and are now on the verge of watching the execution. I'm sure you've already formed an opinion; if you still have any niggling doubts left, the sight of the execution will eliminate them. And now I put this request to you: Help me defeat the commandant!"

The traveler allowed him to speak no further. "How could I do that," he exclaimed. "It's absolutely impossible. I can't help you any more than I can hinder you."

"Yes, you can," replied the officer. With some alarm, the traveler noticed that the officer was clenching his fists. "Yes, you can," the officer repeated more urgently. "I have a plan that is bound to succeed. You don't believe you have sufficient influence, but I know that you do. However, even granting that you're right, isn't it necessary for the sake of the old system's preservation that we try everything, even things that are potentially ineffective? So listen to my plan. In order for it to succeed, it is extremely important that you say as little as possible in the colony today concerning the conclusions you've drawn about the procedure. Unless asked directly you should on no account comment. What you do say, however, must be brief and noncommittal, it should appear that you find the matter difficult to speak about, that you're embittered over it, that if you were to speak freely you would almost be tempted to curse. I'm not asking you to lie, by any means; you should just answer curtly: 'Yes, I have seen the execution,' or, 'Yes, it was all explained to me.' Just that, nothing more. Your bitterness, which should be made obvious, is sufficiently justified, although not in the way the commandant imagines. He will completely misunderstand its meaning of course and interpret it to suit his own needs. My plan's success hinges on this. Tomorrow there's to be a large conference of all the high administrative officials at the commandant's headquarters, presided over by the commandant himself. Naturally the commandant has turned these meetings into public exhibitions. He has built a gallery that is always packed with spectators. I am compelled to participate in these meetings, though they sicken and disgust me. No matter what the case, you are sure to be invited to this meeting; if you behave today as I have outlined, the invitation will become an urgent request. But if you are not invited for some obscure reason, you'll have to ask for an invitation—that will ensure your getting one without a doubt. So now tomorrow you're sitting in the commandant's box with the ladies. He keeps looking up to make sure you are there. After discussing various ludicrous and unimportant issues, introduced solely for the benefit of the audience—usually it's some harbor works, it's always harbor works!—our judicial procedure is brought to the agenda. If the commandant fails to introduce it, or fails to do so soon enough, I'll make it my business to get it mentioned. I'll stand up and report on today's execution. A very brief statement:

only that it has taken place. A statement of this sort is not quite standard at these meetings, but I will make it anyhow. The commandant thanks me, as always, with a friendly smile and then can't restrain himself; he seizes the fortunate opportunity. 'It has just been reported,' he will say, or words to that effect, 'that there has been an execution. I should merely like to add that this execution was witnessed by the great scholar who as you all know has done our colony an immense honor by his visit. His presence here today lends further importance to this occasion. Shouldn't we now ask the great scholar his opinion of our traditional mode of execution and the whole process surrounding it?' Of course there's applause and general approval all around, of which mine is the loudest. The commandant bows to you and says: 'Then I put the question to you in the name of all assembled here.' And now you step up to the balustrade—keep your hands where everyone can see them, otherwise the ladies will press them and play with your fingers—and now you can speak out at last. I don't know how I'll be able to endure the tension while waiting for that moment. You mustn't put any restrictions on yourself in your speech, let the truth be heard out loud, lean over the railing and roar, yes, roar your judgment, your immutable judgment, down on the commandant. But perhaps that is not what you wish to do, it's not in keeping with your character; perhaps in your country one behaves differently in such situations. That's fine, that'll work just as well. Don't stand up at all, just say a few words, in a whisper so that only those officials below you can hear. That will be enough. You don't even have to mention the lack of public support, the screeching gear, the torn strap, the repulsive felt; no, I'll take care of all that and, believe me, if my speech does not hound him from the hall, it will force him to his knees in confession: 'Old Commandant, I bow down before you. . . . ' That is my plan, will you help me carry it out? But of course you will, what's more, you must." And the officer seized the traveler by the arms and, breathing heavily, stared into his face. He had shouted his last sentences so loudly that even the soldier and the condemned man were paying attention; though they couldn't understand a word, they stopped eating for a moment and looked over, still chewing, at the traveler.

The answer that he was obliged to give was absolutely clear to the traveler from the very beginning. He had experienced far too much in his lifetime to falter here; at heart he was honorable and without fear, all the same he did hesitate now for a beat, in the face of the officer and the condemned man. But at last he said what he had to: "No." The officer blinked several times but kept his eyes locked on the traveler's. "Would you like an explanation?" asked the traveler. The officer nodded dumbly. "I am opposed to this procedure," the traveler then continued, "even before you confided in me—and naturally under no circumstances would I ever betray your confidence. I had already been considering whether I would be justified in intervening and whether any such intervention on my part would have the slightest chance of success. It was clear to me whom I had to turn to first: the commandant, of course. You helped make this even clearer, although you did not strengthen my resolve; on the contrary, your sincere conviction has moved me, even though it cannot influence my judgment."

The officer remained mute, turned and approached the machine, took hold of one of the brass rods, and leaning back a little, gazed up at the designer as if to check that all was in order. The soldier and the condemned man seemed to have become quite friendly; the condemned man was gesturing to the soldier, though movement was difficult for him due to the tightly binding straps; the soldier bent down to him and the condemned man whispered something in his ear; the soldier nodded.

The traveler followed the officer and said: "You don't know what I plan to do yet. I'll certainly tell the commandant my thoughts on the procedure, but I will do so privately, not at a public meeting. Nor will I be here long enough to attend any such meeting; I'm sailing early tomorrow morning, or boarding my ship at the least."

It did not look as if the officer had been listening. "So you weren't convinced by the procedure," he muttered to himself, smiling the smile of an old man listening to a child's nonsense while pursuing thoughts of his own.

"Well, then the time has come," he said at last, and looked at the traveler suddenly with bright, somewhat challenging eyes, apparently appealing for some kind of cooperation.

"Time for what?" the traveler inquired uneasily, but got no answer.

"You are free," the officer said to the condemned man in his own language. He did not believe this at first. "You are free now," repeated the officer. For the first time the face of the condemned man was truly animated. Was it true? Was it just a whim of the officer's that might pass? Had the foreigner obtained this reprieve? What was it? His face seemed to be asking these questions. But not for long. Whatever the reason might be, he wanted to be really free if he could, and he began to thrash about as far as the harrow would allow.

"You'll tear my straps," barked the officer. "Be still! We'll undo them." He signaled to the soldier and they both set about doing so. The condemned man laughed quietly to himself without a word, turning his head first to the officer on his left, then to the soldier on his right, and not forgetting the traveler either.

"Pull him out," ordered the officer. This required a certain amount of care because of the harrow. Through his own impatience, the condemned man had already sliced up his back a little.

But from here on the officer paid little attention to him. He went up to the traveler, drew out his small leather folder again, thumbed through the pages, finally finding the one he wanted, and showed it to the traveler. "Read it," he said. "I can't," said the traveler, "I already told you that I can't read these scripts." "Take a closer look," the officer insisted, stepping around next to the traveler so they could read it together. When that proved just as futile, he tried helping the traveler read by tracing the script with his little finger, though he held it far away from the paper as if that must never be touched. The traveler did make every effort in an attempt to please the officer at least in this respect, but it was impossible. Now the officer began to spell it out letter by letter, and then he read it all together. " 'Be just!' it says," he explained. "Surely you can read it now." The traveler bent down so close to the paper that the officer, fearing he would touch it, pulled it farther away; the traveler said nothing more, but it was clear that he still could not decipher it. " 'Be just!' it says," the officer repeated. "That may be," said the traveler, "I'm prepared to take your word for it." "Well then," said the officer, at least partly satisfied, and climbed the ladder with the sheet; he inserted the sheet into the designer with great care and seemed to completely rearrange all the gears; it was very difficult and intricate work that involved even the smallest gears, for the officer's head sometimes disappeared into the designer entirely, so precisely did he have to examine the mechanism.

The traveler followed this activity closely from below; his neck grew stiff and his eyes ached from the blaze of sunlight glaring across the sky. The soldier and the condemned man were absorbed with each other. The condemned man's shirt and trousers, which had already been dumped in the pit, were fished out by the soldier with the point of his bayonet. The shirt was filthy beyond belief, and the condemned man washed it in the bucket of water. When the condemned man donned the shirt and trousers, neither of the men could help bursting out laughing because the garments had been slit up the back. Perhaps the condemned man felt obliged to amuse the soldier, he twirled around again and again in his slashed clothes while the soldier squatted on the ground, slapping his knees in merriment. They did, however, control themselves somewhat out of consideration for the gentlemen's presence.

When at long last the officer had finished his work up above, he surveyed each part of the entire machine with a smile and closed the cover of the designer, which had remained open until now. He climbed down, looked into the pit and then at the condemned man, noting with satisfaction that he had taken back his clothes, then went over to wash his hands in the water bucket, realizing only too late how revoltingly dirty it was, and disheartened that he could no longer wash his hands, he ultimately thrust them—this alternative did not please him, but he had to accept it—into the sand. He then rose and began to unbutton his tunic. As he did this, the two ladies' handkerchiefs that he had tucked behind his collar fell into his hands. "Here, take your handkerchiefs," he said, and tossed them over to the condemned man. And to the traveler he said by way of explanation: "Presents from the ladies."

Despite the obvious haste with which he removed the tunic and then the rest of his clothing, he handled each garment with the utmost care, even running his fingers over the tunic's silver braid and shaking a tassel into place. But all this care was in direct contrast with the fact that no sooner was he finished removing a garment than he hurled it unceremoniously into the pit with an indignant jerk. The last thing left to him was his short sword and its belt. He drew the sword out of the scabbard and

broke it, then gathered it all up, the pieces of sword, the scabbard, the belt, and threw them into the pit so violently they
clanked against each other.

Now he stood there naked. The traveler chewed his lip and
said nothing. He knew without a doubt what was going to happen, but he had no right to prevent the officer from doing anything. If the judicial procedure that was so dear to the officer
was truly near its end—possibly due to the traveler's intervention,
to which he felt quite committed—then the officer's actions were
proper; the traveler would have done the same in his place.

The soldier and the condemned man understood nothing at
first, they weren't even watching. The condemned man was delighted to have his handkerchiefs returned, but he was not allowed to enjoy them for long, as the soldier snatched them with
a sudden, unexpected motion. Now the condemned man tried in
turn to grab at the handkerchiefs, which the soldier had tucked
under his belt for safekeeping, but the soldier was on his guard.
So they half jokingly wrestled with each other. Only when the
officer was totally naked did they begin to pay attention. The
notion that some drastic reversal was about to take place seemed
to have struck the condemned man in particular. What had happened to him was now happening to the officer. Perhaps it would
be seen through to the end. The foreign traveler had probably
ordered it. This, then, was revenge. Without having suffered to
the end himself, he would be avenged to the end. A broad, silent
grin now appeared on his face and stayed there.

The officer, however, had turned to the machine. It had previously been clear enough that he understood the machine well,
but now it was almost mind-boggling to see how he handled it
and how it obeyed him. He had only to reach out a hand toward
the harrow for it to raise and lower itself several times until it
found the proper position to receive him; he merely nudged the
edge of the bed and it started to vibrate; it was plain that he was
rather reluctant, when the felt gag came to meet his mouth, to
receive it, but his hesitation only lasted a moment; he promptly
submitted and received it. Everything was ready; only the straps
still hung down at the sides, but they were evidently superfluous;
the officer did not need to be strapped in. But the condemned
man noticed the loose straps, and in his opinion the execution
was not complete unless the straps were fastened; he eagerly

beckoned to the soldier and they both ran over to strap the officer down. The latter had already stretched out one foot to push the crank that would start the designer, then he saw the two men approaching; he withdrew his foot and allowed himself to be strapped in. But now he could no longer reach the crank; neither the soldier nor the condemned man would be able to find it, and the traveler was determined not to lift a finger. It wasn't necessary; hardly were the straps in place when the machine started to operate: The bed shook, the needles danced over the flesh, the harrow gently bobbed up and down. The traveler had already been staring at it for some time before remembering that a gear in the designer should be screeching, but everything was still, not even the slightest whirring could be heard.

Because the machine was working so silently, it became virtually unnoticeable. The traveler looked over at the soldier and the condemned man. The condemned was the livelier of the two, every facet of the machine interested him—one moment he was bending down, the next reaching up, his forefinger always extended to point something out to the soldier. This made the traveler extremely uncomfortable. He was determined to stay here till the end, but he couldn't bear the sight of those two for long. "Go on home," he said. The soldier might have been willing to do so, but the condemned man considered the order a punishment. With clasped hands he begged to be allowed to stay, and when the traveler, shaking his head, did not relent, he even went down on his knees. The traveler realized that giving orders was useless and was at the point of going over to chase the pair away. Just then he heard a noise in the designer above him. He looked up. Was it that troublesome gear after all? But it was something else. The cover of the designer rose slowly and then fell completely open. The teeth of a gear wheel emerged and rose higher, soon the whole wheel could be seen. It was as if some monumental force were compressing the designer so that there was no more room for this wheel—the wheel spun to the edge of the designer, fell, and rolled a little ways in the sand before it toppled onto its side. But a second wheel was already following it, with many others rolling after it—large ones, small ones, some so tiny they were hard to see; the same thing happened with all of them. One kept imagining that the designer was finally empty, but then a fresh, particularly numerous group would come into view, climb

out, fall, spin in the sand, and lie still. In the thrall of this spectacle, the condemned man completely forgot the traveler's order.
He was fascinated by the wheels and kept trying to catch one,
urging the soldier at the same time to help him; but he always
drew back his hand in alarm, for another wheel would immediately come speeding along and frighten him, at least when it
started to roll.

The traveler on the other hand was deeply troubled—the machine was obviously falling apart—its silent operation was an illusion. He had the feeling that it was now his duty to take care
of the officer, since he was no longer capable of looking after
himself. However, while the chaos of the gear wheels claimed all
his attention, he had failed to keep an eye on the rest of the
machine; now that the last wheel had left the designer, he went
over to the harrow and had a new and even less welcome surprise. The harrow wasn't writing at all but just stabbing, and the
bed wasn't rolling the body over but thrusting it up, quivering,
into the needles. The traveler wanted to do something, bring the
whole machine to a stop if possible, because this was not the
exquisite torture the officer had wished for; this was out-and-out
murder. He reached out, but at that moment the harrow rose
with the body already spitted upon it and swung to the side as it
usually only did at the twelfth hour. Blood flowed in a hundred
streams—not mixed with water, the water jets had also failed to
function this time—and the last function failed to complete itself,
the body did not drop from the long needles: It hung over the
pit, streaming with blood, without falling. The harrow tried to
return to its original position, but as if it also noticed that it had
not unloaded its burden, it stayed where it was, suspended over
the pit. "Come and help!" the traveler shouted to the soldier and
the condemned man, and grabbed the officer by the feet. He
wanted to push against the feet from this side while the other
two took hold of the head from the other side so the officer could
gently be removed from the needles. But the others couldn't
make up their minds to come right away; the condemned man
had even turned away. The traveler was compelled to go over to
them and force them to get in position by the officer's head. And
from this vantage point he had to look, almost against his will, at
the face of the corpse. It was as it had been in life (no sign of
the promised deliverance could be detected). What all the others

had found in the machine, the officer had not; his lips were clamped together, the eyes were open and bore the same expression as in life, a quiet, convinced look; and through the forehead was the point of the great iron spike.

As the traveler, with the soldier and the condemned man following, reached the first houses in the colony, the soldier pointed to one of them and said: "That's the teahouse."

On the ground floor of this house was a deep, low, cavernous room whose walls and ceiling were blackened with smoke. It was open to the street along the whole of its width. Although the teahouse differed very little from the other houses in the colony, which, except for the palatial buildings of the commandant's headquarters, were all very dilapidated, it gave the traveler the impression of being a historic landmark, and he felt the power of earlier times. Followed by his companions, he went closer, passed between the empty tables that stood on the street in front of the teahouse, and breathed in the damp, cool air that came from the interior. "The old man is buried here," said the soldier. "The priest wouldn't allow him in the cemetery. For a while no one knew where to bury him, they ended up burying him here. The officer didn't tell you about it because, naturally, it's what he's most ashamed of. A few times he even tried to dig the old man up at night, but he was always chased away." "Where's the grave?" asked the traveler, finding it impossible to believe the soldier. Both the soldier and the condemned man immediately ran in front of him, pointing with outstretched hands to where the grave was. They led the traveler to the far wall, where several customers were sitting at tables. They were apparently dock workers, strong men with black, glistening, full beards. They were all in their shirt-sleeves and their shirts were raggedy: These were poor, humble people. As the traveler approached, some of them rose and edged back against the wall, staring at him. "He's a foreigner," was whispered around him, "he wants to see the grave." They pushed one of the tables aside, and under it there actually was a gravestone. It was a simple stone, low enough to be hidden beneath a table. It bore an inscription in very small lettering; the traveler had to kneel down in order to read it. It read: "Here lies the old commandant. His followers, who must now remain nameless, have dug this grave and set this stone. It has been prophesied that after a certain number of years he will rise again and lead his followers out of this house to reclaim the colony. Have faith and wait!" When the traveler read this, he rose to his feet. He saw the men surrounding him smile, as if they had read the inscription with him, found it absurd, and were inviting him to agree with them. The traveler pretended not to notice, distributed a few coins among them, and waiting until the table was pushed back over the grave, left the teahouse and made for the harbor.

The soldier and the condemned man were detained in the teahouse by some acquaintances. But they must have broken away from them relatively quickly because the traveler had only descended half the long flight of stairs that led to the boats when they came running after him. They probably wanted to force the traveler to take them with him at the last minute. While he was down below negotiating with a ferryman to take him to the steamer, the two men charged down the steps in silence, as they did not dare shout. But by the time they arrived at the foot of the steps, the traveler was already in the boat and the ferryman was casting off. They could still have jumped aboard, but the traveler hoisted a heavy, knotted rope from the floor of the boat and threatened them with it, thereby preventing them from attempting the leap.

*A Country Doctor**

*Originally published in 1919 under the German title "Ein Landarzt."

I WAS DISTRAUGHT: AN urgent journey awaited me; I had to visit a gravely ill patient in a village ten miles away; a thick blizzard filled the distance that separated us; I had a trap,* a light one with large wheels that was perfect for our country roads; I stood in the courtyard, wrapped in furs, holding my bag of instruments, all ready to go, but the horse was missing—no horse. My own horse had died the night before from the exertions of this icy winter. My maid was now running around the village trying to scrounge up a horse, but it was utterly hopeless. I knew it. I stood there aimlessly, more and more covered in snow, less and less able to move. The girl appeared at the gate, swinging the lantern, alone of course. Who would lend his horse for such a journey and at a time like this? I paced the courtyard once more; there was nothing I could do. Frustrated, I distractedly kicked at the flimsy door of the long-vacant pigsty. It flew open and was flung back and forth on its hinges. Steam and the smell of horses emerged. Inside, a dim stable lantern was hanging from a rope, swaying. A man, crouching in the low shed, revealed his open, blue-eyed face. "Shall I harness the horses to the trap?" he asked, crawling out on all fours. I could think of nothing to say and merely bent down to see what else was in the sty. The maid was standing beside me. "You never know what you'll find in your own house," she said, and we both laughed.

"Greetings brother, greetings sister!" cried the groom, and two horses, mighty creatures with powerful flanks, pushed themselves, one after the other, their legs close to their bodies, their shapely heads dipped down like camels', propelling themselves, with the sheer force of their writhing bodies, through the doorway they completely filled. But they promptly stood upright on their long legs, their coast steaming thickly. "Give him a hand,"

*Light, two-wheeled carriage.

123

I said, and the willing girl hurried to hand the harnesses to the groom, but she was hardly near him when the groom threw his arms around her and shoved his face against hers. She screamed and ran back to me for safety, two red rows of tooth marks imprinted on her cheek. "You brute," I yelled furiously, "I'll give you a whipping, I swear," but then I immediately remember that he is a stranger, that I don't know where he comes from, and that he is helping me of his own free will when all others have refused me. As if he has read my thoughts, he takes no offense at my threat, but, still busy with the horses, only once turns around to look at me. "Get in," he then says, and everything is actually ready. I note to myself that I have never ridden behind such a magnificent pair of horses, and climb in cheerfully. "I'll drive though, you don't know the way," I say. "Of course," he answers, "I'm not going with you at all. I'm staying here with Rosa." "No," shrieks Rosa, and runs in the house with a justified presentiment of her inescapable fate. I hear the door chain rattle into place, I hear the lock click shut, I watch as she extinguishes the lights in the hall and in each room as she runs through, trying to hide her whereabouts. "You're coming with me," I inform the groom, "or I won't go, urgent as my journey is. I do not intend to hand the girl over to you in payment for my passage." "Giddap!" he cries, clapping his hands, and the trap is swept away like a twig in the current. I hear my front door splinter and burst as the groom attacks it, and then my eyes and ears are swamped with a blinding rush of the senses. But even this lasts only a moment, for, as if my patient's courtyard opens just outside my gate, I am already there. The horses stand quietly; it has stopped snowing and there's moonlight all around; my patient's parents hurry out of the house, his sister behind them. I am nearly lifted out of the trap; I glean nothing from their confused babbling. The air in the sickroom is barely breathable; smoke is billowing out of the neglected stove. I need to open a window, but first I must examine the patient. Gaunt but with no fever, neither warm nor cold, with vacant eyes and no shirt, the boy hauls himself out from under the bedding, drapes himself around my neck, and whispers into my ear: "Doctor, let me die." I take a swift look around the room; nobody heard him. The parents are silently leaning forward, awaiting my diagnosis; the sister has brought a chair for my medical bag. I open the bag and search through my instruments. The boy keeps grabbing at me from the bed to re-mind me of his request. I seize a pair of pincers, examine them in the candlelight, and throw them back. "Yes," I think cynically, "the gods help out in cases like these. They send the missing horse, add a second owing to the urgency, and even supply a groom. . . ." Only now do I remember Rosa again. What should I do, how can I save her, how can I pry her from under that groom ten miles away when an uncontrollable team of horses is driving my trap? These horses, who have now somehow slipped their reins, push the windows open from the outside—how, I don't know. Each pokes its head through a window and, unper-turbed by the family's outcry, they stand gazing at the patient. "I'll drive back home at once," I think, as if the horses were summoning me for the return journey, and yet I allow the pa-tient's sister, who imagines that I'm overcome by the heat, to remove my furs. I am handed a glass of rum, the old man claps me on the shoulder, a familiarity justified by the offer of this treasure. I shake my head; the narrow cast of the old man's thoughts would sicken me; for this reason only I refuse the drink. The mother beckons me from the side of the bed, I come forward and, while one of the horses neighs loudly to the ceiling, lay my head on the boy's chest. He shivers under my wet beard. I con-firm what I already know: The boy is healthy. He has rather poor circulation and has been saturated with coffee by his anxious mother, but he's healthy and would be best driven from bed with a firm shove. But I'm not here to change the world, so I let him lie. I am employed by the district and do my duty to the utmost, and perhaps beyond. Though miserably paid, I'm both generous and ready to help the poor. But Rosa still has to be taken care of, and then maybe the boy will get his wish, and I'll want to die too. What am I doing in this eternal winter? My horse is dead and no one in the village will lend me his. I have to drag my team out of the pigsty; if they didn't happen to be horses, I would have to drive sows. That's how it is. And I nod to the family; they know nothing about it, and if they did know, they wouldn't be-lieve it. It's easy to write prescriptions, but it's tougher to really get through to people. Well, that about wraps up my visit; once again I've been called out unnecessarily, but I'm used to it. The whole district torments me with the help of my night bell; but that I had to forsake Rosa this time, that beautiful girl who's lived in my house for years, almost unnoticed by me—this is too much of a sacrifice, and I shall have to try and painstakingly arrange my thoughts with great care and subtlety so as not to attack the family, who even with the best intentions in the world could not restore Rosa to me. But when I shut my bag and gesture for my coat, the family is standing around in a group, the father sniffing at the glass of rum in his hand, the mother probably disappointed in me—why, what do people expect?—tearfully biting her lip, the sister twisting a blood-soaked handkerchief; I am somehow ready to concede that the boy might be sick after all. I go to him, he smiles at me as if I were bringing him the most nourishing broth—alas, now both horses are neighing; the heavens, I'm sure, have ordained that this noise shall facilitate my examination— and now I discover: Yes, the boy is sick. On his right side, by his hip, a wound as big as the palm of my hand has opened up: various shades of rose-red, deeper red further in, paler at the edges, finely grained but with uneven clotting, and open like a surface mine to the daylight—so it looks from a distance. But closer inspection reveals a further complication. Who wouldn't let out a whistle at the sight of that? Worms, as long and thick as my little finger, rose-red too and blood spattered, caught in the depth of the wound wriggle toward the light with their small white heads and hundreds of tiny legs. Poor boy, you are beyond all help. I have unearthed your great wound; this bloom on your side is destroying you. The family is pleased, they see me being busy; the sister tells the mother, who tells the father, who tells some guests as they come tiptoeing in through the moonlight in the open door, their arms stretched out from their sides for balance. "Will you save me?" the boy whispers, sobbing, completely blinded by the life in his wound. This is typical of the people in my district, always asking the impossible of the doctor. They have lost their old faith; the minister sits at home and picks apart his vestments, one by one, but the doctor is expected to fix everything with his fine surgical hand. Well, if it pleases them; I haven't foisted myself on them; if they misuse me for sacred ends, I'll let that pass too; what more could I want, an old country doctor robbed of his maid! And so they come, the family and the village elders, and undress me; a school choir, led by a teacher, stands before the house and sings this verse to a very simple tune:

> First undress him, then he'll cure us,
> If he doesn't, then we'll kill him!
> He's a doctor, just a doctor.

Then I'm naked, calmly surveying the people, with my fingers in my beard, my head bowed. I am quite composed and feel fairly superior to the situation and remain so, but still it doesn't help me, for they pick me up by the head and feet and carry me to the bed. They lay me down next to the wall, on the side of the wound. They all leave the room and shut the door, the singing stops, clouds obscure the moon, the bedding lies warm all around me, the heads of the horses sway like shadows in the open windows. "You know," a voice says in my ear, "I don't have much confidence in you. You just blew in here, you didn't even come on your own two feet. Instead of helping me, you're crowding my deathbed. What I'd love best is to scratch your eyes out." "You're right," I say, "it's disgraceful. But I am a doctor. What should I do? Believe me, it's not easy for me either." "Is that excuse supposed to satisfy me? Oh, I suppose it must. I'm always supposed to be satisfied. I came into the world with a gorgeous wound, that was my sole endowment." "Young friend," I say, "your trouble is that you have no sense of perspective. I have been in sickrooms far and wide, and I tell you this: Your wound isn't that bad—made at angles with two sharp blows of the ax. Many offer up their sides and barely hear the ax in the forest, let alone that it's coming closer." "Is it really so, or are you deluding me in my fever?" "It is really so, I give you my word of honor, the word of a public health official." He took me at my word and lay still. But now it was time for me to think of my own salvation. The horses were faithfully standing their ground. I quickly collected my clothes, furs, and bag, as I didn't want to waste time dressing. If the horses sped back as fast as they had come, I would more or less be jumping from this bed into mine. One of the horses obediently drew back from the window; I flung my bundle into the trap; the fur coat, flying too far, caught on a hook by only one sleeve. Good enough. I swung myself up onto the horse. The reins trailed loose, one horse was barely hitched to the other, the trap swayed wildly behind, and, last of all, the fur coat dragged in the snow. "Giddap!" I shouted, but the horses didn't gallop. We crawled slowly through the wasteland of snow like old men; for a long time the sound of the children's new but incorrect song followed us:

> All you patients now be joyful,
> The doctor's laid in bed beside you!

I'll never reach home at this rate; my thriving practice is lost; my successor will rob me of it, but in vain, for he cannot replace me; that foul groom is raging through my house; Rosa is his victim; I don't want to think of it anymore. Naked, exposed to the frosts of this most unfortunate era, with my earthly carriage and unearthly horses, old man that I am, I am buffeted about. My fur coat hangs from the back of the trap, but I cannot reach it, and not one of my agile pack of patients lifts a finger. Betrayed! Betrayed! A false ring of the night bell, once answered—it can never be made right.

*An Old Leaf**

*Originally published in 1919 under the German title "Ein altes Blatt."

IT WOULD SEEM THAT there is much about the defense of our fatherland that has been neglected. We have not been overly concerned about this until recently and have gone about our daily work, but lately certain events have caused us concern.

I have a shoemaker's workshop in the square in front of the imperial palace. Scarcely have I opened up shop at daybreak when I see armed men posted at the end of every street leading into the square. These, however, are not our soldiers but clearly nomads from the north. They have somehow, just how is inconceivable to me, penetrated the capital, although it is really quite a long distance from the border. In any event they are there, and every morning it seems that there are more of them.

As befits their nature, they camp out in the open because they loathe housing. They occupy themselves by sharpening swords, whittling arrows, practicing their horsemanship. This peaceful square, which has always been kept scrupulously clean, has been transformed by them into a veritable sty. We do, every now and then, dash out of our shops and clear away at least the worst of the trash, but this happens less and less frequently, as the effort is futile; besides, in doing this we risk being trampled by horses or lashed by whips.

Conversation with the nomads is impossible. They don't speak our language and in fact barely have one of their own. Among themselves they communicate much as jackdaws* do; this jackdaw squawking constantly fills our ears. They neither understand nor have any desire to understand our way of life, our institutions, and so as a result even our sign language is willfully incomprehensible to them. You can dislocate your jaw and wrench your wrists out of joint and they still have not understood you, nor will

---

*Glossy, black European birds belonging to the crow family that nest in towers and ruins.

131

they ever understand. They often grimace, then flash the whites of their eyes and foam at the mouth, but they don't actually mean anything by it; it's not even a threat, they just do it because that's their nature. They take whatever it is they need. You can't say that they employ force; when they grab at something, you simply stand aside and leave them to it.

From my own stores they have taken quite a lot. But I can hardly complain when I see, for example, how the butcher across the street fares. He's barely brought in his supplies when they're snatched away and the nomads are all over it. Even their horses feed on meat; a horseman and his horse frequently lie side by side, gnawing at the same piece of meat, one at either end. The butcher is afraid and does not dare stop his meat deliveries. We understand this, however, and we take up a collection to support him. Who knows what the nomads would be capable of if they didn't get the meat—for that matter, who knows what they're capable of even when they do get meat every day.

The other day the butcher thought he might at least spare himself the trouble of slaughtering, so he brought out a live ox in the morning. He must never be permitted to do this again. For a full hour, I lay flat on the floor at the very back of my workshop; I had covered myself with all my clothes, blankets, and pillows, just to drown out the horrifying braying of that ox; the nomads were leaping on it from all sides to rip off pieces of its warm flesh with their teeth. All had been quiet for a long time before I ventured out again. Like drunks around a wine cask, they were lying glutted around the remains of the ox.

It was just then that I thought I saw the Emperor himself in one of the palace windows; ordinarily he never enters these outer rooms but keeps strictly to the innermost garden; but at that moment he was standing, at least it seemed so to me, at one of the windows, gazing down, with head bowed, at the activity before his palace gates.

We all ask ourselves, What will happen? How long can we endure this burden and torment? The imperial palace has attracted the nomads, but it does not know how to drive them away again. The gates stay shut; the sentries, who before always marched in and out with pomp, now hide inside behind barred windows. The salvation of our fatherland is left to us craftsmen and tradespeople, but we are not equal to such a task, nor indeed have we ever claimed to be capable of it. This is a misunderstanding, and it is proving the ruin of us.

A Hunger Artist*

*Originally published in 1922 under the German title "Ein Hungerkünstler."

IN RECENT DECADES THERE has been a marked decline in the public's interest in professional fasting. It was formerly very profitable to mount large, privately managed productions of this kind, while today this is entirely impossible. Those were different times. There was a time when the whole town was entranced by the hunger artist; during his fast, enthusiasm grew from day to day, everyone wanted to see the hunger artist at least once a day; during the latter stages people would reserve special seats in front of the small barred cage all day long, there were even night exhibitions by torchlight for a more extreme effect; on fine days the cage was carried out into the open and then it was a particular treat for children to see the hunger artist, while for the elders he was often mostly a joke in which they participated because it was fashionable; the children stood around in open-mouthed wonder, holding each other's hands for security, and watching as he sat on the spread-out straw, spurning even a chair, a pale figure in black tricot,° his ribs protruding hideously; sometimes he nodded politely, answering questions with a forced smile, occasionally proffering an arm through the bars for them to feel how skinny it was but then sinking down and retreating completely into himself, paying attention to nothing and no one, not even the all-important striking of the clock, which was the only piece of furniture in the cage, but staring straight ahead through narrowed eyes and taking an occasional sip from a glass of water to moisten his lips.

Aside from the milling spectators, there were also constant teams of watchmen selected by the public; oddly enough these were butchers more often than not, whose task it was to watch the hunger artist night and day, three at a time, so that he did

---

°Worsted, or twisted, fabric often used to make garments; the hunger artist's wearing of tricot is certainly for an ascetic purpose.

not partake of somehow secreted nourishment. This was nothing more than a formality instituted to reassure the masses, because as initiates very well knew, during the period of the fast the hunger artist would under no circumstances, including duress, swallow the tiniest morsel; the honor of his profession forbade it. Of course, not every watchman was capable of comprehending this; frequently there were groups of night watchmen who were very lax in their duties and deliberately sat in a far corner absorbed in a card game with the obvious intention of allowing the hunger artist the opportunity of a little refreshment, which they assumed he could procure from some hidden stash. Nothing was more hateful to the hunger artist than watchmen like these, they made him miserable, they made his fast excruciatingly unbearable; sometimes he was able to overcome his weakness enough to sing during their watch for as long as he could to show these people how unjust their suspicions were. This was of little use, however; they only wondered at his skillful ability to eat while singing. He very much preferred the watchmen who sat right up against the bars and who were not satisfied by the dim night-lighting in the hall and so trained on him the beams of electric torches provided by the impresario. He was not at all disturbed by the harsh light, as he was unable to sleep in any case and he could always doze off a bit no matter the light or the hour, even when the hall was packed with noisy people. He was quite prepared to pass a sleepless night with such guards; he was happy to swap jokes with them, tell them stories from his nomadic life and listen to their stories in turn, anything to keep them awake and to show them again and again that there was nothing edible in his cage and that he was fasting as not one among them could fast. He was happiest however when morning came and a lavish breakfast was brought to them at his own expense; they threw themselves on it with the keen appetite of healthy men after the wearying night's vigil. Of course there were people who even misconstrued this breakfast as a bribe for the guards, but that was really going too far, and when asked if they would take over the night watch without breakfast just for the sake of the cause, they slunk away but stuck to their insinuations nevertheless.

But suspicions of this nature are inseparable from fasting. No one was capable of spending all his days and nights keeping watch over the hunger artist, therefore no one person could be absolutely certain from firsthand knowledge that the fast had truly been constant and flawless; only the hunger artist himself could know that, and so at the same time only he could be a satisfied spectator of his own fast. And yet for other reasons he was never satisfied; perhaps it was not just the fasting that emaciated his body to such a point that many people regretfully could not attend his demonstrations because they could not bear the sight of him, perhaps he was so reduced through dissatisfaction with himself. For he alone knew what no other initiate knew: How easy it was to fast. It was the easiest thing in the world. Nor did he make a secret of this though no one believed him; at best they thought him modest, but mostly they chalked it up to publicity or thought him a fraud for whom fasting was easy because he had figured out some scam to make it easy and then had the audacity to more or less admit it. He was forced to endure all this and he even grew accustomed to it over the years, but his own dissatisfaction gnawed at him inwardly, and yet never, not after a single fasting period—one had to grant him that much— had he left his cage voluntarily. The impresario had fixed the maximum period of fasting at forty days, he would never allow a fast to exceed this limit even in great cities, and for good reason. Experience had proved that public interest in any town could be roused by steadily increased advertising for about forty days, but the public lost interest after that and a substantial drop in attendance was noted; naturally there were small variations in this between one town or country and another, but as a rule forty days was the prescribed limit. So on the fortieth day the flower-festooned cage was opened, an enthusiastic crowd of spectators filled the hall, a military band performed, two doctors entered the cage to take the necessary measurements of the hunger artist, announced these results to the audience through a megaphone, and finally two young ladies came forward, pleased to have been selected for the honor of assisting the hunger artist from the cage and down the first few steps toward a small table laden with a carefully prepared invalid's meal. And at this very moment the hunger artist always turned stubborn. He would go so far as to surrender his bony arms to the outstretched hands of these solicitous ladies as they bent down to him, but stand up—that he would not do. Why stop now, after just forty days? He could have gone on longer, infinitely longer; why stop now when he was in his best fasting form, or rather, not yet in his best form? Why should he be robbed of the glory of fasting longer, not only for being the greatest hunger artist of all time, which he probably was already, but for surpassing his own record to achieve the inconceivable, because he felt his powers of fasting knew no bounds. Why did his public, who claimed to so admire him, have so little patience with him; if he could endure fasting longer, why couldn't they endure it? And besides, he was tired, he was comfortable sitting in the straw, and now he was expected to haul himself up to his full height and proceed to a meal the mere thought of which nauseated him to such a point that only the presence of the ladies and enormous effort prevented him from expressing it. And he gazed up into the eyes of the ladies, who were seemingly so friendly but in reality so cruel, and shook his head, which felt too heavy for his enfeebled neck. But then, what always happened, happened again. The impresario came forward silently—the band music made speech impossible—he raised his arms over the hunger artist as if inviting heaven to look down upon its handiwork in the straw, this pathetic martyr, which the hunger artist certainly was but in a completely different sense; he grasped the hunger artist around his emaciated waist with exaggerated delicacy to accentuate the fragile condition he was in, and committed him—not without giving him a secret shake or two so that the hunger artist's upper body and legs lolled and swayed about—to the care of the ladies, who had grown quite pale. Now the hunger artist submitted to everything, his head lay on his chest as if it had rolled there by chance and was inexplicably stopped, his body was hollowed out, some instinct of self-preservation squeezed his legs tight at the knees but they scraped at the ground as if it were not the solid earth they sought, and the entire weight of his body, however modest, was supported by one of the ladies, who looked around for help, panting a little—this was not how she had pictured her post of honor—first she craned her neck as far back as she could to prevent her face from touching the hunger artist, but then, when this was not successful and her more fortunate companion did not come to her aid but merely extended a trembling hand, which held the small bundle of bones that was the hunger artist's hand, she burst into tears, much to the delight of the spectators, and had to be replaced by an attendant who was standing in readiness. Then came the meal, a tiny bit of which the impresario spooned into the virtually comatose hunger artist, amid cheerful patter designed to divert the audience's attention from the artist's condition; afterward a toast that the artist allegedly whispered to the impresario was drunk to the public, the band capped everything with a grand flourish, the crowd dispersed, and no one had any cause to be dissatisfied with the show; no one, that is, but the hunger artist, always only him.

So he lived for many years in apparent splendor and with regular periods of rest, honored by the world, yet despite all that, mostly in a black mood that grew all the darker because no one took it seriously. And indeed, how could he be comforted? What more could he wish for? And if once in a while a kind-hearted soul came along and felt sorry for him and tried to point out that his melancholia was probably due to his fasting, it sometimes happened, especially if the fast were well advanced, that the hunger artist responded with a furious outburst and began to rattle the bars of his cage alarmingly, like a beast. But the impresario had a method of punishment that he was fond of employing for these outbursts. He begged the assembled audience's pardon for the artist's behavior, which he admitted was to be excused only as an irritable condition brought on by the fasting, a condition incomprehensible to well-fed people, and then he would make the transition to the hunger artist's equally outlandish claim that he was able to fast for much longer than he already had; he praised the high aspirations, the goodwill, and the great deal of self-denial undoubtedly implicit in this claim, but then he would seek to refute this claim simply enough by producing photographs, which were simultaneously offered for sale to the public, showing the artist on the fortieth day of a fast, lying on a bed, near dead from exhaustion. This perversion of the truth, though familiar to the hunger artist, always unnerved him anew and was too much for him. What was a consequence of the premature termination of his fast was presented here as its cause! To fight against this idiocy, this world of idiocy, was impossible. He stood clinging to the bars of his cage listening to the impresario in good faith time and time again but always let go as soon as the photographs appeared and sank back down onto his straw with a moan, and the reassured public could approach again and stare at him.

When the witnesses to such scenes reflected on them several years later, they often could not comprehend their own behavior. Meanwhile the aforementioned decline of public interest had already taken place; it seemed to happen almost overnight; there may have been deeper reasons for it, but who wanted to dig around for them; in any event, one day the pampered hunger artist found himself deserted by the crowds of pleasure seekers, who streamed past him toward other, more popular exhibitions. The impresario chased halfway across Europe with him one last time to see if the old interest were still alive here and there, all in vain; it was as if a secret pact had been made and everywhere there was evidence of a veritable revulsion for professional fasting. Naturally it could not realistically have happened so suddenly, and in retrospect a number of warning signs that were not adequately noted or sufficiently dealt with in the intoxication of success now came to mind, but it was too late at present to engage in any countermeasures. Of course fasting would make a comeback someday, but that was no comfort to the living. What was the hunger artist to do now? When he had been lauded by thousands he could never deign to appear as a sideshow in village fairs, and as for embarking on a different career, the hunger artist was not only too old but above all too fanatically devoted to fasting. So he took leave of the impresario, his partner throughout an unparalleled career, and found a position in a large circus; in order to spare his own feelings, he avoided reading the terms of his contract.

A huge circus, with its personnel, animals, and apparatus constantly being shuffled, replaced, recruited, and supplemented, could always find a use for anyone at any time, even a hunger artist, provided of course that his wants were few, and in this particular case it was not just the hunger artist that was hired but also his long-famous name; indeed in light of the peculiar nature of his art, which was not impaired by advancing age, it could not even be said that this was a superannuated artist who was seeking refuge in a quiet circus job; on the contrary, the hunger artist avowed very credibly—and there was every reason to believe him—that he could fast as well as ever; he even claimed that if he were allowed to do as he pleased, and this was promised him without further ado, he would truly astound the world with the results for the first time, although this assertion, owing to the prevailing attitude that the hunger artist, in his zeal, was wont to forget, only provoked a smile from the experts.

The hunger artist had not however lost his sense of fundamental reality and accepted it as a matter of course that his cage was not placed in the middle of the ring as a star attraction but outside by the stables in a spot that was, after all, still accessible. Large brightly painted placards framed his cage and proclaimed what was to be seen inside. When the public came pouring out during intermissions to see the animals, they almost inevitably passed the hunger artist's cage and stopped there for a moment; they might have loitered longer if the crowds pressing them from behind in the narrow passageway, who did not understand the delay in seeing the keenly anticipated menagerie, did not render further contemplation unfeasible. This was also the reason why the hunger artist, who had naturally been looking forward to these visiting hours as the culmination of his life's work, trembled at their prospect. At first he could hardly wait for the intermissions; he had delighted in watching the crowds surge toward him, until all too quickly it was firmly impressed upon him—and even the most obstinate and half-deliberate self-deception could not obscure the fact—that these people, judging from their actions at least, were again and again without exception on their way to visit the stables. And that first sight of them from a distance remained the most cherished. For as soon as they reached him he was promptly deafened by the shouting and cursing that welled up from the two contending factions, the ones that wanted to pause and stare at him—and the hunger artist soon found them the more distasteful of the two—out of no true interest but from nastiness and defiance, and the others, who only wanted to go straight to the animals. After the first rush was over, along came the stragglers, and although there was nothing to prevent them from stopping as long as they liked, these folks hurried by with long strides and nary a glance at him as they hastened to reach the stables in time. And all too rarely he had a stroke of luck when the father of a family arrived with his children, pointed to the hunger artist, and gave a detailed explanation of the phenomenon, telling tales of earlier years when he had attended similar but far grander exhibitions, and the children, since neither their lives nor their schools had sufficiently prepared them for this, remained uncomprehending—what was hunger to them?—

but the gleam in their inquisitive eyes spoke of new and better and more merciful times to come. The hunger artist sometimes remarked to himself that perhaps things might look a little brighter if he were not located quite so near the stables. That made it too easy for people to choose their destination, not to mention how the stench of the stables, the restlessness of the animals at night, the conveyance of raw slabs of meat for the beasts of prey, and the roars at feeding time all continually oppressed him. But he did not dare complain to the management; after all he had the animals to thank for the numerous visitors who did pass his cage, among whom there always might be the one who was there just to see him, and lord knew where they might tuck him away if he called attention to his existence and thereby to the fact that, strictly speaking, he was no more than an obstacle in the path to the animals.

A slight obstacle to be sure, an obstacle growing slighter by the day. One has grown accustomed in this day and age to finding it strange to call attention to a hunger artist, and in accordance with this custom the verdict was carried against him. He might fast as well as only he could, and indeed he did, but nothing could save him, everyone passed him by. Just try to explain the art of fasting to someone! Without a feeling for it, one cannot be made to understand it. The colorful placards became dirty and illegible, they were torn down and no one thought to replace them; the little signboard tallying the number of days fasted, which was at first carefully altered each day, had long remained unchanged, for after the first few weeks the staff had already tired of even this small task, and so the hunger artist just fasted on as he had once dreamed of doing, and it was indeed no trouble for him, as he had always predicted, but no one counted the days, no one, not even the hunger artist himself, knew the extent of his achievement, and his spirits sank. And once in a while when a random passerby lingered, ridiculed the outdated number posted, and hinted at fraud, it was the stupidest lie in a sense, born of malice and brute indifference, for the hunger artist did not cheat; he worked with integrity, but the world cheated him of his reward.

However, many more days passed and that too came to an end. An overseer happened to notice the cage one day and asked the help why this perfectly useful cage with rotten straw in it was left unoccupied; no one knew the answer until someone, with the help of the signboard, recalled the hunger artist. They prodded the straw with sticks and found the hunger artist buried inside. "Are you still fasting?" asked the overseer. "When on earth do you plan on stopping?" "Forgive me, everyone," rasped the hunger artist; only the overseer with his ear pressed against the bars could understand him. "By all means," said the overseer, tapping his finger at the side of his forehead to indicate the hunger artist's condition to the others, "we forgive you." "I always wanted you to admire my fasting," said the hunger artist. "And so we do admire it," said the overseer accommodatingly. "But you shouldn't admire it," said the hunger artist. "So then we don't admire it," said the overseer, "but why should we not admire it?" "Because I must fast, I cannot do otherwise," answered the hunger artist. "What a character you are," said the overseer, "and why can't you do otherwise?" "Because," said the hunger artist, lifting his head a little and puckering his lips as if for a kiss, and he spoke directly into the overseer's ear so that nothing would be missed, "because I could never find food I liked. Had I found it, believe me, I would never have created such a ruckus and would have stuffed myself like you and everyone else." These were his last words, but in his glazing eyes there remained the firm if no longer proud conviction that he was still fasting.

"Now clear this out!" barked the overseer, and they buried the hunger artist together with his straw. Then they put a young panther into the cage. It was refreshing, even to the least sensitive, to see this wild creature leaping around the cage that had been dreary for so long. He wanted for nothing. The guards brought him the food he liked without hesitation; he did not appear to miss his freedom; his noble body, full to almost bursting with all he needed, also seemed to carry freedom with it; this freedom seemed to reside somewhere in his jaws, and the joy of life burned so fiercely in his throat that it was not easy for the onlookers to bear it. But they steeled themselves, surged around the cage, and wanted never to leave it.

Josephine the Singer, or The Mouse People*

*Originally published in 1924 under the German title "Josefine, die Sängerin oder Das Volk der Mäuse."

OUR SINGER'S NAME IS Josephine. Anyone who has not heard her does not know the power of song. There is not one among us who is not swept away by her singing, and this is indeed high praise—higher still as we are not generally a music-loving people. Peace and quiet is the music most dear to us; we have a hard life and even on the occasions when we have tried to shake free from the cares of our daily life we still cannot raise ourselves up to something so lofty and remote from our routine lives as music. But we don't much mourn this, we never even get that far; we consider a certain pragmatic cunning, of which we are sorely in need, to be our greatest asset, and with a smile born of this cunning we are wont to console ourselves for all our woes even if—but it never happens—we were once to yearn for the kind of happiness such as music might provide. Josephine is the sole exception, she loves music and also knows how to give voice to it; she is the only one, and with her demise music will disappear—for who knows how long—from our lives.

I have often wondered what this music of hers truly means— after all, we are entirely unmusical, so how is it that we understand Josephine's singing or, since Josephine denies that, at least believe we understand it? The simplest answer would be that the beauty of her song is so great that even the dullest ear cannot help being touched, but this is not a satisfying answer. If this were really so, her singing would necessarily give one the immediate and lasting impression of something extraordinary, the feeling that something is pouring forth from this throat that we had never heard before, something we did not even have the capacity to hear, something that this Josephine alone and no one else could enable us to hear. But this, in my opinion, is precisely what does not happen; I do not feel it, nor have I observed that others feel it. Among our circle we freely admit that Josephine's song, as song, is nothing out of the ordinary.

Is this in fact singing at all? Despite our lack of musicality, we do have a tradition of singing, for our people sang in ancient times; this is spoken of in legends, and some songs have survived, although it is also true that now no one can sing them. So we do have some ideas about what singing is, and Josephine's art does not correspond to these ideas. Then is it really singing? Isn't it perhaps merely piping?[16] Piping is something we all know about; it is the true artistic forte of our people or, rather than our forte, more a characteristic expression of life. We all pipe, but of course no one dreams of presenting this as an art form; we pay no attention to our piping or even notice it, and there are many among us who are quite unaware that piping is one of our characteristics. So if it were true that Josephine does not sing but only pipes and may not, as it seems to me at least, even rise above the level of our usual piping—and may not even have the stamina required for this usual piping, whereas a common fieldhand can effortlessly pipe all day long while hard at work—so if it were all true, Josephine's supposed artistry would certainly be refuted, but that would open up the larger riddle of the enormous influence she has.

However, it is not just piping that she produces. If you position yourself quite far away from her or, better yet, put yourself through the following test—say, Josephine were singing along with others and you tried to pick out just her voice—you will undoubtedly identify nothing more than rather ordinary piping, distinguishing itself, if at all, by its fragility or weakness. Yet if you are directly before her, it is no mere piping. For a full understanding of her art it is necessary to see her as well as hear her. Even if this were only our everyday piping, a certain peculiarity must be considered: Here is someone creating a solemn spectacle of the everyday. It is truly no feat to crack a nut, and therefore no one would think to gather an audience for the purpose of entertaining them with nutcracking. But if he should do so, and if he should succeed in his aim, then it cannot be a matter of mere nutcracking. Or alternatively, it is a matter of nutcracking, but as it turns out we have overlooked the art of nutcracking because we were so proficient at it that it is this new nutcracker who is the first to demonstrate what it actually entails, whereby it could be even more effective if he were less expert in nutcracking than the majority of us.

Perhaps it is much the same with Josephine's singing: We admire in her what in ourselves we do not admire in the least. In this last respect, I must say, she agrees with us wholeheartedly. I was once present when someone, as often happens of course, called attention to the ubiquitous folk piping; it was the most passing reference, but it was more than enough for Josephine. I have never seen a smile so sarcastic and so arrogant as the one she then displayed; she, who is the very embodiment of delicacy—uncommonly so among a people rich in such feminine ideals—seemed positively vulgar at that moment; she must have realized this at once, owing to her great sensitivity, and controlled herself. In any event, she denies any connection between her own art and piping. For anyone of the opposite opinion, she has only contempt and, most likely, unacknowledged hatred. Nor is this simple vanity; for the opposition, to which I myself partly subscribe, certainly admires her no less than the rest of the crowd, but Josephine does not desire mere admiration, she wants to be admired in precisely the manner she dictates; mere admiration is of no merit to her. And seated before her, one understands her: Opposition is only possible from a distance; seated before her one knows: This piping of hers is not piping.

Since piping is one of our unconscious habits, one might suppose that there would be some piping from Josephine's audience as well. We are made happy by her art, and when we are happy we pipe. But her audience does not pipe, we are as quiet as mice, as if we were partaking of the peace we long for, and this somewhat restrains us from our own piping, we keep silent. Is it her singing that enchants us, or isn't it rather the solemn stillness that envelops that tiny frail voice? Once while Josephine was singing, some foolish young thing also began, in all innocence, to pipe. Now it was just the same as what we were hearing from Josephine; out in front of us was this piping that was still tremulous despite all the practice, and here in the audience was this unselfconscious infantile piping. It would have been impossible to define the difference, but we at once hissed and whistled to quiet the troublemaker, although this wasn't really necessary for she would surely have crept away in fear and shame; meanwhile Josephine, quite beside herself, sounded her most triumphal piping with her arms outflung and her neck thrown back as far as she could.

But she is always like that; every little thing, every chance incident, every nuisance—a floorboard creaking, teeth grinding, or a lamp flickering—she considers cause to heighten the effect of her song. In her opinion her singing falls on deaf ears anyway; there is no lack of enthusiasm and applause, but she has long since given up hope of genuine understanding as she conceives it. In this way every disturbance is more than welcome to her; any external influence conflicting with the purity of her song that can be defeated easily, or defeated without struggle but by confrontation alone, can help to raise the awareness of the crowd and teach it, if not understanding, at least awed respect.

And if small events serve her so well, great ones serve her even better. We lead very uneasy lives; each day brings its surprises, anxieties, hopes, and fears; it would be impossible for any individual to bear it all without the constant support of his comrades. But it often becomes difficult anyway; sometimes a thousand shoulders quake under a burden meant just for one. It is then that Josephine believes her moment has come. There she stands, the delicate creature, racked with frightful trembling especially beneath the breast; it is as though she has focused all her strength in her singing; as though everything in her that does not directly serve her song, every power, nearly every means of sustenance, has been stripped away; as though she were laid bare, abandoned, entrusted to the care of kind spirits; as though, while she is so absorbed and entirely given over to her song, a single cold breath passing over her might kill her. But it is precisely when she makes just such an appearance that we, her alleged detractors, tend to remark: "She can't even pipe. See how she strains herself horribly to force out, not song—let's not even speak about song—but a mere approximation of our customary piping." So it seems to us; however, as I already mentioned, this impression is an inevitable yet fleeting one that quickly fades. Soon we too are submerged in the feeling of the audience, which listens, body pressed warmly to body, with reverently held breath.

And in order to gather a crowd of our people around her—a people almost constantly on the move, scurrying here and there for reasons that are frequently unclear—Josephine mostly needs to do no more than adopt her stance: head thrown back, mouth partially opened, and eyes turned heavenward, to indicate that she intends to sing. She can do this where she pleases; it need not be a place visible from very far away—any secluded corner chosen on the spur of the moment will serve just as well. The news that she is going to sing spreads immediately, and whole processions are soon on their way. Now sometimes obstacles do intervene. Josephine prefers to sing in turbulent times, and then a slew of anxieties and dangers force us to travel by devious routes, and even with the best intentions in the world we cannot assemble as quickly as Josephine would like; she occasionally stands there, striking her imperious pose, for quite some time without a sufficient audience—then she flies into a rage, stamps her feet, and swears in a most unmaidenly fashion; she actually even bites. But even this type of behavior cannot damage her reputation. Instead of trying to moderate her excessive demands, people go out of their way to meet them: Messengers are dispatched to gather new listeners but she is kept ignorant of this practice; along all the routes, sentries can be seen waving on the newcomers and urging them to hurry. This continues until enough of an audience is gathered.

What drives the people to exert themselves to such an extent on Josephine's behalf? This question is no easier to answer than the one about her singing, with which it is closely connected. If it were possible to assert that the people are unconditionally devoted to Josephine on account of her singing, then one could cancel out the first question and combine it with the second. This, however, is emphatically not the case; unconditional devotion is rarely found among us; our people—who above all else love cunning, of a harmless nature of course, and who childishly whisper and idly chatter over innocent gossip—are a people who cannot buy into unconditional devotion. Josephine feels this as well, and it is against this that she fights with all the force in her feeble throat.

It would certainly be a mistake to take these broad generalizations too far, however; our people are indeed devoted to Josephine, just not unconditionally. We would never be capable, for example, of laughing at Josephine. It can be said that there are many things about Josephine that invite laughter, and we are always close to laughing for laughing's sake. Despite the misery of our lives, a quiet laugh is always close at hand, as it were, but we do not laugh at Josephine. I am sometimes under the impression that our people see their relationship with Josephine this way: that this fragile creature in need of protection and somehow worthy of distinction (in her own opinion worthy of distinction because of her song) is entrusted to their care and must be looked after. The reason for this is not clear to anyone; it seems only to be an established fact. But one does not laugh at what is entrusted to one's care; to laugh would be a breach of duty. The utmost spite that the most malicious of us is capable of directing at Josephine is to occasionally say: "We stop laughing when we see Josephine."

So the people look after Josephine in the same way that a father assumes the care of a child whose hand—whether in appeal or command one cannot tell—is stretched out to him. One might not think that our people are equipped to fulfill these paternal duties, but in reality we do perform them, at least in this case, in an exemplary manner; no one individual could do what in this respect the people as a whole are able to do. To be sure, the disparity in strength between the people and any individual is so great that the charge need only be drawn into the warmth of their presence and he will be protected enough. Certainly no one dares to mention such things to Josephine. "I pipe at your protection," she says then. "Yes, you pipe, don't you," we think. Besides, she is not seriously refuting us when she rebels like this—rather it is childish behavior and childish gratitude—and it is a father's place to pay no attention.

And yet something more is going on here that is less easily explained by the relationship between the people and Josephine; namely, Josephine is of a different opinion: It is her belief that it is she who protects the people. When we are facing trouble, be it political or economic, it is her song that supposedly saves us, nothing short of that; and if it does not drive out the misfortune, it at least gives us the strength to bear it. She does not express it in these words or in any other words; as a matter of fact she never says much at all, she is silent amid the chatterboxes, but it flashes from her eyes, and from her clamped mouth (there are not many among us who can keep their mouths closed—she can) it is clearly decipherable. Whenever we get bad news—and many days we get hit with it thick and fast, lies and half-truths included—she rises at once, whereas usually she's sunk wearily on the floor, she rises and cranes her neck to look out over her flock like a shepherd before a storm. Of course children do make similar claims in their wild, impulsive fashion, but Josephine's claim is not quite so groundless as theirs. She certainly does not save us, nor does she give us strength; it is easy to pose as the savior of a people who are inured to suffering, unsparing of themselves, swift in decisions, well acquainted with death, timid in appearance only as they must dwell in an atmosphere of constant and reckless danger, and who in any case are as prolific as they are brave; it is easy, as I say, to hold oneself up as the savior of this people who have somehow always saved themselves at the cost, however, of many sacrifices the likes of which strike historians—generally we ignore historical research completely—cold with horror. And yet it is true that during times of emergency we cling closer to Josephine's voice than at any other time. The threats hanging over us make us quieter, more humble, more compliant to Josephine's commands; we are happy to gather together, happy to huddle close to one another, especially because it is an occasion so far removed from the preoccupying torment; it is as if in all haste—yes, haste is necessary, as Josephine is all too likely to forget—we were drinking a communal cup of peace before battle. It is not so much a song recital as a public gathering, and moreover a gathering that is completely silent except for the faint piping up front; the hour is too serious for us to spend it chatting.

Josephine, of course, could never be content with a relationship of this kind. Despite all the nervous tension that overtakes her because her position has never been clearly defined, there is much that she does not see, blinded as she is by self-conceit, and she can be made to overlook a great deal more without much effort; a swarm of flatterers is always hovering about her working toward this end, in effect performing a public service—however, to be an incidental and unnoticed singer in the corner of a public gathering (although it would be no small thing in and of itself), for that she certainly would not sacrifice her song.

Nor is she obliged to do this, for her art does not go unnoticed. Even though we basically concern ourselves with quite other matters, and the silence that prevails is not due to her singing alone (some listeners do not look up at all but bury their faces in their neighbors' fur, so Josephine seems to be exerting herself in vain out there in front), something from her piping—this cannot be denied—inevitably does come through to us. This piping, which rises up when silence is imposed on all others, emerges almost like a message from the people to each individual; Josephine's thin piping amid grave decisions is almost like our meager existence amid the tumult of a hostile world. Josephine asserts herself; this mere nothing of a voice, this mere nothing of a performance, asserts itself and makes its way through to us; it does us good to think of that. At such moments we could never endure a true singer, should one ever be found among us, and we would unanimously reject any such performance as absurd. May Josephine be spared from perceiving that the very fact we listen to her is proof that she is no singer. She must have some suspicion of this—why else would she so passionately deny that we do listen to her—but she keeps singing and piping away her suspicion.

But she could draw comfort from other things: We really do listen to her to some extent, probably in much the same way one listens to a true singer; she manages to affect us in ways that a true singer would strive in vain to bring about, ways that produce their effect in us precisely because her means are so inadequate. The manner in which we lead our lives is no doubt responsible for this.

Youth does not exist among our people, and childhood only lasts a moment. Demands are regularly made to guarantee the children special freedom and protection, to grant them their right to be a little carefree, to engage in a little lighthearted foolishness, a little play, and to ensure that these rights be acknowledged and steps taken to secure them. Such demands are made and nearly everyone approves them; there is nothing one could approve of more, but there is also nothing less likely to be conceded given the reality of our daily lives; one approves of these demands and one attempts to implement them; but we soon lapse back into the old ways. To be frank, our life is such that as soon as a child can run around a bit and distinguish his surroundings a little, he must likewise look after himself like an adult. The regions over which we are dispersed and in which we are forced to live, for economic reasons, are too vast, our enemies too numerous, the dangers facing us everywhere too incalculable—we cannot shield the children from the struggle for existence; if we did, it would mean a premature end for them. These depressing facts are further reinforced by another more uplifting one: the fertility of our race. One generation—and each is numerous—comes on the heels of the preceding one; the children don't have time to be children. Other peoples may raise their children with great care; they may erect schools for their little ones and from these schools the children, the future of the race, may come streaming out every day; but among those peoples, it is the same children who come pouring out like that day after day, over a long period of time. We have no schools, but bounding forth from our people are the continuous swarms of our children arriving at the briefest intervals, cheerfully peeping or chirping for as long as they can't yet pipe, rolling along or forced forward in the tumult for as long as they can't yet run, clumsily sweeping everything before them by their sheer mass for as long as they can't yet see—our children! And not the same children as in those schools—no, always new ones, again and again, without end, without pause. Hardly does a child appear than it is no longer a child; new childish faces are already pressing through, so many and so fast that they are indistinguishable, all rosy with happiness. Truthfully, however delightful this may be and however much others may envy us for it, and rightly so, we simply cannot give our children a proper childhood. And that has its consequences. A certain deeply rooted and indelible childishness pervades our people; we sometimes behave with the utmost foolishness in direct opposition to our best quality, our infallible common sense; this brand of foolishness is the same as that of children—a senseless, extravagant, grandiose, frivolous foolishness, and often all for the sake of a little fun. And although our pleasure naturally cannot be the wholehearted pleasure of a child, without a doubt there is still something of this in it. Josephine has also profited from our people's childishness since the beginning.

But our people are not only childish, we are also in a sense prematurely old; childhood and age come to us differently than to others. We have no youth, we are grown up all at once and then stay grown up for too long; a certain weariness and hopelessness marks the nature of our people, though we are fundamentally tough and confident. Our lack of musicality is probably connected to this—we're too old for music; exultation does not suit our gravity, we wave it away wearily; we content ourselves with piping, a little piping here and there, that suits us fine. Who knows, there may be some musical talent among us; however, if there were, the character of our people would suppress it before it could develop. Josephine, on the other hand, can pipe to her heart's delight or sing or whatever she wants to call it; that doesn't bother us, that's fine by us, that we can put up with; if there is anything musical contained within, it is so reduced as to be barely traceable; a certain musical tradition is preserved but without having to be the least burden to us.

But our people, given what they are, still get something more from Josephine. At her concerts, especially in troubled times, only the very young are interested in the singer as such, only they gaze in astonishment as she purses her lips, expels the air between her dainty front teeth, swoons in admiration and wonder for the sounds she herself is producing, and uses this lowered position to propel herself to fresh peaks of achievement that are continually incredible to her. Meanwhile, the majority of the audience—this is plain to see—has retreated into itself. Here in these brief gaps between their troubles our people dream; it is as if the limbs of each were loosened, as if every last uneasy individual were for once allowed to stretch out and relax freely in the great warm bed of the people. And into these dreams drops Josephine's piping, bit by bit; she calls it purled,* we call it forced; but at any rate here it is in its rightful place, as nowhere else, finding just the moment that awaited it, as music hardly ever does otherwise. Something of our meager and foreshortened childhood is in it, something of a lost and irretrievable happiness, but also something of our active everyday life, these incomprehensible but actual moments of gaiety that cannot be suppressed. This is all expressed not in large and imposing tones, but softly, breathlessly, confidentially, and sometimes a little hoarsely. Of course it is piping. How could it not be? Piping is the vernacular of our people; only many pipe their whole lives long without knowing it, while here piping is free from the fetters of everyday life, and so it also sets us free for a short time. We would certainly not want to relinquish these performances.

But it is a very long way from there to Josephine's assertion that she renews our strength during such times and so on and so forth; at least it is for ordinary people, even if it is not for Jose-

---

*To purl is to flow with a murmuring sound.

phine's flatterers. "What other explanation could there be," they
say with rather shameless audacity. "How else could you explain
the huge crowds, especially when there is imminent danger and
when these crowds have sometimes even hindered our taking
proper precautions to avert the danger in time." Now this last
point is unfortunately true but can hardly be counted among
Josephine's claims to fame, particularly if one adds that when
such gatherings have been unexpectedly ambushed by the enemy
and many of our people have lain dead as a result, Josephine,
who is entirely to blame and most likely attracted the enemy by
her piping, invariably occupies the safest position and is the first
to be whisked quickly and quietly away under cover of her escort.
Everyone is well aware of this, yet they come running to whatever
spot Josephine arbitrarily decides upon to strike up her singing
and whenever she so pleases. From this one might conclude that
Josephine almost stands beyond the law, that she may do whatever she likes even if it endangers the community, and that she
will be forgiven everything. If this were so, then even Josephine's
claims would be comprehensible; yes, in the freedom allowed to
her, a privilege granted by the people to no one else and in actual
contravention of our laws, one might detect an admission of the
fact that our people—just as she alleges—do not understand Josephine, that they gape helplessly at her art, feel unworthy of it,
and try to assuage the pain they must cause her by making a
desperate sacrifice: to place her person and her wishes as far
outside their jurisdiction as her art is beyond their comprehension. Well, this is just categorically untrue; perhaps the people
individually capitulate to Josephine too readily, but collectively
they capitulate unconditionally to no one, and so not to her either.

For a long time now, perhaps since the very start of her artistic
career, Josephine has been fighting to be excused from all work
on account of her singing; she should be relieved from the burden of earning her daily bread and anything else involved in the
struggle for existence, and the slack should, presumably, be taken
up by the people as a whole. A hasty enthusiast—and there have
been some—might conclude that this demand is inherently justified, owing to its strangeness and the mental state needed to
conceive it. But our people draw other conclusions and quietly
refuse her. Nor do they bother much to refute the arguments on

which it is based. Josephine argues, for example, that the strain of work is bad for her voice, that the strain of work cannot, needless to say, remotely compare to the strain of singing, but it does render it impossible to rest sufficiently after singing and recuperate for further singing, so she must exhaust herself entirely and within these confines never perform at her peak. The people listen to her arguments and pay no attention. This people, so easily moved, will sometimes not be moved at all. Their refusal is sometimes so severe that Josephine is taken aback; she appears to comply, does her proper share of work, and sings as well as she can, but this only lasts awhile. Then with renewed strength— her strength for this purpose seems inexhaustible—she takes up the fight again.

Now it is clear that what Josephine is really aiming for is not literally what she demands. She is reasonable, she does not shy from work—shirking is quite unknown among us anyway—and even if her petition were granted, her life would go on as before; her work would not impede her singing, nor would her singing improve; what she is aiming for is an unambiguous public recognition of her art that would last forever and far surpass any known precedent. But while everything else seems to be within her grasp, this persistently eludes her. Perhaps she should have taken a different tack from the beginning, perhaps she understands her mistake by now, but she cannot back down; any retreat would be tantamount to self-betrayal; now she must stand or fall by her demand.

If, as she contends, she truly had enemies, they could be greatly amused, without having to lift a finger, by the spectacle of this battle. But she has no enemies, and even if she does meet with criticism here and there, no one is amused by this battle of hers for the mere fact that in this circumstance the people exhibit a cold, judicial manner that is rarely seen otherwise. And even if one approves of it in this case, the mere thought that such an attitude might be adopted toward oneself dispels any pleasure. What is important here is not the people's refusal of Josephine's demand or the demand itself but the fact that the people are capable of presenting such a stony, impenetrable front to one of their own, and it is all the more impenetrable because this particular citizen is in every other sense treated with fatherly—actually more than fatherly—with deferential concern.

Imagine that instead of an entire people there were one individual: One might suppose that this man had been giving in to
Josephine but at the same time desperately wishing to put an end
to all this indulgence; that he had been superhuman in the con-
cessions he granted, firm in the belief that there would be a
natural limit to them; yes, that he had conceded more than was
necessary for the sole purpose of hastening the process, to spoil
Josephine and push her to ask for more and more until she did
reach this ultimate demand, at which point he could, being prepared well in advance, reply with a final, curt refusal. Now this
is absolutely not how things stand, the people have no need of
such guile; besides, their admiration of Josephine is sincere and
deeply rooted, and Josephine's demand is so outrageous that any
simple child could have told her the foreseeable outcome. However, it may be that considerations such as these do enter into
Josephine's thinking on the matter and so add a further sting of
bitterness to the pain of refusal.

But even if she does entertain these ideas, she does not allow
them to deter her from her campaign. Recently the campaign
has even been intensified; where she once fought with words
alone, she is resorting to other methods that she thinks will prove
more effective but in our opinion will be more dangerous for her.

Some feel that Josephine is becoming so desperate because
she feels she is growing old and her voice is weakening, and so
it seems high time to wage the final battle for recognition. I don't
believe it. If it were true, Josephine would not be Josephine. For
her, there is no getting old, no weakness in her voice. If she
demands something, it is not due to outward forces but to an
inner logic. She reaches for the highest laurels, not because they
are hanging slightly lower for a moment but because they are the
highest; if it were in her power she would hang them higher still.

This disregard of external difficulties certainly does not prevent her from employing the most unworthy methods. She feels
her rights are beyond question, so that how she secures them
does not matter, especially in this world where, as she sees it, it
is the worthy methods that fail. Perhaps this is why she has trans-
ferred the fight for her rights from the arena of song to another
that she cares very little about. Supporters have passed around
statements of hers to the effect that she feels thoroughly capable
of singing at such a level that every strata of the people, even

the furthest reaches of the opposition, would find true pleasure in it—a true pleasure not by popular standards, for the people maintain they have always found pleasure in her singing, but a true pleasure by Josephine's standards. But, she adds, since she can neither falsify higher standards nor pander to lower ones, her singing must stay as it is. Yet when it comes to the fight to be freed from work, that is another matter; it is also, of course, on behalf of her singing; however, in this case she is not using the precious weapon of song directly, therefore any means she employs is good enough.

So, for example, a rumor spread that if her petition were not granted, Josephine intended to shorten her trill notes. I know nothing of trill notes and have never noticed any sign of them in her singing, but Josephine is going to shorten her trill notes; for the time being she is not going to eliminate them, just shorten them. She has purportedly carried out her threat, although I, for one, have perceived no difference in her performance. The people as a whole listened as always without commenting on the trill notes and did not budge an inch in response to her demand. Incidentally, it is undeniable that Josephine's thoughts can sometimes be as pleasing as her figure; for instance, after that performance, as if her decision with regard to the trill notes had been too harsh and too sudden a blow to the people, she announced that the next time she would again sing the trill notes in their complete form. But after the next concert she changed her tune once more: there was definitely to be an end to the elongated trills and they would not recur until a favorable decision on her petition was reached. Well, the people let all these announcements, decisions, and counterdecisions go in one ear and out the other, much like a preoccupied adult with the chattering of a child: well disposed at heart but unmoved.

But Josephine does not give up. She recently claimed, for example, that she injured her foot while working, so that it was difficult to stand and sing, and since she can only sing while standing, her songs would now have to be cut short. Although she limps and leans on her group of supporters, no one believes she is really injured. Even allowing for her exceptionally sensitive constitution, we are a working people and Josephine is one of us; if we were to start limping at every little scratch, the entire population would never stop limping. But although she may permit herself to be led around like a cripple, although she may display herself in this pathetic condition more often than usual, the people still listen gratefully and appreciatively to her singing just as before and don't bother much about the abridgment of the songs.

Since she cannot continue limping forever, she invents something else: She pleads exhaustion, disaffection, faintness. And so now we get a theatrical performance as well as a concert. Behind Josephine we see her supporters entreating and imploring her to sing. She would be happy to oblige, but she cannot. They comfort her and caress her with flattery, they practically carry her to a previously chosen spot where she is supposed to sing. Finally, bursting inexplicably into tears, she relents, but when she prepares to sing, clearly at the end of her tether, drooping, her arms not outspread as usual but hanging limply at her sides, giving the impression that they are perhaps somewhat too short—as she prepares to strike a note, no, it's no use after all; a reluctant shake of the head tells us as much and she swoons before our eyes. Then she does indeed rally again and sings, much the same as ever in my opinion; perhaps a more discerning ear might detect a slight increase in feeling that does, however, heighten the effect. And in the end she is actually less tired than before and departs with a firm tread, if such a term can be used to describe her rapid, mincing steps, refusing all assistance from her supporters, her cold eyes measuring the crowd, who respectfully make way for her.

That was just a few days ago. But the latest news is that she has disappeared, just at a time when she was expected to sing. It is not only her supporters who are looking for her, many others have devoted themselves to the search, but all in vain; Josephine has vanished, she does not wish to sing, she does not wish to be invited to sing; she has deserted us for good this time.

It is curious how seriously she miscalculates, the clever creature, so seriously that one must believe that she did not calculate at all but is only being driven onward by her fate, which can only be a sad one in our world. She abandons her singing of her own accord and of her own accord destroys the power she has gained over our hearts. How could she ever have acquired that power when she knows so little of our hearts? She hides herself away and does not sing. In the meantime our people—calmly, without visible disappointment, a proud, self-sufficient people, who in all truth and despite appearances can only bestow gifts, never receive them, even from Josephine—our people continue on their way.

But Josephine's path can go nowhere except down. Soon the time will come when her last note sounds and fades into silence. She is a small episode in the eternal history of our people, and the people will overcome their loss. This will not be easy for us though; how can we gather together in utter silence? And yet, weren't we silent even when Josephine was present? Was her actual piping significantly louder and more lively than the memory of it will be? Was it ever more than simply a memory, even during her lifetime? Had not the people rather, in their wisdom, so dearly cherished Josephine's song precisely so that in this way it would not be lost?

So perhaps we shall not miss very much after all. While Josephine, delivered from earthly torment—in her opinion the privilege of chosen spirits—will happily lose herself in the countless number of our people's heroes, and soon, since we are not students of history, will be even further delivered by being forgotten like all her brothers.

Before the Law *

*Originally published in 1919 under the German title "Vor dem Gesetz"; the parable is part of Kafka's novel *The Trial*.

BEFORE THE LAW STANDS a doorkeeper. A man from the country comes to this doorkeeper and asks to be admitted to the Law. But the doorkeeper informs him that he cannot grant him admittance at this time. The man ponders this and then asks whether he will be admitted at some point in the future. "It is possible," says the doorkeeper, "but not at present." Because the gate stands open—as always—and the doorkeeper steps aside, the man stoops down to look through the gateway to the interior. On seeing this, the doorkeeper laughs and remarks: "If it's so enticing, then just try going in despite my interdiction. But take note: I am powerful. And I am only the lowliest doorkeeper. In hall after hall stand other doorkeepers, each more powerful than the last. The mere sight of the third doorkeeper is more than even I can endure." The man from the country never anticipated such difficulties. The Law, he thinks, should be accessible at all times and to everyone, but when he now takes a closer look at the doorkeeper in his fur coat, with his large, pointed nose and his long, skinny, black Tartar beard, he decides that he had better wait for permission to enter after all. The doorkeeper gives him a stool and allows him to set it to one side of the door. There he sits for days and years. He makes many attempts to be admitted and exhausts the doorkeeper with his pleas. The doorkeeper often conducts little interviews with him, asking him about his home and many other things, but the questions are put indifferently, much as highranking officials would put them, and he always concludes by repeating that he cannot yet admit him. The man, who came well equipped for his journey, uses everything he has, however valuable, for the purpose of bribing the doorkeeper. The doorkeeper accepts everything but says as he does so: "I'm only accepting this so you won't think there's something you haven't tried." Throughout the many years he observes the doorkeeper fixedly with almost no interruption. He forgets the other doorkeepers and this first one seems to him the sole obstacle between himself and the Law. He curses his miserable fate, loudly and recklessly in the early years, but later, as he grows old, he just grumbles to himself. He becomes childish, and since he has come to know even the fleas in the doorkeeper's fur collar during the long years of studying him, he begs the fleas to help him and to help win the doorkeeper over to his side. Eventually his eyesight begins to fail, and he does not know whether his eyes deceive him or whether it is really growing darker around him. But through the gloom he can now definitely make out a radiance that pours unendingly from the doorway of the Law. Now he no longer has much time to live. Before his death, all the experiences of these long years come together in his head to form one question that he has not yet put to the doorkeeper. He beckons to him because he can no longer raise his cramped and stiffening body. The doorkeeper has to bend down to him, since the difference in their heights has changed drastically, much to the man's disadvantage. "So, what is it that you still want to know?" asks the doorkeeper. "You are insatiable." "Surely everyone strives to reach the Law," says the man, "so how is it that no one but me has ever begged for admittance?" The doorkeeper recognizes that the man is near the end and, in order to penetrate his failing senses, shouts: "No one else could ever be granted admission here, as this gate was just for you. Now I am going to close it."

Translator's Afterword

IT WOULD BE IDEAL if each of us could read all the world's literature in the language in which it was originally written. Since that is not a realistic possibility, every reader, sooner or later, comes to rely on the interpretive skills of a translator.

Being an act of interpretation, a translation is also an act of criticism. At any given point several options are available and critical choices must be made. These choices will obviously reflect the translator's understanding not only of the text but of the author's intentions. What the translator sees or reads into the text—bringing to bear all of his or her knowledge and experience—invariably influences these decisions to some degree. But one hopes that the portion of this understanding that might be called "biases" can be kept to a minimum.

By nature, a translator must be flexible and approach each work as a separate challenge, although there are larger principles that guide translation in general. The foremost of these is to stay true to the text. This entails adhering to the author's intentions, insofar as the translator can discern them, and being able to view the text as a distinct entity while not losing sight of the context in which it was written. The translator must decide how best to serve the not always compatible demands of the author, the reader, and the text. He or she must choose what to stress and what to sacrifice; some authors are noted for their particular use of language—Henry James and Ernest Hemingway come to mind; some are known more for the content of their work, the historical moment that they chronicle—Aleksandr Solzhenitsyn and Harriet Beecher Stowe might be examples; and some, like Jorge Luis Borges and Franz Kafka, for creating a new kind of story altogether—familiar yet strange, rich in its specifics yet timeless in its reach.

There is always compromise in translation because every language affords different possibilities and imposes unique limita-

171

tions. Still other problems arise when dealing with texts that were written long ago or in circumstances alien or unfamiliar to the contemporary reader or translator. If one completely modernizes a text, one risks losing the delicious essentials of time and place; if one adheres strictly to the language and knowledge of an earlier time, one may obscure the reader's access to the timeless appeal of the original work. Although great literature often outlives its author, it is written at a specific time and in a specific place, and this must be taken into consideration when translating.

The stories of Franz Kafka largely address the human condition and are therefore timeless, but Kafka was also a German-speaking Jew in early twentieth-century Prague. One way that I have attempted, in this translation, to make his work accessible to the modern reader is to update his language, particularly in the dialogue, where modern idiom and phrasing have been employed with some regularity. On the other hand I've also maintained some of the vocabulary of the time in which Kafka lived. For example, the furniture, money, and clothing of his time and place are very different from those of ours, as are the words used to signify them. Using the English equivalents for the original European terms for these things, rather than convert them into their modern, American incarnations, helps to establish the actual historical time and setting in which the events take place and thus allows the reader to savor the ambience of the original instead of merely surveying its outlines. In this case it seems to me that this is an aspect of these texts that the reader need not and ought not be excluded from.

This translation attempts to present the stories of Franz Kafka in as readable a version as possible and in much the same way as they would be read and understood by the German reader. The singular situations Kafka's characters find themselves in, the turns these situations take—at times uncanny, at times all too frighteningly routine—the sensation of being pressed to the existential brink without knowing how one got there (or whether one will be permitted to return) all have far more immediate impact than his diction. His language is, in fact, quite simple and straightforward; it is his verbal structure that is often complex. This is due, in part, to the structure of the German language, which builds sentences—often of astounding length—in modular units. Kafka did make diligent and sometimes amusing—and subversive—use of this aspect of his native tongue. But some of the older English translations have become mired in those structural complexities. As a result, the stories have been made less available to the reader than they might otherwise have been.

In an effort to cope with such difficulties, a proclivity has developed in contemporary American translation for rendering the original text as it might have been constructed if written by a contemporary American. Toward that end, modern idioms and rhythms are introduced. Sentence lengths and even paragraphs are restructured to embrace the American ear. Translators who employ this style feel this is the best way to bring the original across and keep it fresh.

For the most part—except where it would interfere with the reader's full understanding of the text—I have maintained Kafka's sentence length and paragraph structure in this translation, as I feel that both are strategic elements of his writing style. At the same time I have tried to alleviate those difficulties within his sentence structure that arise merely because normal German and English word order are substantially different. I didn't find it necessary to sacrifice the rhythm and length of Kafka's sentences for the sake of clarity.

Once the structural dilemmas have been resolved in English, the stories speak for themselves, but when Kafka does use a particular storytelling device I have tried to incorporate it into the English translation. In "The Metamorphosis," for example, Kafka first—and almost continually thereafter—refers to Gregor's parents and sister as "the mother," "the father," and "the sister." Other translators have employed personal pronouns here (i.e., "his mother," etc.), probably because it seemed less formal and awkward in English. But it is awkward in the German text, and meant to be. It is an intentional device, serving to make immediately apparent Gregor's alienation from his family. And it soon comes to seem—under Kafka's skillful guidance—appropriate. At one point later in the story, however, it is "his father" who kicks Gregor into the room; this usage is also intentional and is introduced because Gregor had previously seen his father as pathetic—it was due to his father's business failure that Gregor had to work as a traveling salesman—and his own father is now the very personal cause of his being banished from the family instead of their helping him, something he could not feel impersonal about.

Similarly, it is the abrupt switch to the present tense that catapults the story "A Country Doctor" forward. From the moment when the groom attacks the maid, the doctor is uncontrollably propelled through the story in the present tense, until he attempts to take matters into his own hands and leaves the patient's house, at which point the tense reverts to the past. While my first priority in this translation has been to maintain clarity for the English reader, I felt it was imperative not to lose sight—as many other translators of this story have—of an author's device that is there for the purpose of enhancing the narrative.

There are also moments when Kafka seems so caught up in the narrative drive of a story that some of its continuity gets lost. In "The Stoker," the maid that Karl impregnates is later referred to as the cook. This may have been an oversight that Kafka would have corrected in future revisions (he planned to include "The Stoker" as the first chapter in a novel he did not complete, posthumously published under the title *Amerika*), but this translation remains faithful to the text. I have not corrected these lapses or reconciled such minor inconsistencies, as they may be of interest to the reader. They are, however, footnoted in the text itself.

Despite the common conception of Kafka as a spurt writer periodically driven by the white heat of inspiration—perhaps the result of the well-known anecdote of Kafka's writing his breakthrough story "The Judgment" in one all-night session in 1912—it would seem that he worked and reworked his stories and, in some cases, held a clear picture of what he planned to write well in advance of the first draft. In 1906 he wrote a story about a man who splits into an insect and a man, the insect self going off to work and the man staying home in bed.* This precursor to "The Metamorphosis" was never published. He also wrote in a letter to his friend and publisher Kurt Wolff that he wished to include "The Judgment," "The Stoker," and "The Metamorphosis" in one volume under the title *The Sons*. This letter is dated April 4,

---

*Donna Freed here refers to Kafka's story "Wedding Preparations in the Country," originally published in 1915 under the German title "Hochzeitsvorbereitungen auf dem Lande."

1913—well before he had written either "The Stoker" or "The Metamorphosis." For whatever reasons, the stories were never published together under that title while Kafka was alive. Kafka's wish that these three stories be published together has in part formed the basis of this collection. All of the stories included, of course, have become classics, but it has been a special pleasure for me that by including "Josephine the Singer" along with "The Judgment," this collection contains both the last and the first stories that Kafka saw published in his lifetime.

—DONNA FREED
1996

ENDNOTES

1. (p. 7) *transformed in his bed into a monstrous vermin*: Translator Donna Freed here follows Stanley Corngold's lead in translating *ungeheures Ungeziefer* as "monstrous vermin" (*The Metamorphosis*, Bantam edition, 1972; see "For Further Reading"). Elsewhere, Corngold also identifies *Ungeziefer* as deriving from a Middle High English word meaning "unclean animal not suited for sacrifice." Willa and Edwin Muir originally had Gregor changing into a "gigantic insect" (see *The Complete Stories*).

2. (p. 7) *held out to the viewer*: Mark Anderson points out the similarity between Kafka's description of this picture, Gregor's one treasured object, and the figure of Venus in Leopold von Sacher-Masoch's 1870 novel *Venus in Furs* (Bloom, *Franz Kafka's "The Metamorphosis"*). In that story, Venus' slave Severin is made to change his name to Gregor, which in Austria was a common name for a manservant. Kafka's Gregor comes into a more sexualized contact with his picture later in the story (p. 33).

3. (p. 15) *visited by great misfortune*: In some Jewish and European cultures, doors and windows are opened after a family member dies so that the spirit of the deceased may leave the house peacefully. Note, however, that through the rest of the story, an effort is made to keep doors and windows shut, perhaps connoting a death that cannot escape.

4. (p. 16) *repelled by an invisible and relentless force*: The head clerk, who has come to intimidate Gregor, is instead threatened by him, and thus his authorial position to Gregor is turned on its head. Though now gifted with power, Gregor fails to recognize his aggressive abilities.

5. (p. 20) *hissing like a savage*: Note that the father behaves more like an animal than Gregor, who at least strives to be articulate.

6. (p. 35) *stood still and gathered everyone around him:* This idea of vigor and vitality being obfuscated by affected frailty stems from Kafka's observation of his own father. In "Letter to His Father" (see *Dearest Father*) Kafka addresses Hermann Kafka: "Your nervous condition . . . is a means by which you exert your domination more strongly, since the thought of it necessarily chokes off the least opposition from others." The same type of attempt at intimidation occurs in "The Judgment" (p. 62).

177

7. (p. 35) *It was an apple*: Walter Sokel argues that "The Metamorphosis" takes on a mythic dimension with the introduction of the apple, which can be seen as symbolizing the guilt of the original parents Adam and Eve, not to mention Gregor's own (Bloom, *Franz Kafka's "The Metamorphosis"*). Thus the lobbed apples can represent death in both the original and the causal senses; in this light, it is possible to see Gregor as a Christlike figure.

8. (p. 41) *"Come on over, you old dung beetle!"*: This is the only time Gregor is referred to as a particular species (*Mistkäfer*), albeit by a fairly unreliable source, the garrulous charwoman. Despite the efforts of scholars like Nabokov, though an able lepidopterist, to pin Gregor to a rigid realism, Kafka remains intentionally vague about Gregor's physical form. When "The Metamorphosis" was going to press, Kafka contacted his publisher in Leipzig. Fearing that Ottomar Starke, the illustrator for the first edition, would be tempted to render a metamorphosed Gregor on the title page, Kafka wrote, "The insect itself cannot be depicted. It cannot even be shown from a distance."

9. (p. 41) *three gentlemen boarders*: Notice how all three boarders possess the same characteristics and dispositions, how, in fact, they all lodge in one room. Kafka employs this technique of fusing multiple characters into one to create an amorphous and unknowable figure—think of the doorkeepers in "Before the Law" and the mouse people in "Josephine the Singer."

10. (p. 48) *Herr and Frau Samsa*: Grete's transformation into "the sister" and finally the Samsas' "daughter" parallels the mother's change into "Frau Samsa." Heinz Politzer argues that the women become mere extensions of Herr Samsa, formerly the feeble father, forming a powerful alliance against Gregor (Politzer, *Franz Kafka: Parable and Paradox*).

11. (p. 50) *three letters of excuse*: This kind of frivolity never would have been tolerated in the days when Gregor was working. Much of Gregor's torture in the first section revolves around the prospect of his missing work. On page 8 the text reads, "What if Gregor reported in sick? This would be extremely painful and suspicious, as he had not once been ill during his five-year employment." In Gregor's own words, his family members have become "healthy but work-shy people."

12. (p. 62) *the monstrous specter of his father*: This reversal of physical strength mirrors Kafka's own perception of himself and his father. In "Letter to His Father" he writes: "I was, after all, weighed down by your mere physical presence. I remember, for instance, how we often undressed in the same bathing hut. There was I, skinny, weakly, slight; you strong, tall, broad. Even inside the hut I felt a miserable specimen, and what's more, not only in your eyes but in the eyes of the whole world, for you were for me the measure of all things" (*Dearest Father*, p. 144).

13. (p. 67) *The arm with the sword*: Donna Freed notes that either by design or in error, Kafka describes the Statue of Liberty this way.

14. (p. 68) *from the Irish especially*: Kafka here pokes fun at Irish immigrants, who were reputed to be rowdy and hard-drinking, and were commonly not allowed in public establishments.

15. (p. 86) *And that cook*: Donna Freed notes that Kafka here refers to the woman, earlier called "the maid," who seduced Karl.

16. (p. 150) *Isn't it perhaps merely piping?*: The narrator of Kafka's "The Burrow" hears a piping or a sort of whistling in his burrow, which he initially attributes to the "smaller fry," among them "field mice." This sound grows louder, and eventually the narrator convinces himself that his burrow will be invaded by something possibly larger—more powerful and sophisticated—than himself.

Literature

In his struggle to escape the sweeping stretch of his father's domain, Franz Kafka cast his own inescapable shadow across the map of literature. He has had an impact on the minds of writers as diverse as Martin Buber, S. Y. Agnon, Walter Benjamin, Jorge Luis Borges, Vladimir Nabokov, Erich Fromm, Theodor Adorno, Albert Camus, Anatole Broyard, Paul Celan, Philip Roth, and Paul Auster.

Many writers have engaged in an active dialogue with Kafka, adapting his writings and ideas to suit their own perspectives. Bruno Schulz, a Polish Jew who was personally acquainted with Kafka, shared many of the cultural experiences that shaped Kafka's life and worldview; he translated *The Trial* into Polish in 1936. Schulz's own writing was greatly influenced by Kafka; in his story "Father's Last Escape" (1937), the narrator's father is dead—in fact, he has died a number of times. His "features" have dispersed, animating at times the wallpaper, a fur coat, and ultimately the form of a crab. The father scuttles around the apartment, not unlike Gregor Samsa in the latter's vermin form, terrorizing his surviving family members until the mother boils him and serves him for dinner. Though jellified, the father manages to escape, never to be seen again.

South African novelist and short-story writer Nadine Gordimer, who in 1991 won the Nobel Prize for literature, wrote a response to Kafka's "Letter to His Father," with her story "Letter from His Father" (1984). The letter is written to Franz, now dead, by his likewise deceased father. The tone is what one might expect from Hermann Kafka—defiant, vigorous, belittling. Herr Kafka, penning his response from an afterworld of some kind, closes with "I've outlived you here, same as in Prague."

Marc Estrin's novel *Insect Dreams: The Half Life of Gregor Samsa* (2002) continues the tribulations of Gregor as if he had survived the end of "The Metamorphosis." In Estrin's book, written with rollicking humor and a deft juggling of historical accounts, the charwoman and the "three ex-boarders chez Gregor" take the crate containing the man-sized beetle to the circus. As part of the freak show, Gregor traces a path among the major cultural events of the early twentieth century and acquaintances that include Austrian novelist Robert Musil, best known for his unfinished work *The Man without Qualities* (3 vols., 1930–1943); Austrian philospher Ludwig Wittgenstein; suffragist Alice Paul; U.S. President Franklin D. Roosevelt and his wife, Eleanor; physicists Robert Oppenheimer and Albert Einstein; and American composer Charles Ives. In Estrin's telling, Gregor is increasingly disenchanted with the trajectory of history, and he becomes a Christlike figure hopelessly dedicated to saving humanity from itself.

"Kafkaesque"

So ubiquitous is Kafka's legacy that the word "Kafkaesque" has been introduced into the English language. The adjective refers to anything suggestive of Kafka, especially his nightmarish type of narration, in which characters lack a clear course of action, the ability to see beyond immediate events, and the possibility of escape. The term's meaning has transcended the literary realm to apply to real-life occurrences and situations that are incomprehensibly complex, bizarre, or illogical.

Film

The flavor of Kafka's unending guilt has made its way into the work of many movie directors. Alfred Hitchcock claimed that all his films revolved around the innocent man wrongly accused. Both Woody Allen's famous insecurity and his complicated view toward his Jewishness echo Kafka's identity. Martin Scorsese's *After Hours* (1985) explores a modern-day *Trial* set in an absurdly comic New York City. David Cronenberg gives a nod to "The Metamorphosis" in two of his films: *The Fly* (1986), his remake of the 1958 classic horror flick, and *Naked Lunch* (1991), his adaptation of William S. Burroughs's 1959 novel. Steven Soderbergh's *Kafka* (1991) centers around Kafka's biography while combining elements of *The Trial*, *The Castle*, *Amerika*, "The Metamorphosis," "Wedding Preparations in the Country," and "Letter to His Father."

It is *The Trial* that has been translated into cinema most often. In Orson Welles's version (1963) the antihero, Joseph K., played by an eccentric and jumpy Anthony Perkins, floats from situation to situation, each more surrealistic than the last. Once the police invade his home, where he is arrested but not charged, K. wanders a bleak, unreal landscape. Much of the nightmarish quality derives from the film's being shot with seamless continuity in several countries. Particularly memorable is K.'s office, where rows of desks, with workers clacking furiously at typewriters, sprawl into an endless distance. Welles not only wrote the screenplay and directed but also played the role of the Advocate to whom K. pleads for help. Because Kafka's novel was left unfinished and the intended order of its chapters is uncertain, Welles, with characteristic ambition, rearranged the story when he wrote the screenplay. The film's experimental style—long shots, labyrinthine and claustrophobic settings, stark angles, swinging lightbulbs, and hammering sounds, along with Welles's trademark, the deep-focus technique—makes for a difficult, intense watch, a factor in its critical and financial failure.

In 1993 British director David Jones attempted a faithful adaptation of the novel based on the manuscript as edited by Max Brod, Kafka's friend and literary executor. Harold Pinter wrote the screenplay, which often quotes directly from the book. Shot in Prague, Jones's version of *The Trial* stars Kyle MacLachlan as Joseph K., supported by Anthony Hopkins and Jason Robards. In a terror-inspiring exchange between K. and the priest, well portrayed by Hopkins, K.'s guilt is confirmed and accentuated. However, while Jones strives to be literal in his rendering of Kafka's work, something is lost in the translation. In Welles's film the overbearing architecture, the constant snickering in the next room, and Anthony Perkins's unpredictable nervous tics combine to convey paranoia. Jones's film lacks such clues and so fails to convey much of the anxiety evoked by the novel. Instead, Jones's *The Trial* focuses on the indignation aroused by the actions of an invasive, all-controlling state.

Opera

Kafka's work has also been adapted into opera. Austrian composer Gottfried von Einem's *Der Prozess* is again based on *The Trial*. First performed in 1953, *Der Prozess* features a libretto by Boris Blacher and Heinz von Cramer. In the course of two acts and nine scenes it follows Joseph K. through his arrest, return to work, and desperate search for help. Von Einem was gifted in his sense of melody but wrote music for *Der Prozess* that, to emphasize K.'s frustration in an unknowable situation, is dissonant and oppressive.

In 2000 Philip Glass premiered *In the Penal Colony*, his operatic adaptation of Kafka's short story centering on a world traveler, an officer, and the "apparatus." *In the Penal Colony*, which features a libretto by Rudolph Wurlitzer, is scored for a tenor and a baritone (the traveler and the officer, respectively). Glass's music, typically minimalistic and repetitive, played by the unamplified string quintet the score requires, is appropriately bizarre. The production was directed by Glass's former wife and frequent collaborator JoAnne Akalaitis, who fashioned the "apparatus" out of tricks of beautiful light and torquing gears. Kafka sits in the foreground, where he scribbles notes and occasionally interrupts the action by reading from his diaries and letters. The author's presence onstage makes him a primary player in such a way that the action between the traveler and the officer can be interpreted as a direct product of, and allegory for, Kafka's imagination.

COMMENTS & QUESTIONS

In this section we aim to provide the reader with an array of perspectives on the text, as well as questions that challenge those perspectives. The commentary has been culled from sources as diverse as reviews contemporaneous with the work, letters written by the author, literary criticism of later generations, and appreciations written throughout history. Following the commentary, a series of questions seeks to filter Franz Kafka's The Metamorphosis and Other Stories *through a variety of points of view and bring about a richer understanding of these enduring works.*

Comments

FRANZ KAFKA

This story, *The Judgment*, I wrote at one sitting during the night of the 22nd–23rd, from ten o'clock at night to six o'clock in the morning. I was hardly able to pull my legs out from under the desk, they had got so stiff from sitting. The fearful strain and joy, how the story developed before me, as if I were advancing over water. . . . Only *in this way* can writing be done, only with such coherence, with such a complete opening out of the body and the soul.

—from a diary entry (September 23, 1912)

FRANZ KAFKA

Great antipathy to "Metamorphosis." Unreadable ending. Imperfect almost to its very marrow. It would have turned out much better if I had not been interrupted at the time by the business trip.

—from a diary entry (January 19, 1914)

WALTER BENJAMIN

To do justice to the figure of Kafka in its purity and peculiar beauty one must never lose sight of one thing: it is the purity and beauty of a failure. The circumstances of this failure are manifold. One is tempted to say: once he was certain of eventual

185

failure, everything worked out for him *en route* as in a dream.
There is nothing more memorable than the fervor with which
Kafka emphasized his failure.

—from *Illuminations* (1969)

CLEMENT GREENBERG

One feels that what Kafka wanted to convey transcended literature, and that somewhere, inside him, in spite of himself, art had
inevitably to seem shallow, or at least too incomplete to be profound, when compared with reality.

—from *Commentary* (April 1955)

PAUL AUSTER

In Kafka's story, the hunger artist dies, but only because he forsakes his art, abandoning the restrictions that had been imposed
on him by his manager. The hunger artist goes too far. But that
is the risk, the danger inherent in any act of art: you must be
willing to give your life.

In the end, the art of hunger can be described as an existential
art. It is a way of looking death in the face, and by death I mean
death as we live it today: without God, without hope of salvation.
Death as the abrupt and absurd end of life.

—from "The Art of Hunger" (1970)

VLADIMIR NABOKOV

[Franz Kafka] is the greatest German writer of our time. Such
poets as Rilke or such novelists as Thomas Mann are dwarfs or
plaster saints in comparison to him.

—from *Lectures on Literature* (1980)

THOMAS MANN

[Kafka] was a dreamer, and his compositions are often dreamlike
in conception and form; they are as oppressive, illogical, and absurd as dreams, those strange shadow-pictures of actual life. But
they are full of a reasoned mortality, an ironic, satiric, desperately
reasoned mortality, struggling with all its might toward justice,
goodness, and the will of God.

—from his "Homage" preceding Kafka's *The Castle:
Definitive Edition* (1954)

MAX BROD

When Kafka read aloud himself . . . humor became particularly clear. Thus, for example, we friends of his laughed quite immoderately when he first let us hear the first chapter of *The Trial*. And he himself laughed so much that there were moments when he couldn't read any further. Astonishing enough, when you think of the fearful earnestness of this chapter. But that is how it was.

—from *Franz Kafka: A Biography* (1960)

FRANZ KAFKA

My writing was all about you.

—from "Letter to His Father" (1919)

Questions

1. In considering Kafka's two diary entries, it becomes evident that the author feels interruptions in the process of composition are detrimental to a writer's work. Given Kafka's dissatisfaction with the end of "The Metamorphosis," and the fact that he failed to complete any of his three novels, what can be said about his notion of resolution? Is a satisfying ending impossible in his fiction? How do you read the ending of "The Metamorphosis"? Does it strike you as particularly superior or inferior to the rest of the tale?

2. Thomas Mann finds Kafka's literature "full of a reasoned mortality." Is this consciousness of death what drives Kafka to have Gregor Samsa regress into an insect, the officer in the Penal Colony condemned to a botched and sloppy death, and Georg Bendemann, in "The Judgment," drown himself on orders from his parents, instead of allowing his characters to overcome their circumstances? Is death itself transcendent in Kafka's work?

3. Max Brod's anecdote about Kafka reading aloud reveals not only the latter's sensibilities, but his intentions. How is Kafka funny? Is Kafka's sense of humor so peculiar that it is inaccessible?

4. Kafka and his critics always talk about his failures. Some of us think that he succeeded brilliantly. What do you think?

5. Teachers often tell students to apply literature to life. "Literature is equipment for living," said American philosopher Kenneth Burke. How would you apply Kafka's fiction to life? Is there any way that reading him might help you to persevere through difficult times?

6. One of Kafka's methods is to make the subjective objective. Instead of giving us the interior life of a character whose circumstances make him feel like an insect, he gives us a character that has literally turned into one. Does this way of reading "The Metamorphosis" account for all the details?

FOR FURTHER READING

Works by Kafka

Amerika. Translated by Willa and Edwin Muir. New York: Schocken Books, 1954.

The Basic Kafka. Edited by Erich Heller; various translators. New York: Washington Square Press, 1979.

The Castle: The Definitive Edition. Translated by Willa and Edwin Muir, with additional materials translated by Ernst Kaiser and Eithne Wilkens. New York: Alfred A. Knopf, 1954.

The Complete Stories. Edited by Nahum N. Glatzer; translated by Willa and Edwin Muir, et al. New York: Schocken Books, 1971.

Dearest Father: Stories and Other Writings. Translated by Ernst Kaiser and Eithne Wilkins. New York: Schocken Books, 1954.

Diaries, 1910–1913. Edited by Max Brod; translated by Joseph Kresh. New York: Schocken Books, 1948.

Diaries, 1914–1923. Edited by Max Brod; translated by Martin Greenberg with the cooperation of Hannah Arendt. New York: Schocken Books, 1949.

The Trial: The Definitive Edition. Translated by Willa and Edwin Muir, revised and with additional materials translated by E. M. Butler. New York: Alfred A. Knopf, 1956.

Biography

Brod, Max. *Franz Kafka: A Biography*. New York: Schocken Books, 1960.

Hayman, Ronald. *K: A Biography of Kafka*. London: Phoenix Giant, 1996.

Neider, Charles. *The Frozen Sea: A Study of Franz Kafka*. New York: Oxford University Press, 1948.

Pawel, Ernst. *The Nightmare of Reason: A Life of Franz Kafka*. New York: Vintage Books, 1985.

Wagenbach, Klaus. *Franz Kafka: Pictures of a Life*. Translated by Arthur S. Wensinger. New York: Pantheon Books, 1984.

Criticism

Benjamin, Walter. "Franz Kafka: On the Tenth Anniversary of His Death" and "Some Reflections on Kafka." In *Illuminations*, edited by Hannah Arendt; translated by Harry Zohn. New York: Schocken Books, 1969, pp. 111–145.

Bloom, Harold, ed. *Franz Kafka's "The Metamorphosis."* New York: Chelsea House, 1988.

Borges, Jorge Luis. "Kafka and His Precursors." In *Labyrinths*. New York: New Directions, 1964, pp. 199–201.

Corngold, Stanley. *The Commentators' Despair: The Interpretation of Kafka's "Metamorphosis."* Port Washington, NY: Kennikat Press, 1973.

Emrich, Wilhelm. *Franz Kafka: A Critical Study of His Writings*. New York: Frederick Ungar Publishing, 1968.

Flores, Angel. *The Kafka Debate: New Perspectives for Our Time*. New York: Gordian Press, 1977.

———, ed. *The Kafka Problem*. New York: New Directions, 1946, pp. 122–133.

Gray, Ronald, ed. *Kafka: A Collection of Critical Essays*. Englewood, NJ: Prentice-Hall, 1962.

Greenberg, Clement. "The Jewishness of Franz Kafka." *Commentary* XIX (April 1955), pp. 320–324.

Gross, Ruth V. "Kafka and Women." In *Approaches to Teaching Kafka's Short Fiction*, edited by Ronald Gray. New York: Modern Language Association of America, 1995, pp. 69–75.

Nabokov, Vladimir. *Lectures on Literature*. New York: Harcourt Brace Jovanovich, 1980.

Udoff, Alan, ed. *Kafka and the Contemporary Critical Performance*. Bloomington: Indiana University Press, 1987.

Other Works Cited in the Introduction

Emrich, Wilhelm. Commentary in *The Metamorphosis*, translated and edited by Stanley Corngold. New York: Bantam, 1972.

Kafka, Franz. *The Metamorphosis*, translated and edited by Stanley Corngold. New York: Bantam, 1972.

Mann, Thomas. Commentary in *The Castle: The Definitive Edition*. Translated by Willa and Edwin Muir, with additional materials translated by Ernst Kaiser and Eithne Wilkens. New York: Alfred A. Knopf, 1954.

Politzer, Heinz. *Franz Kafka: Parable and Paradox*. Ithaca: Cornell University Press, 1962.

Sokel, Walter. Commentary in *The Metamorphosis*, translated and edited by Stanley Corngold. New York: Bantam, 1972.

Thorlby, Anthony. "Kafka's Narrative: A Matter of Form." In *Kafka and the Contemporary Critical Performance*, edited by Alan Udoff. Bloomington: Indiana University Press, 1987.

Wenniger, Robert. "Sounding Out the Silence of Gregor Samsa: Kafka's Rhetoric of Dyscommunication." *Studies in Twentieth Century Literature* XVII (Summer 1993): pp. 263–286.